EXILE AND EMBRACE

KIRA COLE

Copyright © 2024 by Kira Cole

All rights reserved.

No part of this book may be reproduced in any form or by any electronic or mechanical means, including information storage and retrieval systems, without written permission from the author, except for the use of brief quotations in a book review.

1

FINN

Just one more week, and I'm out of this hell hole.

"Are you listening to me?" Dad scoffs through the contraband phone, his tone disapproving. "This is your one chance to prove to this family that you are capable of doing something useful with your life, Finnigan. Have you made any progress with finding a woman to be your fiancée?"

Because it's so easy finding women from behind bars. I barely hold the snort threatening to escape.

Breathing deep, I stare up at the cement ceiling, the metal of the bunk chilling me through the thin mattress.

"I've talked to a few women I used to know, but they're either married or about to be. I've got a couple more people to ask. I'll find someone before I'm out."

"You better." His voice is a low growl. "The second you're released, you're on your way to Oregon. You need to have all the pieces in place before you leave. I won't be arranging this entire thing for you."

"I understand. I'm not going to fail you. I know the plan."

Except I'm running out of options.

"Good. I'm not having you fuck up our family any more than you already have."

The line goes dead as I squeeze my eyes shut and take a deep breath.

Getting inside the Oregon mob, knowing all the players, and then killing the mob leader in Oregon so my father can take over is the last thing I want to do. Besides, it won't be a quick kill and exit. It will take time and really getting involved with the man one-on-one. Gaining his trust.

However, if it's going to put distance between me and my dad, then I will be more than glad do it.

As much as I don't want to be in Oregon, I want to be around him even less.

God, what I really wanted was to be out there, in the free world, preferably with a loving family. A family of my own, where I can love and be loved and maybe a few little ones running around.

But that's a pipe dream. With my family, any chance of a family goes down the drain because they would be nothing more than weapons to be used against me.

A soft whistle echoes through the thick stone walls of the prison.

I almost miss it above the noise from the other prisoners.

Moving swiftly, I sit up and remove the small shelf off the wall to reveal the hidden hole. I turn the phone off before slipping it inside.

The shelf is barely back in place when a guard appears in front of my door.

He smacks the bars with his baton. "Get up."

Another thing I won't miss.

Three years of being told what to do and when to do it is enough to drive a person insane.

Maybe I would be less annoyed by it all if I had done the crime. At least then I would deserve it.

Officer Topp smacks the baton against the bars again, the metal clang a subtle reminder to hurry up. "Work detail, Finnigan. Get your ass in gear. I won't have you wasting my time."

I swing my legs out of bed and hop down from the top bunk.

Off to scrub floors I go. Great.

At least if Ava's working, I get to see a friendly face. A face I see so many times in impossible dreams.

My lips press into a thin line as a loud buzz rises above the noise of the other prisoners.

The door slides open, and Officer Topp nods to the hall, remaining silent.

In the years that I've been here, he's the only officer that doesn't look like he's stepped in dog shit when he sees me.

The silence follows us all the way to the infirmary where the cleaning supplies and Ava are waiting.

If things were different, I might ask her to be my fake fiancée.

Though she doesn't seem elated to see me, she still offers a polite smile as she braids her dark hair back from her face. "Hey, Finn. How's your day going?"

She's just as beautiful as she was when she was dating my brother all those years ago. More so now, that she has lost that teenage innocence and is all woman now. A woman that in a different universe, I wouldn't mind getting to know better. Maybe even see if any of my impossible dreams had a chance to come true.

Too bad in this one, our paths outside these walls will never cross.

I pull the bottle of cleaner and a scrub brush out of the

bucket, setting them on a small table just inside the infirmary door. "It's alright. Getting a break from the cell at least."

Officer Topp heads for the door. "I'm going on break. Officer Richards is in the hall. No funny business, Finnigan."

"Yes, sir." The scent of ammonia fills the room as I drag the bucket to the sink.

"You're not going to be here much longer, are you?" Ava leans back in her chair, bouncing her leg. "Your release date's coming up."

"Thank fuck."

I turn away, knowing that if I look at her too much longer, my heart will take off like a runaway train. There is no denying that Ava is beautiful, but she's not the kind of woman who should hold my interest. She's too good.

Exhibit A. Working in a prison with some people who could be considered the scum of the earth.

I'm definitely not dragging her into my shit.

"What are you going to do when you get out?"

As I lift the spraying hose from the sink and aim it at the bucket on the ground, I consider whether or not to tell her the truth. I doubt that she is really interested.

Fuck it. It might be nice to have someone interested in me for once.

"I'm going to Oregon." As I glance over my shoulder at her, she smiles like she's won the lottery.

"Will you take me with you?"

The bucket nearly overflows as I stand there, not knowing how to respond to her.

My first instinct is saying, "Hell, no. Are you crazy?"

My second instinct is screaming, "Hell, yes!" She would be the perfect fiancée. She already knows about the mob. I wouldn't have to hide what I'm doing from her, and I'd be able to protect her.

She could be the answer to all my problems.

But this is Ava we're talking about.

"No. You can't come with me." *I'm not going to put you in danger.*

"Please, Finn. I know we're not friends, but we're friend*ly*. We could travel to Oregon together."

"Not going to happen, Ava."

As far as I'm concerned, this conversation is over.

Officer Carlson walks into the room, putting a more effective end to the conversation.

"What's going on?" Ava turns to him, crossing her arms and standing taller.

Carlson pulls out cuffs and walks over to me.

Officer Richards follows him into the room as I set the mop aside. He gives her a thin-lipped but polite smile as he stomps across the floor. "We're just here for Finn."

"Hands, Finnigan." Carlson unlocks the handcuffs and holds them out.

As I extend my arms and present my wrists, I glance at Ava.

She glowers at the two men, and those full lips stay pressed together.

I bite back a curse as the guard snaps the cuffs on my wrists a little too tight.

The cool metal bites into my skin as he nudges me out of the infirmary.

I move with them. "Where are you taking me?" Though I may not be the most liked inmate, I haven't done anything to anger anybody. At least, not lately.

"You have another visitor. No visitors for three years and then when you're due to be released, people start appearing?" Richards sneers, that thin lip curling up to his pig nose.

Carlson leads the way down the hall to the stairs, favoring his left leg. "I suspect we'll be seeing you in here soon enough."

"Or maybe I'm just making arrangements for my parole with a friend, ever think of that?"

Snapping at the guards is stupid, but with a week left of my sentence, I don't care.

They might be able to look the other way while I'm beat up again, but they can't touch me. Powerful friends make sure of that.

Still. I need to watch it. I don't want them to find a way to extend my sentence.

"We'll be seeing you back in here before you know it." Richards smirks as we descend the stairs. "Men like you don't make it long on the outside before they come crawling back."

"I'm not coming back." I stand still as Carlson reaches the bottom floor and holds open the door.

Richards nods, and I walk through the door, stepping to the side of the hallway and waiting for both of them to take their positions again.

We continue down the hall before stopping outside one of the visitation rooms.

Richards pats me down, checking for contraband. When he comes up empty, there is a flash of disappointment on his face.

Christian Herrera looks up as I enter the room, his eyes narrowing.

The door shuts behind me, both guards still outside.

I glance up to the top corner of the room.

The camera's there, but the red light's missing.

No witnesses. It's amazing what kind of power you have when you run a cartel.

"You're getting released next week." Christian nods to the metal chair across the table from him.

I take a seat, stretching out my legs in front of me as Christian leans forward.

"I've done my best to protect you over the last three years, but once you're outside of these walls, there's not much more I can do."

His body is tense, and his presence seems to pull all the air from the room.

If I weren't on good terms with Christian, I would be terrified of what he's capable of.

"I understand. I want to thank you for all that you have done over these last few years. If it hadn't been for your kindness, I would've been dead."

Christian nods and drums his fingers on the wooden table. "Yes, you would. The assassin for the Irish mob is sure to make a lot of enemies. I don't want to become one of those enemies, but I will if you stay in Tennessee. I will not put my people at risk for the wrath of your father if you decide to hide out here."

His message comes across loud and clear. If I had any plans to stay in Tennessee, I would be changing them starting right now.

"You don't need to worry about that. I have no intention of staying. As soon as I get out of here, I'm heading to another state. The same plan I had as when we spoke a week ago."

"Good." Christian sits back in his chair, some of the stiffness from his shoulders fading. "This will be my final visit with you. With that comes the reminder that Georgia and Florida do not want you either. An assassin has no business disturbing the peace Jovan, Alessio, and I have worked so hard to create."

I nod. "I understand. I can assure you that I'll be heading to the other side of the country."

"Good. See that it stays that way."

Christian jerks his chin in the direction of the door.

I dip my head toward him before getting up and raising my joined hands to knock on the door.

It opens a few seconds later, and the guards appear.

Neither guard says anything on the long walk to the infirmary.

Ava is busy, thank fuck, and I finish my shift before being escorted back to my cell.

I suppose whatever bribe the guards would've gotten is enough to silence them because they don't utter a single word.

Good.

We stop outside my cell, and one of the guards takes my cuffs off.

The second they're off, I rub my wrists, trying to ease away the red marks and the dull throbbing.

The guards exchange a look before stepping back.

Seconds later, a fist collides with my face, sending me stumbling back into the wall.

I groan and push myself upright.

Though I want to fight back against whoever they got to attack me, it's not worth it. I'm not going to risk getting my sentence extended.

Instead, I put my arms up to protect myself as best as I can and take another punch, this one to the side of the face.

Pain radiates in my cheek. The skin splits open with another punch, blood trickling down my eye and cheek.

As the man takes a step back, the guards disappear.

"Bastards." I spit a mouthful of blood onto the ground before running my tongue over a cut in my lip.

The man smirks, his beady eyes flashing with amusement, and slams his fist into my gut.

I shove him back a step as other inmates start to gather around. The last thing I need is for this to turn into a situation where the other guys think this is a free for all.

The red panic button glows on the wall, but I ignore it. If that button is pressed, the beating is only worse the next time.

The other prisoners don't take too kindly to snitches here.

After another punch to my gut, leaving me feeling like I'm going to throw up, the man takes a step back.

He reaches up to wipe some of the sweat from his forehead.

"*That's* what you get," he says, his voice booming for the others to hear.

I slump against the wall, the air knocked from my lungs with another punch.

"You think that you're better than us because you're getting out? Fuck you."

I spit another mouthful of blood onto the floor once I can finally breathe again. My torso aches as I pull myself off the bars.

His gaze locks with mine, and he takes a step forward in a silent challenge.

Before I make a bad decision, the guards come back around the corner, and the crowd starts to disperse.

Officer Richards looks at me with a shit-eating grin before pulling out his cuffs and snapping them back on my wrists. He makes sure they dig into my wrists.

I press my lips together, not saying a word as they shove

me into the elevator and up several floors, back to the infirmary.

When the elevator comes to a stop on the top floor, my heart comes to a screeching halt with it.

I wish I could have locked myself in my cell instead of coming up here.

The guards lead me down the long hall, past walls with windows on one side and offices on the other.

Ava laughs at something one of the other nurses says to her as he leans against the desk. Her long braid sways, the overhead lights making the lighter strands in her chocolate-colored hair shine.

Richards pushes the door to the infirmary open. "Look who's back."

He nudges me inside as Ava stands up, her warm brown eyes widening as she looks at me.

Coming up here and having my heart crash through my chest as she looks at me with what appears to be disappointment is hell.

This is just further proof I can't take her with me. It's too dangerous. And I will not put her in danger. I can't.

"Over there," Ava says, nodding to one of the hospital beds. "And the two of you can step out of the room. I will handle this. Carter, Doctor Marsden wanted to see you too."

The other nurse looks between me and Ava with a scowl as the guards head out of the room. "You shouldn't be alone with him."

"The guards are right outside the door as they are with every other patient I have. Now go. I can handle this, and I'll shout for the guards if anything happens."

Carter glares at me before leaving.

I roll my eyes and head over to the bed.

Ava follows me over, takes the chain attached to the metal frame of the bed, and snaps it onto my cuffs.

"What happened?" Her cool fingers grip my chin and turn my head. "You've got multiple lacerations your cheekbone and a split lip. There's going to be some bruising here too."

"Fell."

She picks up my hands and examines my knuckles. "These are clean. Not a single scratch. You didn't fight back?" That last past was barely a whisper as her eyes widen.

I shrug. "Like I said, fell."

Ava's eyes narrow, and she arches one of her slender eyebrows. "You know I've worked here long enough to not believe that bullshit, right?"

"Then you've also worked here long enough to know that I'm not going to tell you anything else."

I try to get comfortable to put her at ease, even though the throbbing in my face is driving me insane.

She goes over to one of the locked metal cabinets as she pulls out a key from the pocket of her scrubs.

My gaze drops to her ass.

The way those scrubs hug her curvy little body should be illegal.

"Have you given anymore thought to my request?"

"To come to Oregon with me? No. But now that you mention it, care to explain why you're going there?"

Ava turns around with antiseptic wipes and some bandages in her hand. "That's my business and I'll answer you... If you take me. So, what's it going to be?"

And there's that fire that was always so entertaining.

I didn't use to be on the receiving end of it back then, though.

She really would make the perfect fiancée.

It's too dangerous, though.

I could keep her safe. I would *keep her safe.*

Shit, it's not like I have any alternative, so why the fuck not?

My mouth goes dry as our gazes connect. "You want to go to Oregon with me?"

She nods.

"Okay. Then you need to be my fiancée."

2

AVA

"Say what?"

I blink a couple times.

This is all just some horrible dream. It has to be.

I wanted to go to Oregon with him, but this? "Absolutely not! I don't know what kind of scheme you're up to, but no way in hell. Not happening. I know you Byrne boys, and I know exactly how this ends for me."

Been there, done that, never happening again.

Finn clasps his hands together, the picture of innocence with his wavy brown hair and big green eyes. "Suit yourself. All I'm saying is you asked to go to Oregon with me, and I need a fiancée. This is a way for both of us to get what we want. It's nothing big."

"You say being engaged to you is nothing big?" I scoff and drop the supplies on the little table beside the bed.

I tear into one of the antiseptic wipes.

"It isn't. It's pretty easy. We go to Oregon, *pretend* that we're a happy couple, and I take care of the business that I need to take care of."

"Yes, because your brother is going to love that so much

when he finds out. I've spent the last few years without Declan in my life. I'd like to keep it that way."

Finn scratches his neatly groomed beard. "We won't be anywhere near him. He'll be in Virginia, and we'll be all the way in Oregon."

"Stop talking like I agreed to do this with you. I'm not going to. Quite frankly, I want nothing to do with your family. I asked to go to Oregon with you because I didn't want to travel alone. Not because I wanted to strike a deal with you."

I dab at his wounds, guilt curling through me as he hisses. I keep dabbing at the blood, getting a better look at the cuts.

"Your cheek needs stitches."

"And I need a fiancée. Please, Ava. You think I'd be asking you if I had anyone else available? If I hadn't already asked everyone I possibly could?"

I go back to the cabinet for suturing supplies, my hands trembling as I look for the right-sized needle. "Not happening, Finn. Find someone else to get all tangled up in your family drama. I'm not doing it again. I have a happy life now, and I plan to keep it that way."

He keeps his mouth shut as I stitch up the wound, trying to ensure that the stitches are small and neat.

It would be a shame to have a scar marring his handsome face.

Finn doesn't say another word to me as I put away the supplies and fill out my paperwork on the incident.

I stay seated at my desk, watching as he leans back against the bed and shuts his eyes.

Dark circles beneath those eyes and hollow cheeks make me think that he hasn't been sleeping well.

I check the overnight stay in the infirmary box on the paperwork before passing it to Officer Richards.

He sighs before handing it to Doctor Marsden as he appears in the hall.

Doctor Marsden reads the paperwork, his wire-framed glasses falling down his nose before he nods. "If this is what Ava recommends, then I am signing off on it. Inmate is to stay the night in the infirmary."

I give Doctor Marsden a quick nod before heading back inside. "Good news, Finn. You get to stay in the infirmary overnight for monitoring. I've reached the end of my shift, but Carter will be staying in here with you, and a guard will be stationed outside the door."

"I don't need to stay in the infirmary." Finn's chains clank together as he stands up from the bed. "I'm fine."

"Take the good night's sleep. You look like you need it, and I doubt that you're going to get one before your release if you don't stay here."

His eyes pierce mine for a few seconds before his shoulders sag. "Thank you." His expression softens as he sits back down. "I appreciate it."

"You're welcome." I head for the door, tossing him a small smile over my shoulder. "Get some rest."

I get changed in my office and leave the prison, going through all of the security checks with my head held high.

As soon as I get in my car, I program the restaurant my mother wants to meet at in my GPS.

My knuckles go white as I back out of my parking space, trying not to think about how disastrous this dinner could be.

One of these days, I need to just cut my losses and move on with my life. Zoe did.

I sigh and run my hand through my hair as I come to a red light.

There's still enough time to turn around and cut ties with my mother without talking to her. I could ignore her calls forever and everything would be alright.

Except I'm going to this dinner to tell her that I'm moving to Oregon. I need to go to my father's birthplace and figure out who the hell he was because he sure wasn't the man I knew.

That much was proven to me after the amount of danger he put Zoe in. Trying to marry her off to protect himself was disgusting. Selling her off to human traffickers was worse.

She might not want to know the truth about the man we both called Dad, but I do.

I turn up the music, drowning out the thoughts that keep circling around in my head with the pounding bass.

By the time I get to the restaurant, I'm as close to calm as I get when it comes to my mother. I park near the door for a quick escape if I need it, before heading inside.

My heels click against the glossy black floor as I make my way past white tables.

Mom stares at me from a table near the middle of the room, a bottle of red wine already open in front of her.

"You're late." Mom's nose wrinkles, her narrowed gaze dragging up and down my body as I sit across from her. "At least you changed out of those awful scrubs for once, but you could have bothered putting a little more effort into your appearance."

"You're the one who has an appearance to uphold." I grab the wine and pour myself a glass, the dark red liquid sloshing up the sides and pooling in the bottom. "Aren't you supposed to be playing the grieving widow?"

How can the woman who birthed you have so much obvious contempt for you? Shouldn't a mother love her children?

What did I ever do to her to deserve this kind of treatment? What did Zoe, for that matter?

Maybe we're not the problem. Maybe she's just incapable of loving.

If I ever have any kids, which I hope I do, from the bottom of my heart, I don't want to be anything like her. I'll show my kids every day just how much I love them.

"I *am* a grieving widow. I miss your father very much, even though I do not agree with some of the choices he made while he was alive."

I take a long sip of my wine. "If you say that a few more times, I might start to believe you. Look, the only reason I agreed to come to the restaurant with you is because it's a public place. I'm done with the abuse. I'm tired of being manipulated by you."

Mom's upper lip curls as she pinches the stem of her wine glass, her red nails shining. "You wouldn't be *anything* without this family. I turned you into the woman you are, and I'll be damned if you turn your back on me just like your sister did. Your father may be dead, Ava, but I am still your mother, and you will obey me and respect me at all times."

"I'm a grown woman, I don't have to put up with this anymore."

"You will do whatever I tell you, you little brat, or so help me god, I'll—"

"And I'm done. Have a nice life." I get up and turn on my heel, striding for the door.

I tried my best. I thought maybe my dad dying would

change her. And it did. For the worst, if that is even possible. So, it's time to cut ties with her and move on.

I don't need her toxicity in my life.

I never gave it much thought to what my life would be, but I always knew I didn't want this for myself. And then my dad sold my sister.

Her loss of choice, of control made me realize I do want something out of my life.

I want to be free. Free to choose if I want to love, who to love, how to love.

I know love is probably not in the cards for me, but I don't want anyone dictating who I have to get married to.

And yet, Finn asked me. He gave me a choice. I can go with him under his condition, but he isn't forcing me one way or the other.

He is letting me choose.

I need to go in order to have closure from my dad's situation, but if I think about it, this is also my chance to get away from my mom. If I stay here, I'm never going to fully slip from her clutches.

I should talk to Finn. Find out exactly what being his fiancée means to him.

Even if the situation is less than ideal, I'm leaving one way or another. Playing along with whatever Finn's game is could help me. Having his contacts could be useful.

Even if the last thing I want is to be associated with the Byrne boys again, he might be able to help get information on my father.

And he is right, we will be far enough away from his big brother that I never have to cross paths with him again.

The person Dad revealed to be in his last few days is a stranger, a dangerous one, so who better off to help me get information than a Byrne.

But should I get entangled with that family again? Those times... No, I won't think about that. I refuse.

I get in my car and head for Zoe's house. I need to tell her that I'm moving on with my life.

It's only a short drive from the restaurant.

She's sitting on the front porch with her guitar when I pull up. Her smile lights up her face as she puts the guitar to the side.

I turn off the car and get out, giving her a dramatic eye roll and sigh.

"That great, was it?" Zoe asks, jogging down the steps and over to me. She pulls me into a tight hug, rocking us back and forth.

I hug Zoe back, squeezing her tight. "Don't know. I was only there long enough to tell her that I was done with her before taking off."

We pull apart slightly, so I can look into her eyes. "I'm moving up the Oregon timeline, though. I need to get out of this state. My last day at work is supposed to be in two days. I think I'm going to leave shortly after that."

"This feels like you're running away." Zoe takes a step back and holds me at arm's length. "That doesn't feel like you, Aves."

"I'm not running away. You know that I want to find out who Dad really was. I just need to get out of here for a while. Tennessee hasn't felt like home in a long time, and to be honest, apart from you, there isn't much holding me here."

"That's on Mom." Zoe loops her arm through mine and guides me over to the stairs, forcing me to sit beside her as we look up at the stars. "You're the best part of our family, Aves."

"You are my family, Zoe. But I need to find out who I

am now. Without the dysfunctional family. I've spent so long rebelling against Mom and Dad that I don't know if that person is who I am, or if she's someone else I invited to keep myself safe."

"I get it." Zoe leans her head on my shoulder. "I'm just going to miss you. Promise to call me whenever you can. I don't know how I'm going to survive without my big sister."

"You'll do just fine, just like you always have. Besides, you have Christian now too. We both know that man would light the world on fire for you."

"Maybe when you're out in Oregon you'll find that for yourself."

Or maybe I'll be tied to the brother of a man I can't stand who may have the connections I might need.

For the last two days, all I've been thinking about is heading to Oregon with Finn. I go back and forth on it in my head every night.

On one hand, I don't want to be tied to Finn and his family again. I already broke away from that, and I have no intentions of going back.

On the other hand, if I need connections to find out how deep my father was in with all his problems, I have that connection with Finn.

I could ask Christian, but I don't know if he would be honest with me.

Zoe is holding things back when it comes to our father, I know she is, and if she tells him to keep his mouth shut, then that's what he's going to do.

As I sit in the infirmary, waiting for the guards to bring

Finn up for his pre-release exam, my heart pounds against my chest.

My hands shake as I pull out the forms I need to complete and attach them to the clipboard.

Everything is going to be fine. I'm going to tell him that I'll go along with his crazy plan and then I'm going to pretend that I'm not going to regret it.

Unless I'm making the wrong choice, and it takes me back to a life I hate.

But at least I have a choice, unlike my sister. So, this is it.

I take a deep breath as the door to the infirmary swings open.

Finn comes in and takes a seat in the hard plastic chair on the other side of my desk. His hands are cuffed together in front of him, and he pushes the metal out of the way as much as he can to rub the red rings around his wrists.

"Take the cuffs off." I nod to the metal around his wrists. "I need to be able to do the exam without him confined."

"One cuff," the guard says as he leans down and unlocks one cuff. He takes the empty cuff and closes it around the leg of my desk. "I'll be right outside, Byrne. Make sure that you don't give the nice nurse a problem."

I scowl.

The patronizing is nothing new. Most of the guards here seem to be on a power trip.

Normally, I would stand up for myself, but right now I need the guard to leave so I can speak to Finn without anyone listening to our conversation.

The guard gives me what I'm sure he thinks is a charming smile before heading for the door.

As soon as it closes behind him, I turn my attention to Finn, glancing toward the door every now and then.

"You're going to be doing my exam?" Finn asks, smirking as he leans back. "If you wanted to see me naked, all you had to do was pretend to be my fiancée."

The low rumble of his voice sends a rush of heat through my body.

It would be lying to say that I hadn't thought about him while getting acquainted with my vibrator. It would be an even bigger lie to say that he wasn't the main source of my latest fantasies.

He had been in the infirmary shortly after he got to the prison, and he looked nothing like the Finn I remembered.

We started to get to know each other again once he got his work detail. Having him invade my space nearly every day to mop the floor and wash the windows made it impossible to avoid him, and he started starring in my dreams.

But I wasn't going to allow a purely physical attraction to ruin my life.

And I'm still not going to. Not a chance in hell.

"Not that I have any desire to see you naked, but do you still need a fiancée?" I lean forward, keeping my voice low. My gaze cuts to the hall where the guard is pacing up and down. "Carter is going to walk in here in a few minutes and do your exam. That means that if you really do want a fiancée, you need to cut to the chase and tell me now."

Finn sits up a little straighter, his eyebrows creeping up his forehead. "Excuse me?"

"You heard me. If you still need a fake fiancée, I'll do it."

"Wow, hold your enthusiasm," Finn says, his tone teasing.

It's a reminder that whatever this is going to be, it won't be anything more than a game to him.

The teasing tension in the room fades.

His face grows serious. "Are you sure?"

Not even a little bit.

"Yes. I may need some connections in Oregon, and if I remember correctly, your family has many."

Finn nods. Right now, he's all business. "Pick me up on release day. I get out at noon. Two days from now. Last chance to back out, Ava."

I should back out. I should tell him that I was temporarily insane and that I didn't know what I was talking about. I should tell him whatever I can to get out of going to Oregon with him.

A smarter woman would. She wouldn't trust him.

I don't have to trust him, though. I just need to benefit from our deal.

"Ava, that nurse with a crush on you is coming back. Are you sure that you want to go through with this?" Finn's tone is unusually soft, his green eyes searching mine.

Don't give another Byrne boy the chance to hurt you.

"I'm sure." I stand up, hoping that the feeling returns to my legs soon.

This entire conversation with Finn has made my body numb. "And for the record, he doesn't have a crush on me."

Finn snorts as the door to the infirmary opens.

Carter walks in, smiling at me. As his eyes land on Finn, his face pinches like something crawled up his ass and died.

I hand off the clipboard to him, not looking back at Finn as I make my way to my office to freak out.

Two days from now, I could be driving away to the biggest mistake of my life.

3
―――
FINN

She's not going to come. She was fucking with your head when she said that she'd do it. It's all some sort of sick form of revenge against Declan for acting like a colossal asshole yet again.

The thoughts spiral through my mind as I stand in the intake room, staring down at a bag full of things that used to be mine. There's a faded wallet with a cracked ID and an expired pack of gum. A few loose coins jingle around in the bottom of the bag. My mother's gold chain tangles around it all.

"Well, hurry up," Officer Topp says as he enters the room and looks at the bag still in my hands. He holds out an envelope. "This is your remaining mail and the payout the prison gives to get you started in your new life."

Topp chuckles like he's told the greatest joke in the world as I take the envelope. I tuck the bag beneath my arm to open the envelope, closing it again after glancing at the new ID and credit cards in there.

I'm not surprised. With how obsessed Dad is with taking Oregon, he would have planned most of the small details. Leaving me to find my own fiancée was to satiate his sick sense of humor.

Three years in prison with no visitors and then I have to ask people for a favor.

Yeah, Dad would get off on that.

I tuck the envelope in my back pocket before opening the bag. The only thing I take out is Mom's gold chain and the wallet. I shove the wallet back with the envelope before putting on the chain and tucking it beneath my shirt.

It's the only thing of hers that I have left.

My body is numb as Topp leads me out of the intake room and outside to a path made of chain link fencing.

The sun shines bright, and the air is warm. The need to keep moving rushes through me.

I don't want to stop long enough for them to tell me that this was all a cruel joke. That I'm not actually free after three long years.

We walk down the length of the passage before coming to a guard booth.

Topp nods to the other guard, and a door in the fence swings open, revealing the parking lot.

I'm one step away from the world outside. One step away from being a free man.

Yet, for a moment, it feels wrong to try to take that step.

Squaring my shoulders, I take it anyway.

As my foot settles on the other side of my home for the last three years, the weight of the prison slides from my shoulders.

No more sleeping in a cement room on a cold bed. No more nights with screams as soundtrack and fear as your bed partner.

Tonight, I get to sleep on a soft bed with a warm blanket covering me.

Tonight, for the second time in three years, I get to sleep.

That reminds me of Ava and her kindness in letting me crash in the infirmary. That was the first night I slept.

But tonight will be different. Tonight, I'll be free.

No more guards coming around in the morning, making sure that the beds are made properly.

I'm finally free.

Outside of the prison walls, the sun on my skin feels different. The rays are warmer, and the breeze is stronger. The scent of the trees surrounding the prison wafts over to me as a shining black sedan comes to a stop along the curb.

The window rolls down, and Ava gives me a tight smile, large reflective sunglasses perched on her slim nose.

She doesn't bother to say anything, rolling her window back up.

I stride away from the prison and around the back of the car.

Am I doing the right thing?

Maybe I should have picked someone else to pretend to be my fiancée. Being trapped in a car with Ava from Nashville to Portland is going to be hell.

Three years without touching a woman, and she is the first one I happen to be around. The woman that I've thought about every night in my bunk for the last three years. The one woman I should stay away from.

I don't know what happened between her and my brother, but knowing Declan, it must have been bad.

No wonder she doesn't want anything to do with me either. She's nice to me, but I doubt that she is ever going to be my friend.

I open the passenger door before taking the envelope

and wallet out of my back pocket. I slide into the leather seat and shut the door. "Thank you for picking me up,"

"I have my reasons for doing it." Ava's tone is hollow as she stares straight ahead. Her knuckles are white as she grips the wheel. "I've got a suitcase in the trunk for you. Picked up everything you said you needed in that message."

"How much do I owe you?" I look at the side mirror as we pull away from the prison. As we go, the massive stone building fades into the horizon.

"Don't worry about it. You can pay me back by doing the first grocery run."

I nod, glancing out the window as we get onto the highway. "We have to make a stop for weapons first. I don't want to be out there and not have any connections to get weapons. I still have a few people who don't hate me here."

Ava keeps her eyes on the road, the corner of her mouth tipping upward as she taps a finger on the wheel. "Lift the backseat."

I raise an eyebrow but do as she says, taking off the seatbelt and turning in my seat to slide my fingers along the bottom edge of the backseat until I find a small button. As soon as it's pressed, a latch releases, and the seat lifts slightly. I push it the rest of the way up, my eyes widening at the small arsenal in the hidden compartment.

"What is all this?"

Ava smirks. "Weapons. You said you wanted some. I happen to have some."

I hate to admit it, but I'm impressed.

The Ava I know is a quiet woman. She stays out of trouble and never carries a weapon. Yet, here she is, several guns in a hidden compartment of her car and a variety of knives stashed among them.

"How did you manage to get those?" I ask, wondering if there is a serial number still etched onto any of them.

"I have connections." She moves into the fast lane and hits the accelerator. "Well, my brother-in-law has some connections, and he was willing to hook me up."

"Does he know you're with me?"

"No. I had him fix up my car a little while ago. I thought that I needed some protection, and he was more than willing to oblige."

My shoulders sag a little. One less thing to worry about. No one can know where I'm headed.

But another question pops up.

"Do you know how to shoot?" I lower the seat back into place. The latch locks, and the arsenal disappears. I turn to sit back properly and buckle up again.

"Yeah. Brother-in-law taught me that too."

Who is this brother-in-law of hers?

I want to ask so bad, but it's clear she's being intentionally vague, so I'll save it for another time.

For now all I can do is assume she's connected to one of the low-level gangs or my father would've mentioned her in recent years.

Declan's ex having cartel ties is not something my father would ever ignore.

"You know, this is the last chance for you to back out of our deal," I say as we leave Nashville in the rearview mirror. "I won't blame you for not wanting to do it. The job I have to get done is dangerous, and while I'll try my best to keep you safe, I can't promise that I'll be able to."

There is a part of me that hopes she does back out of the deal. The last thing I want to do is play house with my brother's ex.

I might not have known her well when she was with Declan, but I saw her often enough.

Often enough to know that she was his, and he was willing to do whatever it took to make sure another man didn't even look at her. He once killed one of our guys for mentioning that Ava was hot.

I had noticed her too, but I was wise enough to keep my mouth shut and my hands to myself. As far as I knew, she loved him. What a waste.

So, being involved with Declan's ex is definitely the last thing I want to be doing. If she backs out now, there might still be time to find a woman to play along.

You'd still want her, though. She is perfect for this.

Ava laughs and pushes her sunglasses on top of her head before glancing over at me. "Look, my father turned out to be a bastard in disguise. I need to figure out exactly who he was so I can put all that shit behind me. Which means, I would be going to Portland either way."

"Your dad?"

"Yeah. Dead now, so don't get yourself worked up over meeting him. He was the Head of State." She focuses on the road, weaving through traffic.

"You never mentioned that when you were with Declan."

Ava gives me a flat look, those brown eyes looking like they're seconds away from rolling to the back of her head. "I knew then what your family did for a living. Did you really think I was going to put my family in jeopardy like that? All Declan needed to know was that my father was a politician in Tennessee."

"Even back then you didn't trust him?"

"I trusted him. I loved him." Ava's hands tighten on the wheel again before she reaches over and turns up the music.

The bass rattles the windows as the crooning voice of a singer I don't recognize fills the car.

I guess we're done talking about this. That's fine, there's going to be plenty of time to find out what else she was hiding back then.

The phone that was in the envelope starts ringing a few minutes later.

I sigh at my father's number on the screen. Even though I want to ignore the call, I'm smarter than that.

When Dad calls, you answer.

"Hello." My tone is low as I reach over to turn the music down.

"Are you on the road?" Dad doesn't bothering to ask how my release went or how it feels to be free. Not that I'm surprised. The parenting gene definitely didn't embed itself into his DNA.

"Yes. We should be arriving in Oregon in a couple days."

"See that you do," he says, his tone stern.

The thud of something heavy shutting comes down the phone.

It's a subtle intimidation tactic, and one he's used many times before. "I don't want to have a problem, Finn. This is your chance to prove yourself to the family. If you fail me one more time, I'll make sure that it's the last."

The line goes dead.

4

AVA

My eyelids grow heavier the longer we drive.

Finn snores softly beside me, his head leaning on the window as I pull into the parking lot of a motel.

Dim lights shine overhead, though one is broken. Glass is shattered on the ground beneath it.

If I squint against the darkness, I think I can see a man leaning against it.

"Wake up." I park the car in front of the office. "We need to go get the key for our room and get some rest."

Finn swats at my hand when I try to nudge him awake.

I sigh and push his shoulder again, hating the way sparks fly at even the simple touch.

He's an attractive man, sure, but that's it. That's all that he is ever going to be to me. Something nice to look at while I spend time in Oregon and a way to get some harder answers that might need his connections.

"Wake up. We're at the motel." I shove him a little harder.

He bolts upright, looking around the car like he is

expecting someone to jump out at him at any moment. His eyes are wide and bright, though they are bloodshot.

"It's just me," I murmur, showing him my hands palms out and facing him. "I'm not going to hurt you. You're not in prison anymore. We're just at the motel. There's a guy under the broken streetlight. I don't want to get the keys to the room alone."

Finn blinks slowly, scrubbing his hands down his face before nodding. "Reservation under your name?"

"Yeah." I unbuckle my seatbelt, getting ready to follow him out of the car.

Finn shakes his head as he opens his door and steps out.

I settle back into my seat. "You have to pay cash when you pick up the key."

He opens his envelope and pulls out a wad of cash, tucking it into his pocket before glancing at the man outside. When he looks back at me, his mouth is set in a thin line.

"Stay here, Ava. Lock the doors, and don't open them until I'm back in the car." Finn shuts the door and points downward.

I press the button for the locks, and they click into place.

As Finn walks to the office, I keep my focus on the broken streetlight and the man beneath it.

The man watches Finn as he walks into the office but doesn't make any move to approach him.

Finn disappears through a set of broken glass doors covered with tape and flyers.

I sit back in the seat, watching as the man looks toward the car.

My heart pounds in my chest, and my breathing quickens. I try to focus on not panicking.

The motel may not be in a good area, but it's a place

that takes cash. Untraceable. A chance for us to get out of Tennessee.

I drum my fingers on the wheel, the soft music still playing.

The man pushes himself away from the streetlight and walks toward the car. He is just about to cross in front of the office doors when Finn steps outside.

Even in the dim light, it's clear that Finn is more muscular than the other man.

Finn stands taller, crossing his arms and looking down at the man, waiting until he turns around. Finn keeps watching the man, waiting until he is out of sight before backing toward the car.

I unlock the doors as Finn reaches the passenger door.

He gets in and hands me the key, pointing to the far end of the motel.

The brick walls are crumbling and more than one of the windows we pass are covered with plywood.

As I park the car in front of our room, I start to think that I should've found a slightly nicer place. Somewhere without prostitutes peeking out windows at us.

The door of the room next to ours opens, and a man walks out, zipping up his pants as he goes.

A woman in tight jeans and a crop top follows him, stuffing several bills into her bra.

"Well, you sure know how to pick a place." Finn's clearly amused as we get out of the car. "I have cards. We could have stayed in a nicer hotel. One without venereal diseases."

"This place takes cash and doesn't have cameras." I look him up and down, my upper lip curling slightly. "As I seem to remember, you used to sleep with anything that moved. I think my chances of catching a disease from sitting next to you in the car are higher than staying one night in the hotel."

Finn laughs, the sound warm and rich, sending a shiver down my spine. "You couldn't have been more than nineteen back then. I was twenty-four. What the hell were you doing paying attention to me?"

"I wasn't paying attention to you. On the rare nights I stayed over at that apartment you shared with Declan in Virginia, I stumbled into your many hookups. One of them had the audacity to drown themselves in my favorite perfume."

He laughs and leans against the car. "You've seen my bloodwork, so you know I'm clean. But tell you what, as a special reward for putting up with my hookups back then, I'll buy you a new bottle of perfume."

I roll my eyes and go to the back of the car to grab a duffel bag. Part of me wants to smile and laugh with him, but the larger part of me remembers who he is, but more than that, who he is connected to.

I can't let my guard down.

Finn watches me, his arms crossed as I take the bag to the backseat and open the hidden compartment.

I pack the guns into the bag quickly before zipping it up and slinging it over my shoulder. There is no way that I'm leaving a bunch of guns in my car in this neighborhood.

Finn grabs the suitcases from the trunk before I lock the car. He crams the key into the lock, exhaling when it doesn't turn the first time. Finn jiggles the key in the lock and twists the handle.

The lock finally turns.

As we stumble into the room, I'm met with the sight of a single bed.

My jaw drops to the ground, and my entire body feels like it's on fire.

I may not want anything to do with Finn beyond what's required of me with our deal, but I'm not stupid. I know that if I share that bed with him, I'm going to stop fighting the attraction between us that's been burning since the first day he walked into the infirmary.

I might give into one of the countless fantasies I've had.

And I can't afford to do that.

"They have to have a room with two beds." I keep the bag of guns over my shoulder as I turn for the door. "I'll head back to the office and see if there's something else."

Finn laughs and drops the suitcases in the corner before shutting the door and locking it behind him. He slides the deadbolt into place before going to pull the ugly floral curtains across the window.

"I don't know why you're laughing about this. There is a single bed which looks like it came straight from my grandmother's house. The two of us are not going to be sleeping together."

Finn sits in the cracked leather armchair and kicks his heels up on the coffee table. He's only going to add to the scuffs and chips in the cheap wood, but he doesn't seem to care. "Ava, this is a prostitute motel. Rooms with one bed are all they have."

I run my hands down my face, groaning as I sit on the edge of the bed. I look around the room, trying not to let the peeling wallpaper bother me. As I take in the white bars of the headboard, I regret booking this motel.

We have to make the best of a horrible situation. It's too late to find somewhere else for the night.

"How many people do you think have been handcuffed to those bars?" Finn asks, nodding to the headboard. "I'm betting that there's been at least one a night since the motel opened."

"Well, damn." I put the bag of guns on the floor and tuck it under the bed. "It looks like we're about to break that streak."

The corner of his mouth tips up, and a small dimple appears in his right cheek. "Damn shame."

"Not the handcuff type." I shrug, taking my sunglasses off the top of my head where they were pushed hours ago and setting them down on the nightstand. "More of a silk restraints kind of girl."

Finn coughs, his face going red. "Good to know, I guess. Do you tell all of your fake fiancés that?"

"Only the ones I'm never going to sleep with," I say with a sweet smile as I get up and crouch near my suitcase.

Opening it, I rummage through it until I find a pair of linen shorts and an oversized black t-shirt. "So, tell me, jailbird, what did you miss the most while you were in prison?"

Finn shrugs and links his hands together behind his head, making his muscled torso press against the thin gray shirt he wears.

Heat floods my core as I stare at him for a couple of seconds too long.

"Come on, there has to be something that you missed more than anything else."

"There is." His gaze drags up and down my body as I stand.

He's not subtle about it, and I don't think he wants to be.

The room grows a thousand degrees hotter as his gaze connects with mine. "But I don't think you want to hear it. And since there's nothing I can do about it, it's better not to say."

"Nothing you could say could shock me. I worked in a prison."

He barks out a laugh. "That's fair. I suppose working in there, you would have heard it all."

"Then come on, out with it." I wave a hand in his direction. "What did you miss the most while you were in prison, jailbird?"

"If that nickname is going to stick, then I'm going to have to think of a good one for you." Finn gets up and heads for the washroom. "Sex and alcohol. That's what I missed the most while I was in prison. That and a hot shower where I didn't have to stare at another man's junk while trying to wash my own."

His tone is low and husky, sending a shiver down my spine. Butterflies erupt in my stomach, and my pussy clenches.

There is no way someone like Finn Byrne is bad at sex.

Down, girl. He is nothing but a bad idea.

It's been a long while since I was with someone. And if we have to pretend to be engaged, it's going to be a longer while until I can sleep with somebody again.

Maybe I could have just this one night. No strings attached.

No. I know what happens when Byrne boys crash into lives. They scorch everything in their paths.

But it would be just once, right? One little night couldn't hurt.

Except, I know it would. It might be a good time—hell, I was sure it was going to be a great time—but it's one that I should avoid.

Although, the way Finn looks at me makes me think that it might not be as easy to resist him as I hope.

There is no denying that he's charming when he wants to be, even if he kills people for a living.

Yet another reason why being involved with him is a bad idea.

I make a show of wrinkling my nose as I kneel back down to the suitcase and pull out a bottle of vanilla whisky and two cups. "Well, lucky for you, I can help with one of those."

Finn's eyes light up as he takes in the bottle and grabs a pair of shorts from his suitcase. "I'm going to head for a shower. When I come out, we are definitely splitting that bottle."

I get up and set the bottle on the coffee table as he disappears into the washroom.

The door closes with a soft click, leaving me in an empty room.

I shed my clothes quickly and pull on the shirt and shorts before turning off the overhead light. I shuffle my way across the floor, reaching for the light on the nightstand.

Warm light fills the room as I settle on the bed and hope that the sheets are clean.

Not that I plan on getting beneath the covers at all.

Especially if we're going to be sharing a bed.

I'm going to make this as cold and clinical as possible.

But when the bathroom door opens and Finn is there wearing nothing but a pair of shorts, lust burns through my body as rivulets of water trail down the defined muscles of his stomach.

I don't know how much longer I'm going to keep up my mental game of pretend.

Finn ruffles his dark hair with a towel before tossing it

back in the bathroom. He grabs the bottle of vanilla whisky before joining me on the bed.

As he cracks open the bottle, not bothering with the cups, I search for the television remote.

Once I find it, I turn on some old show and turn down the volume.

Finn takes a swig of the whisky before passing the bottle to me.

I take a drink, leaning back against the pillows and crossing one leg over the other.

"If we're going to pretend to be married, then we're going to need to get to know each other." I take another sip from the bottle before passing it to him. "You already know that I'm a nurse, and I went to university in Virginia where I met you."

Finn swallows more of the alcohol, wincing as it goes down. "Is there really more we need to cover? That seems like enough."

"People are going to want to know how you asked me to marry you. How long we were dating before you popped the question. How you knew I was the one, that kind of thing."

His fingers tighten around the neck of the bottle as he twirls it, sloshing around the liquid inside. "I don't know. This fake relationship is the most serious one I've ever been in."

"Thirty-two and you've never been in a serious relationship?" I take the bottle from him and take a long sip, enjoying the burn as it goes down.

Finn nods. "Never met any woman that was worth my time. And women expect things of you. And then there's the biggest problem. Nobody wants to marry a killer. Nobody except you, apparently."

"Well, I've always liked living a little on the wild side." I snort and drink more of the whisky, the edges of my mind starting to blur.

My body begins to relax as Finn takes another drink before setting the bottle to the side.

"You were always too good for my brother. I'm glad that you came to your senses and left him."

My chest constricts, but the alcohol flowing through my veins keeps me from launching into full-scale panic.

I hate talking about Declan. My plan was to leave everything involving him in my past but then Finn came around and messed that up for me.

"I'd rather talk about anything else." I roll onto my side and face him.

My shorts rise higher up my thighs, and Finn's gaze drops.

When he looks back up at me, there is a heated look in his eyes.

And the alcohol has me believing that one little night with him wouldn't hurt.

Just to see what I've been missing out on.

"Well, if you want to talk about anything else, we could talk about those silk restraints." He smirks, his muscles flexing as he rolls onto his side and faces me.

That's it. I'm a fucking goner.

Maybe it's the alcohol that fuels me or maybe it's the strange attraction that's been building up over the last three years. It could be danger lingering just beneath the surface that lures me in like the most addictive drug.

Honestly, I don't know what it is about Finn.

One moment, there's inches between us, and then the next, there's not even enough room for air.

His mouth moves against mine, his kiss slow and soft despite the raging boner that's pressing against my stomach.

The imprint of his hard cock has my pussy dripping as I roll on top of him. My legs frame his hips as he lays back into the bed.

The only thing I know I'm going to remember about this moment is that Finn Byrne tastes like vanilla whisky and bad decisions.

Finn's tongue tangles with mine as his hands move up and down the curves of my body.

He groans into the kiss as he nips my bottom lip before plunging his tongue back into my mouth again.

His cock presses against my pussy, building a delicious friction through the thin layers that separate us.

His fingers dig into my hips as I rock my hips back and forth, grinding my core against his hardened length.

He hisses as I kiss his jawline before grazing his pulse point with my teeth.

"Fuck," he says, breathless as he flips us over. "There is no way that I'm going to last long with you."

I smirk and run my fingers through his wet hair. "This is the first and last time we're doing this, so you better make it count."

"Yes, ma'am." His voice is husky as he pulls my shirt over my head and tosses it to the side.

Finn sucks on the sensitive skin at my hip, marking it before hooking his fingers in my shorts and pulling them down my legs.

He sucks in a sharp breath as I spread my legs wider and dip my hand between my legs.

My finger circles my clit as he kisses his way up one leg and down the other.

I moan as he returns to my pussy.

His broad shoulders spread my legs wider as he slides his tongue up my wet slit.

My hips buck as he sucks my clit into his mouth before pressing two fingers into my core.

As he thrusts his fingers, massaging my inner walls, tension starts to build in my body.

My back arches off the bed as his fingers move faster, driving me closer to the edge.

I run my fingers through his hair, pulling on it slightly and guiding him to exactly where I need him.

"Fuck yes, Finn. Just like that." I roll my hips as his fingers thrust deeper into me. "Don't stop. Please don't stop."

He chuckles and sucks on my clit again, before flicking his tongue over the little bundle of nerves. When he crooks his fingers and drives them against the spot that drives me wild, I come.

"You taste like the best dessert I've ever had." He licks his fingers clean.

Fuck. I didn't think that would be as hot as it is.

He flips us over, and I slide down his body until my knees are back on either side of his hips.

I rub my soaking wet pussy against his throbbing cock.

Finn grabs my hips and drags me down onto his cock.

I moan, rolling my hips as I get used to the way he stretches me.

He thrusts from below as I rock my hips, riding him while another orgasm starts to build.

Finn wraps my hair around his hand and pulls my head back.

His cock slams deeper into me as my back arches.

"I'm going to come," he says, his voice raspy as he thrusts harder.

I move my hips faster as my legs start to shake.

My pussy clenches down around him, miking his cock as he comes. Another orgasm rocks through me, leaving me slumped against his chest.

Finn chuckles, his hands working their way to my back. "Fuck this being the only time, Ava. I'm done with you when the fucking sun comes up."

As he flips us over and takes a nipple into his mouth, I'm sure that I'm going to regret agreeing to his terms in the morning.

But right now, I'm going to enjoy orgasms from a man who knows exactly what to do with his tongue.

5

FINN

Fucking hell. I'm stupid.

She's going to want to end the deal we have and then I'm going to be screwed.

The sun is streaming through the thin curtains and casting a hazy glow over Ava's naked body when I swing my legs to the side of the bed and sit up, rubbing my hands down my face in a desperate attempt to wake up. Maybe when I do, I'll realize that last night was a dream, and I didn't sleep with my brother's ex.

As I get out of bed, I try not to look at Ava. I know that if I do, I'm going to want to get back in that bed and wake her up only to give her another orgasm.

If I do that, if I get another taste of her, I'm never going to want to leave her bed.

That will only cause more problems for me.

I stumble to the washroom and shut the door behind me.

When the lights come on, they flicker overhead, reminding me of a cheap horror film.

The sooner we get out of here, the better.

After splashing water on my face, I go back into the room and pull on some clothing.

While Ava is still sleeping, I load the guns and my suitcase back into the car. For a few minutes, I stand outside, trying to figure out if I've just ruined everything.

I probably did. The same way that I ruin everything else.

I sigh and stare at the wispy clouds drifting across the sky, trying to focus on something other than my mind spiraling out of control.

Even though it was a night that we both agreed to, it feels like the guilt is eating me alive.

Ava said that she wanted nothing to do with me. She said that she was never going to sleep with me, and then we slept together.

She's going to think that I took advantage of her.

THE DOOR TO THE ROOM OPENS, AND AVA STEPS OUT, keys in one hand and her suitcase in the other. She's dressed in a pair of leggings and a crop top that hug her curves. The swell of her breasts visible thanks to the low neckline sends all the blood in my body rushing straight for my cock.

"I'll drive today." I already have the car keys since I used them to unlock it.

My tone is cold, and I do my best to look indifferent as I take her suitcase and load it into the sedan.

"I'm fine driving." Ava tries to take the keys from me. "I got more than enough sleep last night to be comfortable driving today. You should get more rest. You've only been out of prison for a day, and I know you weren't getting a lot of rest in there."

Even after last night, she is still acting like she gives a

shit. We both know that she shouldn't. We both know that all I'm going to do is complicate her life.

"I'll drive."

I get into the driver's seat, knowing that if I don't have something to do with my hands, I won't be able to keep them off her. Not after last night.

Especially not after she wrapped those full lips around my cock and made my soul feel like it was leaving my body.

Stop thinking about fucking her and start thinking about the job you have to get done. You can't afford any distractions.

Ava rolls her eyes but rounds the car and gets in the passenger side.

She's silent as I drive us over to the office. She heads inside to drop off the key while I sit behind the wheel, drumming my fingers against the leather.

When she returns to the car, she reclines her seat and closes her eyes, sliding her sunglasses off the top of her head and over her face.

I frown, watching her dark eyes disappear behind the mirrored lenses.

Ava crosses her arms behind her head and stretches her long legs out in front of her. "So, what's the plan once we get to Oregon? Other than pretending that we like each other enough to get engaged."

"Yeah, that's going to be a tough sell." I mentally kick myself for being a jackass, but it's for the best.

I need to remember that this is fake, and if making her hate me does that, then that is what I'm going to do.

As I head for the highway, I try not to think about how much this entire job is going to suck my soul from my body. I know that I'm going to be fighting myself every step of the way, and I need to take Ava out of that equation.

I don't need any temptation to say fuck it all and spend days with her in bed instead of doing my job.

"Alright, crank-ass. Why don't we talk like civilized people? Just because we slept together, things don't have to get weird."

"It's better if we talk to each other as little as possible."

Ava sighs, her gaze burning into the side of my head. "Finn, I'm sorry about last night. We shouldn't have gone there, and I shouldn't have teased you. Doesn't mean I didn't enjoy myself, because I did, but it was a line that we shouldn't have crossed."

Somehow, hearing her say the words out loud hurts more than having them circle through my mind over and over again.

"When we get to Oregon, there is going to be a house ready for us. It's going to be small, but it's in a nicer neighborhood. I have to get close to the leader of the mob there."

"Do I want to know what you're going to do to him once you get close to him?" Ava's tone is hesitant.

She knows who I am. Who my father trained me to be.

"I'm not going to tell you that. It's better if you have as little involvement with the mob as possible. I told you before and I meant it, I don't want to put you in danger. You're going to have to interact with them a little to keep up our act, but I'm not going to let you get too deep into that world."

Ava scoffs and when I glance over at her, she's glaring at me over the top of her sunglasses. "I appreciate that you want to protect me, but I'm already in that world. My father wasn't a good man. I don't know how deep his ties run, but I'm no stranger to how horrible people can be. If you need me to do something, I will try to do whatever I can to help you."

"Ava, you don't know what you're saying."

Except, there's a part of me that knows she is saying exactly what she means. She wouldn't be able to get her hands on that many guns without having ties to the underground. Whatever her brother-in-law is involved in taints her life too.

"Yes, I do. I need you to be there for me until I have my answers, so I'm vowing to be there for you. We are in this together no matter what. We are only done when both of us are done. Can I count on you to be there for me? To be there for me even after you have done your job if I'm not done yet?"

I want to be the one person who doesn't send her life spiraling out of control. I don't want to drag her any deeper than she has to be.

But I also want to be there for her. I want to show her that I'm nothing like my brother. I want her to count on me.

She is a light in my life and selfish as it may be, I want her there, even if it is better if she wasn't. Safer.

"Do we have a deal, Finn?"

I sigh. "Fine, we have a deal." I just hope I'm doing the right thing.

Because if my father or brother find out who is playing this game of pretend with me, there is going to be hell to pay.

It's not really my world I'm protecting her from. It's my family.

"WE'VE BEEN DRIVING FOR FOUR HOURS," AVA SAYS as we pull into a gas station. She stretches and gets out of the car, bending over to look at me. "Sooner or later, you're going to have to give up control and let me drive again."

"I'm good."

I get out of the car and slide the keys into my pocket.

She pushes her sunglasses on top of her head, pinning those dark waves back.

"Finn, there is no way that you're going to be the one doing all the driving for the rest of the trip. Once we're done here, let me take a turn. Get some rest."

"Not going to happen. You drove yesterday. My turn today."

Ava rolls her eyes to the sky. Her chest rises and falls with the slow inhale. "You're going to drive me insane. You've barely said a word to me since we left the motel. Now, you're talking to me in as few sentences and syllables as possible."

Even though I know I shouldn't, I smirk. "Yup." The pop I put at the end of the word makes her eye twitch.

Ava storms away from me, yanking open the door to the gas station.

It swings shut behind her while I hit the button to pop open the gas tank.

I've barely finished filling the car when she comes out with a bag full of snacks. Not a word leaves her mouth as she settles back into the passenger seat and rifles through her bag.

It's only when she produces a chocolate bar that my stomach starts to growl.

I can't remember the last time I had a good chocolate bar.

"Are you going to give me a piece of that?"

She glares at me as I slide back into the car before cramming the remaining half of the chocolate bar into her mouth.

I smother the smile that tugs at the corners of my mouth. Smiling right now would only piss her off more, and I really want some of her snacks.

"Come on. I'm hungry. Please tell me that there's something for me to eat in that bag." I twist the key in the ignition, still not quite used to driving a car again. When it rumbles to life beneath me, I clench the wheel a little tighter.

Ava opens a small bag of chips and tilts it upside down, dumping half the bag into her mouth.

"Fuck." I reach over and snag the bag away from her. "You're so fucking stubborn. I'm sure that stubbornness is going to be the reason I throw myself off a cliff while we're in Oregon."

She shrugs and looks out the window. "Well, maybe your ghost will talk to me more than you do."

I set the bag in the cupholder and pull out a few chips. "Maybe."

Ava's face darkens to a bright shade of red. She reaches for the bag, aiming to steal the snack back, but I swat her hands away. "You don't get snacks if you're not going to play nice."

"And who said that I was ever going to play nice?"

She pulls her sunglasses out of her hair and settles them back on the bridge of her nose. "We're trapped together for the foreseeable future. If us getting tipsy last night and fucking is going to make you act like someone who's never touched a woman and is absolutely terrified of them, then this is going to be a long fake engagement."

Just the mention of what happened last night is enough to send the blood in my body rushing south.

I grunt at her, shifting in my seat just enough to relieve some of the ache.

"So..." I draw out the word until she glances over at me. "What's the situation with your father?"

Even though we should clear the air about what happened last night, I don't want to. Not if it means driving to Oregon with a raging boner.

Ava rolls her bottom lip into her mouth. "It's a long story."

"Good thing it's a long drive."

"My father sold my sister to a sex trafficker. Well, would you look at that. Not that long of a story after all."

My knuckles turn white as I picture her father's throat instead of the steering wheel. "Is there more to that story?"

"Not a whole lot. He always seemed like the doting father, which is why this doesn't make sense. It's why I need to get to Portland and get some answers. Going to my mother and asking about who my father really was isn't an option."

I nod. I know all about complicated relationships with parents. "Well, since I've already promised to do everything I can to help you find the truth about him, why don't you fill me in on some of the finer details."

She's silent for so long that I'm sure she isn't going to start speaking.

When she does, it's clear that a momentary truce has been called.

Though I don't know how long it will last, I'm going to bask in it while I can.

6

AVA

When we enter our hotel room in Wyoming and two beds greet us, I'm equal parts relieved and disappointed.

Looks like it's back to the vibrator for me.

The thought only disappoints me more. My little vibrator is nothing compared to the feeling of his mouth and his hands on my body. But it's better this way. It has to be better this way. We can't get lost in booze and each other again.

Except, if there was only one bed in the room, I don't think that I would be able to avoid a repeat of our night in the motel.

I don't think I would want to.

Finn sets our bags on the desk near the window. "I'm going to go pick up dinner and then take a shower."

Did not need to know that. This room is too small to whip out ol' reliable without him hearing the buzzing.

Or the sound of his name on my lips when I come.

Finn checks his pockets for his wallet. "Is there anything specific you want for dinner?"

"I'm good with whatever. Not that hungry."

He twirls the keys around his finger. "Okay. Well, keep this door locked while I'm gone. Don't leave the room. Don't open the door for anyone other than me."

"Got a problem if I go out on the balcony?" I cringe and give him a small smile. "Sorry, that sounded bitchy. I guess I am a little hungry."

Finn laughs and gestures to the doors on the other side of the room. "Out there is safe but if you see anything weird, head back inside and lock the door. Okay?"

I nod and cross the room, unlocking the balcony door. "I think I'm going to be out here for a bit. It's a nice night."

"Good. Don't leave the room. I'll be back soon."

Finn's steady gaze watches me for a moment before he heads back out of our hotel room.

As soon as he's gone, I step out onto the balcony and shut the door behind me.

More than once today, I've thought that we should turn back. Especially when he asked about my father. Though I kept most of the details light, it is still more than I've opened up to anyone about the entire situation.

And then there is what happened last night and this morning.

I thought that we were making progress. We could open up a little to each other while still keeping our secrets guarded.

After three long years of fantasizing about his hands on my body, I finally got to experience it. And he's ruined me for other men. There is no way that I'm going to be able to sleep with another man and not think about Finn. Crave him.

But we shouldn't go there again. He's a Byrne boy. They're nothing but heartache and pain.

I know better than to give them my heart and trust them with it.

I slump into one of the egg chairs, kicking my feet up on the glass panel in front of me. No sooner do my eyes start to drift shut, than my phone screams, the shrill noise breaking the peace of the sunset.

"Hey." I lift the phone to my ear, reclining deeper into the chair. "I didn't think that I was going to be hearing from you this soon."

Zoe's soft laugh makes me homesick. "Well, I wanted to call and see if you changed your mind. It's not too late to come home and drop the entire situation with Dad."

As much as I miss home, her words are the reason why I'm here. She isn't willing to tell me whatever it is that she knows.

So, I have to go to Oregon.

"I don't want to drop it. I need to know what was going on with him. You can understand that, can't you?" I tap my feet on the glass panel, tapping out the beat of a song stuck in my head. "I need to do this, and I need your support."

"I do support you." Her voice cracks a little. "This is just hard. I don't want you to see the same side of him that I saw. You're going to get hurt, Aves. It's not worth it."

The familiar feeling of being in the dark creeps up on me. "Zoe, is there a reason that I shouldn't go digging deeper into this? Honestly, it feels like you're hiding something from me."

She clears her throat. "No. Everything is fine. He's just not a good man, and if I can spare you that heartbreak, I want to."

I've known my sister for her entire life. She is amazing at a lot of things, but she's never been a good liar.

I shift in my seat, holding the phone a little tighter. "I'm supposed to be the big sister here. I should be the one looking out for you."

A warm breeze toys with the ends of my hair. Down below, people head to and from the hotel. Cars whizz by on the street as the sun dips lower.

Zoe sighs. "Oh, Aves. You are the big sister. Dad just wasn't a good man. It's going to hurt you to find out things about him. I'm sure that he was hiding more than we ever knew about."

"I still feel like I have to do this. If I don't, then I'm going to spend the rest of my life wondering who he was and what he was hiding from us. I need closure."

"I hope you get it." Zoe sighs as a door closes in the background.

"What else are you doing with your evening?" I shift in my seat, pulling myself up straighter.

"I've got a new song to work on. Well, a new album, actually." Excitement fills her voice as her speaking speeds up. "I've been thinking about doing this tragic album. Something low and haunting that really cuts people to the core. But then I've got the other album to work on that's a little more upbeat. It's a lot."

Smiling, I get up and move to the edge of the balcony, leaning over the railing. "What I'm hearing is that you're going to work on both albums until you're practically falling asleep in that studio every night."

"Maybe."

Chuckling, I turn around and lean against the railing. "I'm so proud of you for chasing your dreams, Zoe. I can't wait to hear them both."

"And I'm proud of you for getting the hell out of this town. You were never meant to be stuck in Tennessee with Mom and Dad, Aves. As much as I've loved having you around since you came home from university, this isn't the place for you."

Her words have a slight pain racing through my chest.

Zoe is right. I never should have moved back to Tennessee when I left Virginia. I should've chased my dreams. I could've gone to be a nurse in any other part of the country.

But at the time, going back home seemed like the only thing I could do.

Hindsight is a wonderful fucking thing.

Although, if I hadn't gone back home, Zoe would have been alone for longer with our parents.

She would have gone through everything alone, and I would have blamed myself more than I already do.

It's a good thing I went home.

"I know it isn't. I feel like I can finally breathe, but there's still a blockade in the rest of my life. I need to know whatever I can find about Dad. Zoe, you're sure that there's not more you aren't telling me?"

Though I know I shouldn't keep pressing my sister, I'm sure that she's hiding from me.

We've spent most of our lives together. If she's avoiding the subject as much as she does, then there is something else going on.

"There's nothing else." Zoe's tone is sharp. "I support your need to know, but I don't want to talk about our father anymore. I know that you need to know the truth, but I want to forget all of that and move on with my life. Please respect that."

I clear my throat, trying to swallow the lump that threatens to choke me. "I'm sorry, I've got to go, Zoe. Love you."

I hang up before she can respond.

As I slip the phone into my back pocket, my eyes burn. My nails dig into my palms as I look up and try to keep the tears from falling.

The balcony door slides open and soft footsteps make their way to me.

For such a large man, Finn is quiet when he moves. Although, I suppose if killing people for a living was my job, I would want to be as silent as possible too.

What the hell am I doing here? This is a mistake. I never should've agreed to come out here and do this with him.

Finn says nothing as he sits on one of the chairs and stretches his long legs out in front of him. He runs his fingers through the damp strands of his hair. Those green eyes flicker over to me before darting away.

I glance down at the rose tattoo on the back of his hand. "Did that hurt?"

He lifts up his hand and flexes his fingers. "Not too much. It could have been worse. I hear the head is pretty bad."

"Right. I only have the two on the back of my arms, just above my elbows. Didn't hurt that much. Not a walk in the park either."

Finn swallows hard, his Adam's apple bobbing. "I know. I saw them the other night."

Warmth spreads through my body.

This is the closest we've come to discussing what happened.

I keep my mouth shut, hoping that he will say more.

Maybe he'll want to pretend that we're back at the other motel, sipping whiskey and making bad decisions.

Instead, Finn does what he does best and changes the subject.

"Why are you out here looking like you're on the verge

of tears?" He shifts in the seat, his legs spread. "We don't have to talk about it if you don't want to, though. I have food waiting inside."

"You infuriate me."

The corner of his mouth twitches. "Yeah. I suppose I do."

"I don't think I can eat right now."

His fingers tap against the dark wicker of his chair. "Then tell me why you're about to cry."

"It's nothing, really. I just had a hard phone call with my sister." My voice breaks a little as I stare at the streaks of orange lighting up the sky. "She's hiding something from me about our dad. I know she is, but I can't even begin to guess at what it could be."

"I don't want to sound like an ass, but have you considered that it's her business and not yours?"

His low rumbling tone is too close to the one I heard last night. My core clenches just thinking about him whispering words to me again as we get lost in each other.

Nothing but trouble, Ava. Keep it together. He'll only hurt you in the end.

"I don't see how." I cross one leg over the other, my foot bouncing. "He was my dad too. He wasn't perfect, but he was better than my mother. She's the real reason why I went to school in Virginia. I just needed to get away from that life."

"And then you met Declan." His tone is bitter. Finn's hands curl into fists as the muscle in his jaw twitches. "I'm sorry about that."

I bark out a sharp laugh. "Yeah. Me too. I had to pick between the lesser of two evils. It's why I went back home to Tennessee. I was barely moved back before you went into prison."

"The lesser of two evils?"

My lips fold together as I get up and stretch, faking a yawn before turning for the door and pulling it open. "It's been a long day. I think I'm going to go inside and get something to eat before I get to bed."

Fierce green eyes freeze me in place.

My heart pounds against my ribcage, threatening to break free.

Finn gets up and nods to the door, his hand brushing against the small of my back.

Bumps raise on my skin at the light touch.

I try not to think much of it as I head inside and sit down at the little dining table beside the kitchenette.

Finn sits opposite me, opening the bag and pulling out a couple different containers.

My stomach growls as he pushes the container of shakshuka over to me.

As I crack open the plastic lid, the scent of garlic and chili powder fills the room.

"I didn't think you knew I liked this." I take a spoon from the pile of utensils he dumps out.

As I spear a poached egg, he shrugs.

I huff. "I see that we're back to barely speaking to each other."

Finn cracks a small smile. "I don't want to get in between you and food. Could get my head bitten off."

"I do not bite heads off." I take the first bite of my food and dance in my seat. "This is amazing."

"A woman who does not bite heads off doesn't dance when she eats." The corners of his eyes crinkle. "The only times I ever used to see you angry back in Virginia is when you were hungry."

"I really don't want to talk about that time in our lives." I shove another spoonful of shakshuka into my mouth.

Finn nods, the table falling silent as we eat.

It's better this way. We should remember what and who we are to each other and leave it at that.

I finish my food as quick as I can. The second I'm done, I get up from the table and grab my pajamas.

Finn keeps eating as I head for the washroom to get ready for bed.

I wasn't lying when I told him it was a long day and I wanted to sleep.

But I wasn't telling the entire truth either.

There is no way that I can sit in a dark hotel room with him, watching a movie, and pretending that everything is the same between us. Not after the events of the last twenty-four hours.

When I finally head for bed, Finn is sitting on the bed closest to the balcony with a gun in his hand. Some old movie plays on the television, soft voices filling the otherwise silent room.

He glances over at me as I crawl beneath the covers, the gun still in his hand. "Good night, Ava."

As soon as the blanket is pulled up to my chin, his attention turns to the window.

A shiver works its way down my spine as his face becomes a blank mask.

Who the hell is he so worried about?

7

FINN

Ava's intake of breath is sharp as I park the car in front of our new house. She turns to me, her eyes as wide as saucers. "There is no way that this is our house. You have to be fucking with me."

No, but I'd like to fuck you again.

"It's our house." I get out of the car and head to the lockbox. As I punch in the code to retrieve the keys, Ava starts taking her bags out of the car.

I understand why she would think that the sleek black house wouldn't be ours. We had to drive through a gate to get here. Gates mean living in the lap of luxury, even if the house is smaller than all the others surrounding it.

Or, to a recently released convict, those gates mean some sick joke at the hands of his father.

"Those windows are massive." She raises her sunglasses to get a better look and brings the suitcases to the door. "And those red-toned woods with the black stone? It's like your father knew what my dream house was and brought it to life."

When I look at the house, I don't see the same thing she does. I can't.

All I see when I look at the house is my father's clutches wrapped around my neck. I'm a puppet, and he continues to pull the strings.

And there's nothing that I'm going to do about it. Nothing I *can* do.

At least, if this is her idea of a perfect home, she's not going to be miserable living here.

Maybe I could even convince Dad to let her buy the house when our arrangement is over.

"This is really your dream house?" I unlock the towering double doors and shove them open. "This is my nightmare. We're too close to other people. I wish that we were out in the woods. I don't want to be able to see my neighbors."

She gives an unladylike snort as I take the suitcases from her. "I'm not surprised by that at all. Assassin wants to live in the woods so nobody knows who his next target is going to be? Sounds very much up your alley."

"You make it sound awful."

She shrugs and leads the way into the house. "I don't know that I could spend my life isolated away from other people. A life in the woods could be nice, but not if it means never seeing anybody again."

I set our bags down in the massive entryway, taking in the gleaming white oak floors and cream walls. Black trim and doors accent the house, making it look like a place I would never live in.

It's too polished and airy. Especially after the cement floors and cinderblock walls. The bars over the windows and lack of sunlight.

This house is too uncomfortable. Too different from the

place I called home for the last three years. I never thought I would miss prison.

Ava wanders into the kitchen as I trail behind her. She runs her fingers along the butcher block countertops and opens several of the black cabinets. "Looks like this place is fully stocked with everything we could need. Not really my style, though. How long are we going to be here?"

"Until I finish the job." I glance around the kitchen, spying a little black dot in the top corner of the room.

That fucker.

I move through the rooms, dodging around suede couches and leather chairs. I pull paintings off the wall, looking behind them for more of the tiny cameras. Each room I tear apart has at least two.

Most of the rooms are covered in them.

Dad can see us from every angle. He can watch whatever he wants. There will be endless hours of footage to use against me if I don't take every single camera out of here.

In all the years that he's controlled my life, I don't know that I've felt more violated than I do right now.

As I make my way into the primary bedroom, I pull out my phone. My thumb stabs against the screen as I dial a number I hoped I could avoid.

The phone rings several times before it connects. The sound of soft breathing comes down the line, but the person on the other end says nothing.

Of course he wouldn't. Yet another fucking mind game from the book of psychotic fathers.

"Hello, Dad." I stand at the foot of the king-sized bed and stare across the room at the dresser. A mirror hangs above it, dried flowers draping along the top rim. "Are you enjoying the show?"

His bitter chuckle has the hair on the back of my neck

standing up. "I was. You look insane going around and checking for cameras."

"I wouldn't have to check for them if you didn't feel the need to spy on me." I cross the room and pull the flowers down. Another camera hides within their petals. "I will not be spied on."

"You will do as I say." I can only imagine the disapproving look on his face. "You have a history of not being trustworthy, Finnigan. You have yet to prove yourself to me. You've spent a lot of years locked away."

"You're spying on the wrong fucking son." I drop the tiny camera to the ground and crush it beneath my boot.

Dad scoffs. "You're the one who betrayed this family."

His words are a sharp knife driven through my heart. After all these years, the reminder of Cormac's death is as jagged edged as ever.

I shake my head and look around the room for more cameras. Another one is inside the closet, pointing straight at the racks. I find yet another in the ensuite bathroom.

There is no way these fuckers are going to see Ava naked.

Dad laughs as I rip the camera down. "Now, Finnigan, don't go getting so upset. You know that this is for your own good. How could you be trusted to get the job done when you've been away for three years? I have no clue what kind of things you might have picked up in that prison."

"I'm going to find all your fucking cameras, and they're coming down immediately. I will not be spied on. Not if you want me to get the job done."

I stab my finger against the red icon to end the call. My chest heaves, and my blood boils.

It's going to take hours to search for every hidden camera my father has. They're all going to come down today, though.

"Is everything alright?" Ava appears in the doorway with her hair piled into a messy bun. She holds our suitcases, the bag of weapons slung over her shoulder. "You sounded like you were on the edge of killing someone."

"Guess you heard about the cameras, then."

She sets the bags on the burgundy duvet and shrugs. "I never liked your father much."

The way she says it feels too casual—like she didn't just find out that we were being spied on in our own home.

Not our home. Our fake home. The fake place we live in while we get through this fake fucking engagement.

I comb my fingers through my hair. "That makes two of us."

"What now?" She unzips the first suitcase and pulls out piles of clothes. "Now that we've established we both don't like your father, what's the next step in the plan?"

"I'm going to find the rest of the cameras if you don't mind unpacking. There's only one bedroom here—the other is an office to keep up with the cover story."

"Which is what?"

I lean against the dresser, crossing one leg over the other at the ankle. "We're a young couple just starting out. I work from home as an accountant. You're planning on being a housewife."

Ava wrinkles her nose. "That doesn't sound like me at all."

"Yeah. Me neither. It is what it is. The sooner I can get this job over with and you have your answers, the sooner we can get back to our normal lives."

I push off the dresser and head for the door. "You can take the bedroom. I'll take the couch."

"Not going to happen." The stubborn set of her jaw makes it clear that she's not going down without a fight.

"I can take the couch. It looks comfy, and I'm small. You have muscles that turn you into a man the size of a house. Sleeping on a couch is only going to fuck up your back."

She brushes past me to the linen closet in the hallway. As she piles blankets and spare pillows into her arms, I roll my eyes.

I snatch the bedding from her. "Thank you for pulling out my sheets." I smirk and spin away from her, heading to the living room.

She follows me, her gaze boring into my back. "Finn, this is ridiculous. I can sleep on the couch and be perfectly fine. You take the bed. I take the couch. It's better this way anyway. The last thing we need is a repeat of the other night."

"Take the bedroom, Ava." I toss the bedding onto the couch and sit down on top of it. "This isn't a fight that you're going to win."

"Back pain. You are going to be in constant back pain from sleeping on a couch that is too small to accommodate you. Do you think that you are going to be able to fool anyone into doing whatever it is that you need to do if you're a cranky asshole?"

"Who says I'm going to be a cranky asshole?"

Those full lips twitch as she smothers a smile. "If you don't get a good night's sleep, you will be. I don't know what it is we need a cover story for, but people don't lie well when they're tired. Take the damn bed."

"Are you going to stop giving me a massive headache?" I get off the couch. "I need to take down the rest of the cameras and then go for a shower. I'll take the bed tonight, but this conversation is far from over."

She rolls her eyes and starts arranging the bedding on

the couch. "I'll finish unpacking once I'm done getting the couch ready."

I nod and take off to start rummaging through the house. I tear apart the rest of the house, digging out all the cameras I can find.

After the first sweep, I do another. I pull nearly a dozen more cameras out of their hiding places. I crush them all, the metal crunching beneath my foot.

By the time I'm done and have the house put back together, I'm exhausted. All I want is a hot shower and to sink onto the couch. Even though I told Ava that I would take the bed, I have no plan of sleeping there.

Yet, as I walk into the living room on the way to the bedroom, I find her already napping on the couch.

Her dark hair fans out on the pillow, and her dark eyelashes dust her high cheekbones.

There is no fucking way that I'm going to survive being engaged to her.

Especially not when those tiny silk shorts creep up her long legs, showcasing the curve of her ass.

Cold shower it is.

A few minutes later, the spray of water is cascading down my chest. All I can think about is the way her body felt against mine the other night.

I groan and brace one arm against the black tiles, one hand gripping my cock.

With a moan, I slide my hand up and down my hardened length. As I brush my thumb over the head, I picture her mouth wrapping around me.

Her lips would slide up and down my length, her tongue flicking over the tip.

She'd graze her teeth along the underside before soothing away the sting with her tongue.

My hand would sink into her hair, guiding her faster.

I'd press my cock to the back of her throat, watching her eyes water.

My groans fill the steamy bathroom as I grip my cock tighter.

As the memory of Ava's moans echo through my mind, my hips rock.

I fuck my fist to the thought of her on her knees for me.

She'd wrap her small hand around my cock. Her touch would be soft as she coated me with spit.

Ava would work her hand and mouth up and down my length, teasing me closer to the edge.

I'd pull her hair harder, my hips rocking as she sucked.

Her soft moans would urge me on, encouraging me to take everything she was willing to give.

My hips would move faster as her big doe eyes would stare up at me.

She's the kind of woman who is eager to please.

I could have her begging for more of my cock.

In the end, I would happily give it to her too.

I'd pull out and tease her. Guide her to her feet with my grip on her hair.

Her breasts would be heavy in my hands, her nipples stiff.

I'd taste those rosy buds, teasing them with my teeth and tongue before telling her to get back on her knees for me.

Her nails would rake down my skin, taunting me and teasing me.

Ava would hollow her cheeks before swallowing every last drop of come I gave her.

My breath hitches, and my cock throbs.

I move my hand faster, twisting it.

I come hard and fast to the thought of the devilish look she would give me as she licked my cock clean.

As the water washes away the evidence of crossing yet another line where Ava is concerned, I hang my head.

Fuck. I've never been more fucked.

8

AVA

The house is quiet during my first morning in Oregon. Though it's a nice house in a stunning neighborhood, it's small. It's the kind of house that a wealthy young couple would buy when they are just starting out.

Finn is nowhere to be found, but it's better that way.

After overhearing him moan my name in the shower last night, I don't know what to think.

He thought I was asleep. He never would have jerked himself off if he knew I was awake.

I run my hand through my hair, glancing at the coffee machine. I'm craving a cup, but I need to start figuring out who Dad was.

He used to talk about Clover Café.

It should be near here.

I can go get a coffee and see if anyone there knows him. Sitting in one of his favorite places might make me feel a little closer to him. Though, I'm not sure if that's a good thing.

I grab my set of keys and slide on my sneakers before heading out the door.

The sun shines bright overhead, warming my skin as I lock the door. My car still sits in the driveway, covered in dirt and bug guts.

I'm going to have to clean that up, eventually, but today is not that day.

People stand in their driveways, watching the people they pay to manicure their lawns.

I shake my head, tucking my hands in the pocket of my jeans.

If I ever get to the point where I stand in my yard and watch somebody else do the work, then I'm going to request to be put out of my misery.

Even though I grew up with money, I still remember Dad in the yard every Saturday morning, mowing the lawn as his security team trailed behind him.

The café is only a short walk from the gates of the community. Its bright orange walls light up the block. A mural of a woman sipping a cup of coffee decorates one of the exterior walls.

I walk through the dark green doors and inhale the scent of lattes and sugar.

"It's amazing in here, isn't it?" A woman in a long, lilac skirt stops in front of me with a wide grin. "You must be new around here. I know all the regulars."

"Yeah. I'm Ava. Just moved here yesterday with my fiancé."

The words feel strange to say out loud, but I'm going to have to get used to them sooner or later.

"I'm Brooklyn. My aunt owns this place." She grins and wanders to the counter. "I run it for her on the weekends. If you're going to try one thing over anything else, I recommend the lemon and white chocolate scones."

"One of those, then." I follow her to the counter and pull out my phone. "And a large latte."

She rounds the counter and punches in the order.

After tapping my phone against the debit machine, I step to the side and try to see the café through my father's eyes.

It's a small little place and almost empty. There is another mural of a family sharing a scone on one wall. The muted colors swirl together, making the building feel warm and cozy.

"Like the mural?" Brooklyn slides the latte across the counter with a scone on a plate.

"It's stunning. The one outside is really good too."

Brooklyn beams and waves the other barista over. "Carla, take care of the counter. I'm going to sit down with my new best friend who loves my murals."

I laugh and take my breakfast over to an empty table. "You do amazing work."

"Thank you. My aunt likes to get them changed every couple years. When I'm not here or painting for her, I have a gallery downtown." Brooklyn drops into one of the chairs across from me. "So, why'd you move to Portland?"

I break off a piece of the scone and take a bite.

Me and Finn haven't gone over that part of our story yet. "My dad is from here. He died recently, and I want to spend more time figuring out who he was when he lived here. He used to come to this café all the time."

"I might know him, then. What was his name?" Brooklyn's smile is warm and comforting as she leans forward.

"Jeremiah Redford."

Her smile only grows wider as she bounces in her seat. "He was my dad's best friend! He used to come out here every couple years to spend some time with Dad, although, I'm sure that you already knew that."

"I didn't." My chest constricts slightly as I sip the latte. "There is a lot that Dad didn't really tell us. I don't even know where his parents live or if they're still alive."

Brooklyn reaches into her pocket, pulling out a piece of charcoal and a slip of paper. Black dust covers her fingertips as she writes out an address.

"This is where your grandparents used to live. I'm not sure if they're still alive, though. I wish that I could be of more help." She passes me the address, black smudges all over the paper. "You're going to have to keep in contact with me. I love a good mystery."

I laugh and fold the paper before sliding it into my pocket. "Thank you. This is more than I thought that I would get when I came here."

The bell above the door chimes, and Brooklyn stands, ready to tend to another customer.

She gives me a bright smile before heading back to the counter to help Carla. The pair of them work in unison as people start to stream into the café.

I finish off my breakfast, savoring the last few moments of peace I have before I tear my life apart at the seams.

My grandparents' house is small and set back from the road. Trees tower high over it. Gravel crunches beneath my tires as I make my way up the driveway.

Sweat beads on my palms as I pull up behind the car already at the top of the driveway.

This is a bad idea.

I should have found a way to call them before showing

up. I should have figured out how to get in contact with them and then I should have spoken to them.

I'm about to throw the car into reverse when a black lab trots around the corner of the house with a dopey doggy smile on its face.

A woman who looks just like my father follows the dog, her narrowed gaze landing on the car.

I guess there's no going back now.

I park the car and turn it off.

When I get out, the woman's jaw drops.

Her eyes are glassy as she walks toward me, the gardening tools dropping from her hands.

"Ava?"

My chest tightens as I stay close to the car, ready to escape if I need to. "Yes."

Her bottom lip quivers as the dog trots over to me. A big block head collides with my leg, sending me stumbling back into the car.

The woman laughs and shakes her head.

"Sorry about Lola, she's a gentle giant, and I don't think she's ever met a person that she didn't like." The woman holds a shaking hand to her mouth. "I'm sorry. I'm Courtney. I didn't think that I would ever get to meet you. Jeremiah always wanted the family to stay away from you and your sister. He used to come back here every now and then, though. He told us about you two."

My stomach twists itself into a tight knot. "He never said anything about you."

She swipes away a tear that tracks down her cheek. "That doesn't surprise me. He always thought that I was trying to stand in his way. I'm his younger sister."

My aunt. I have an aunt.

An aunt that I knew nothing about. One that I never heard Dad speak of.

For the entire twenty-seven years of my life, I've thought that my dad was an only child.

"Are my grandparents here?" My voice wavers as I reach down and rub Lola's fluffy head.

Her pink tongue lolls to the side as she looks up at me with big brown eyes.

Courtney gives me a sad smile as she shakes her head. "No. They died nearly a decade ago. It's just me now."

"You know that Dad died?"

She nods and gestures toward the house. "I know this is a lot. Why don't you come in and we talk?"

My legs feel numb as I follow her into the little stone house, but my mind is spinning. Even something so simple about my dad's life was hidden from me.

It's only my first full day in Oregon, and I'm already starting to question everything I know.

Everything I *thought* I knew.

Courtney leads the way through a small living room and into a slightly bigger kitchen. She takes a seat at the table and nods to the other seat.

As soon as I'm sitting, Lola puts her big head in my lap, her tail slapping against the white cabinets.

I run my hand along the dog's head, using it as something to distract myself from spiraling too far.

Courtney leans forward and clasps her hands together. "What do you want to know?"

Pictures of my dad when he was younger stare back at me from the walls.

A lump in my throat threatens to choke me. I keep running my hands along Lola's silky fur, trying to figure out what I want to know first.

There are so many different places we could begin.

I force down the lump. "What was he like as a child?"

"Difficult." A soft smile creases the lines on her face. As she speaks, her gaze is a million miles away, lost to a different time. "He was never an easy child. I used to think that maybe one day my parents would finally be done with his antics."

"He was that bad?"

"Jeremiah was in trouble a lot. He hung around with a bad crowd, and everyone knew they were only going to cause trouble. Especially in high school. There were times when I was sure that he was going to die at seventeen. Everyone was surprised when he decided to become a politician."

Lola licks my hand when I pause in her pets.

Despite the turmoil raging a war inside me, I smile. If nothing else, Lola is at least helping calm my nerves.

Maybe I should go home tonight and try to convince Finn that we need a dog.

He would never go for it, but once our arrangement is over, I'm going to get myself a dog.

I need something to share my life with. Love. A man is only going to disappoint me.

All the men in my life have so far. But a dog's love is unconditional. And I have so much love to give back.

I glance at the pictures of my dad as a teenager, scowling at the camera. "How bad were these people that he was hanging out with?"

"I'm amazed that he made it out of Portland without getting arrested." Courtney's voice is strained as she takes a peek at the picture. "He was sixteen in that one. Told Mom that he was going to leave Oregon and never come back.

Insisted that the rules weren't for him and that he was going to be out the door the moment he turned eighteen."

"And then he went on to become a politician?" I scoff. The dad I knew loved rules. He was rigid in them most of the time.

He was also a loving father who never would've sold his youngest daughter to sex traffickers.

"Yeah. He graduated high school. Spent the summer smoking pot and waiting for his birthday. He came home one day, said that he was going to be a politician, and then took off. He never was able to stay out of trouble, though. He just did a better job of hiding it."

"What do you mean?"

Courtney shifts in her seat, her gaze flitting around the room. "I can't talk about that. Not right now. It's difficult, and there are a lot of other people involved. I don't want to get on the wrong side of those people."

"That's it, then?"

Lola nudges her wet nose against my hand.

I can't hide the disappointment in my voice. "That's all that you can tell me about Dad?"

"Right now. That's all that I can tell you right now." Courtney reaches out to take my hand. "I promise that there is more I will tell you, but I need some time to figure out how. Seeing you here was unexpected."

"I understand."

The clock in the corner of the room chimes at the top of the hour.

I sigh. "I have to get going. Can I have your number? Maybe see you again?"

"Absolutely." She smiles, pulling her phone out, and hands it to me.

I send myself a quick message before passing it back to her. "Thank you."

Courtney stands with me, walking me to the door. When she gives me a quick hug, her floral perfume wraps around me.

Tears gather in my eyes as I hold her tight.

I don't know why Dad kept his family from us growing up, but I'm going to find out.

When I get home later that evening, Finn is sitting at the kitchen island. Papers spread out in front of him, barely legible writing making my vision blur.

I head to the fridge and pull out a bottle of white wine.

He raises an eyebrow as I pull out a stemless glass and pour myself a healthy serving.

The bottle trembles slightly in my hand before I set it back down.

Finn's look is fleeting before he skims through the papers again. "How was your day?" His voice is low and robotic.

Yet another reminder that his only going through the motions with me.

It's the same way that his brother used to ask me about my day. The tone makes it obvious that though he is asking, he doesn't care.

"It was fine. Met an aunt I didn't know I had." I finish the glass of wine and pour another. "Found out that my grandparents are dead."

Finn hums and grabs a paper from the other side of the counter. "That's interesting."

I can tell he isn't paying any attention. He doesn't care.

And I shouldn't care that he doesn't. But I do. And it hurts.

Getting involved with Finn was a bad idea, but I need him. We agreed to stay together until we both have what we need.

And there's the added issue that needing him comes with the risk of getting involved with Declan again. Or maybe a carbon copy of him that's been hiding all this time.

Would Finn be able to hide his real personality for years in prison?

Do I know the person sitting across from me at all?

He was sweet when we were younger. Cold—like his dad and brother—but the sweet moments were there.

Now, his disinterest is blatant.

I take another sip of my wine. "How was your day? You were gone before I woke up."

He blows out a long breath. "Yeah. I needed to get an early start. I've got a lot going on."

"Like what?"

Finn glances at me, his head still dipped down over the papers. "Nothing that important. Just part of the shit I need to get done while we're here."

He doesn't say anything else, and I don't ask. He's tight-lipped and I have no desire to change that.

Instead, I take my bottle of wine and the glass and go sit in the backyard. Watching the stars sparkle against the night sky is better than trying to force a relationship of any kind with Finn.

The more distance we keep between us through the course of this fake engagement, the better.

9

FINN

I'm going to fuck this up royally.

Nobody is going to believe that we're engaged if I keep avoiding her.

Except that's all I've done since we got to Oregon three days ago. It's all that I can keep doing.

If Ava gets too close to me, then she's closer to the danger.

I promised that I was going to do everything I could to keep her out of it, and I intend to keep my word.

Ava glances up as I walk into the bedroom. Her legs are stretched out in front of her. The tiny shorts she always wears to bed are climbing up the legs I want draped over my shoulders.

A silky crop top shows off a sliver of her stomach.

My mouth waters at the thought of licking that peeking skin until she's begging me for more.

Now is not the time to get a fucking boner. I have shit to do.

Clearing my throat, I cross the room and yank open the

closet. The scent of laundry detergent and her perfume is a punch in the face.

Although, it's the perfume and the thought of her beneath me that sends all my blood rushing to my cock.

She sets the book she's reading to the side. "Going out?"

I pull my leather jacket out of the closet and shrug it on. "Yeah. I have some business I need to take care of tonight."

"Oh."

After three days of watching Cillian O'Reilly and his mob, I finally have a plan in place to intersect with him.

That plan took more time that I would like to put in place, but once it's all over, I should have my in with the O'Reilly mob.

And then I can begin their destruction.

Ava picks up her book again. Tendrils of her hair fall from her bun and into her face as she tilts her head forward to read.

Fuck going out tonight. I should get into bed with her and never leave.

Which is exactly why I turn around and stride out of the room.

I don't need another cold shower before I go.

Although, as I head to the front door, the urge to turn around and go back to the bedroom it's almost impossible to resist. I force myself to keep moving, engaging the security system before heading outside to meet the taxi.

The drive to the club is short and silent.

I run over the plan several times in my mind before the taxi comes to a stop.

After tossing a large tip over the seat, I get out and head for the front of the line.

The people behind me complain and mumble to themselves.

The bouncer nods to me as I pull out a hundred dollars and hand it to him.

The second the blue velvet rope is out of the way, I head inside.

Pounding bass shakes the floor, the speakers pulsing with the music. Bright strobe lights swirl around the room. Sweaty bodies shine beneath the lights as they writhe together.

The VIP lounge is on the other side of the club.

Cillian O'Reilly and several of his men are sitting at a table.

Women wrap themselves around the younger men, whispering in ears and kissing cheeks. Roaming hands and short dresses make this the last place I want to be in.

I would much rather be at home, on the couch and watching a movie with Ava.

My night would be a thousand times better, but it's not going to happen.

I'm here to do a job, and I need to remind myself Ava is just another piece to the massive puzzle.

As I weave through the writhing bodies, men in black clothing move around the edges of the room.

They get closer to Cillian's table, avoiding the looks of the men around him.

Although, none of his men seem interested in anything other than the women in their laps.

Even at the safe distance I keep, their bloodshot eyes are visible. Though I knew they would be drinking, I didn't think that they would be too drunk to protect their leader.

As one man stands and stumbles, the men in black surge forward.

Women scream and run away from the table as I push through the crowd.

The men wearing black slit the throats of two of Cillian's guards.

I leap over the frosted glass railing that separates the VIP lounge from the rest of the club.

One of the men holds a knife to Cillian's throat while other men pull guns.

I blend in with the people running away from the scene as I make my way to the shadowy areas of the club.

Though the men I hired know what is about to happen, none of them flinch. They hold their positions as planned while I sneak up behind the man with a knife to Cillian's neck.

The man shouts as I grab him by the hair and the wrist, snapping the bones.

The knife drops to the ground.

Shouts continue as I haul the man away by his hair and slam his face into one of the glass tables.

Blood pours from the man's face as I drop him and lunge for another.

Guns lower as I knock one man unconscious.

Blood gushes from a cut on my hand as I slam my fist into the final man's face.

The man drops to the ground.

Cillian's guards grab the three men, dragging them into one of the back rooms.

Cillian stands from the leather couch and nods to me. "Thank you for that. I need to have a long discussion with my men."

Cillian cracks his knuckles, making it clear that it is going to be more than a discussion.

I wrap the hem of my shirt around my bloody knuckles. "Saw them when I came in. They've been hovering around the edges of the club."

"What's your name? Where did you learn to fight like that?" Cillian's thick eyebrows pull together as he crosses his arms over his chest. "You didn't flinch when it came to stepping between me and those men."

"Finn. Took mixed martial arts for years. Thought about making it my career at one point. Then the marines seemed like a better option."

Though I did study mixed martial arts for years, the rest of the story is a lie. Part of the last three days has been trying to come up with a believable cover story.

The marines is as close as I'm going to get to believable.

Interest shines in his eyes as he looks me up and down. "And now what are you doing with your life?"

"Accounting. Me and my fiancée moved to Portland recently. I was looking for a change of pace, and I've always been pretty good with numbers."

Cillian gestures to the couch beside him. "Sit. Talk with me for a few moments."

Staff weaves around us, not saying a word as they clean up the broken glass and spilled drinks. None of them acknowledge the blood as they put the VIP lounge back together.

It's the kind of silence that the mob demands when they own a club.

I take a towel one of the waitresses holds out, replacing my shirt with it as I sit. "What else is there to talk about?"

"Why Portland?" Cillian leans back, his arms still crossed. "It's a nice city, but you don't exactly seem like the kind of man who wants to live in the middle of a city."

"You're right about that." I chuckle and dab at the blood. "My fiancée's family is from here. She thought that it would be a nice place to live. After the trouble I got myself into, there was no real arguing with her about it."

Cillian laughs, the tension in his shoulders fading. "I know that life all too well. What kind of trouble did you get yourself into?"

"Nothing too bad, but nothing great either." I shrug, the corner of my mouth curling up. "Just the kind of trouble where you piss off the wrong people with some powerful connections."

"So, you ran."

"No. I did what I could to smooth things over, and once I was given the okay, I whisked my fiancée away from all that. Except, it seems like there are still some problems following me. Nothing that getting another job won't fix."

Cillian rubs his hand along his jaw.

His dark eyes pierce through me, but I don't flinch. I'm confident in my cover story.

"Tell you what." Cillian stands and tilts his head to the door. "Come with me, and we can talk about your real skills. I get the feeling that there is a lot you aren't saying and with good reason."

Cillian leads the way through the VIP lounge and to a door hidden in the back. A set of stairs lined with soft white lights sits in front of me.

Cillian climbs the stairs as I trail behind him.

The office we step into a few moments later is small but built for whatever conversation he wants to have.

There are no cameras and only a few pieces of furniture.

He locks the door behind us. "What is it that you were really doing for work before you came here?"

I perch on the edge of the desk. "I was an assassin."

Cillian looks like he's won the lottery. "Were you? I have no knowledge of you."

The corner of my mouth twitches. "Isn't that the point? What kind of assassin would I be if everyone knew me?"

Cillian tucks his hands in his pockets, his head bobbing. "Alright, Finn. You say that you need a job. Which means that you are no longer employed as an assassin. That would lead me to believe that the story you just fed me about your problems is likely bullshit."

The way he blocks the door has my palms sweating.

I avoid wiping them on my jeans. The last thing I need to do is give him reason to be suspicious of me.

I tap my foot against the floor, keeping time with the dull beat of the music.

It can barely be heard through the office door, but it's still there.

The room isn't entirely soundproofed, even though it is hidden away from the rest of the club.

"It was mostly bullshit. Can you blame me, though? I'm not going to announce to an entire club that I used to illegally kill people for a living."

Cillian smirks. "Hence the marines. Was that part true?"

"Yes." I push off the desk and stand up taller. "I had a job to do, and I got it done. However, there were a lot of people involved who didn't take too kindly to that. I had to leave Nevada because there were people coming after me. I love my fiancée. I'm not about to get her killed because I pissed people off."

"Admirable." Cillian's mouth presses into a thin line. "But that will be the first and the last time that you get away with lying to me. I will not tolerate it if you are to be employed by me."

"You're going to give me a job?"

It should be harder than this. Though, if he is offering me a job, I'm going to have to prove myself to him.

I'm in this for the long haul.

This job is going to take a long time, and I knew that when planning the move to Oregon.

Taking down Cillian O'Reilly is my only priority.

That and keeping Ava safe. No matter what I get involved with here, I have to keep Ava safe.

Cillian nods and wanders over to the desk, hitting a button to the right of the computer.

A low buzz sounds through the room as the door unlocks.

Another man walks in, keeping to the corner.

"I have a few people I need taken care of." Cillian opens a drawer in the desk and pulls out a folder. "This is for the first man. Dawson here is going to show you the ropes."

The man in the corner of the room nods. He stands a little shorter than me, but he looks like someone I might have a hard time killing which doesn't happen often.

I'm going to have to keep my eyes on him.

I step forward and take the envelope. "You're serious about this? You're really giving me a job?"

"I am." Cillian sits down behind the desk and stretches his legs out in front of him. "You do the work, and I'll pay you. You'll have the protection offered to all my employees."

"Thank you." I force a smile that stretches from one side of my face to the other. "I'm not going to disappoint you."

Cillian waves a hand to the door. "You better not, Finn. Your job starts tonight. Do not fail me."

10

AVA

Even though it's almost two in the morning, I can't sleep.

A tingle crawls down my spine as I throw the covers off the couch and head into the kitchen. Yet another glass of water isn't going to fix my sleepless night, but at least it gives me something to do with my hands.

Finn left several hours ago, and he still hasn't come back.

I can't shake the feeling that something bad is happening to him. Though, I wouldn't know.

Finn is making it clear that we're nothing to each other beyond two people who happen to live in the same house.

Which is what I should want, right? All I need are his contacts, not him. Not his body on mine.

The front door chimes as I pour myself the glass of water.

The icy drink is a shock to the system, but it's not nearly as shocking as the man covered in blood.

My scream echoes through the room as the glass drops

to the ground. It shatters, broken glass and water going everywhere.

"Don't move, Ava. You'll cut up your feet." Finn's voice comes from within the blood-covered person, but in the dim light, it doesn't look like him.

"What the... Finn?" My voice cracks as I take a step back.

Finn lets out a low growl as he flicks on the light in the front hall and locks the door behind him. "I told you to stay still, Ava. You're going to cut yourself."

Finn takes off his shoes and socks before stripping down to his black boxers in the entryway, leaving his bloody clothes in a pile.

"Is that... Are you hurt?" My heart races, my brain stuck in fight or flight mode, unable to process anything.

So much blood.

I'm going to be sick. This is so much more than I signed up for.

With another step back, something sharp jabs me in the foot, a zing running up my leg.

I yelp and grab onto my foot, looking down at it.

Blood. I'm bleeding.

I hop up onto the edge of the counter, lifting my bleeding foot into my lap.

The dim light reflects on the shard that has embedded itself deep into my skin and is now sticking out of my heel.

Shit.

Finn's bloody state is momentarily forgotten as I pinch the piece of glass and pull it out. I wince.

"Shit, that hurt."

He takes a step in my direction.

"Wait! You'll hurt yourself further."

He huffs but stops. "I need to see if you're okay."

"Just give me a second, no need for both of us to get cut."

I need to stop the bleeding to make sure the glass is all out, so I grab a wad of paper towel from the roll and hold it against my foot, that's bleeding even more now. I gasp at the sting.

"Damn it, Ava. Please say something. Is it bad?" He's pacing back and forth but not coming any closer to where the broken glass is littering the floor. Good.

"Don't worry about me. Tell me why you're standing here looking like you're straight out of a fucking horror movie?" My voice rises as I gesture my free hand at him. "Is that your blood? Are you hurt? Where the hell were you?"

"Ava, you need to calm the fuck down. It's been a long night already, so fighting you is the last thing I need right now."

"Calm down? Look at you! You're a walking crime scene." With a sharp inhale, I pull away the paper towel and stick my foot in the sink letting the water run over the gash. "What happened?"

"That's my business."

"You're wrong. It's *my* business too. I can't tell if that's your blood or not. If it's someone else's, then you're putting us both in danger. I said that I would help you, Finn, but I'm not going to fucking jail for you."

The cool water runs pink until all the blood is washed from my skin. I grab a clean towel and wrap it around my foot. Some blood is still trickling out, but not much anymore.

I crawl to the other side of the counter and check for glass before hopping down.

He pulls a plastic bag out of the front closet and stuffs

the clothes inside. "It's mostly not my blood and I've got this."

"Mostly? That means some of it is yours? Where are you hurt?" My eyes scan his body, but the blood in the clothes has seeped inside, and he is covered in it.

"Doesn't matter, it's not that bad. Is your foot better?"

I sigh and pinch the bridge of my nose. "Yes, now, go to the washroom. I'll grab my medical kit and help you patch up."

Finn stares at me for a moment before heading down the hall.

I leave the glass and water on the floor for now. It doesn't matter.

Not when I need to know what the hell I've gotten myself into.

"I won't tell you what happened. It is better if you don't know, for both our sakes." Finn perches himself on the edge of the tub as I follow him into the washroom, careful to stay out of my injured heel.

I pull out the medical kit from beneath the sink and put it on the counter before pointing at the tub. "Get in. You need to wash some of the blood off so I can see what's going on."

He swings his legs to the side, a soft groan coming from deep in his chest.

And my heart speeds. How bad is he hurt?

Finn leans back against the sloped edge of the white tub as I pull the sprayer off the hook. His eyes close, and his head tilts back.

I adjust the water until it's warm before waving the soft spray along his body.

The water is red with the blood as it circles the drain.

My chest constricts as cuts appear on his chest, rivulets of blood running from them.

"Still don't want to tell me what the hell you were doing out there?" I turn off the water once it runs clear.

Finn pulls himself out of the tub and sits on the edge. "Like I said, it's better if you don't know."

I grab a bottle of antiseptic and some cotton rounds. "I know what you did for a living, Finn. I spent enough time around your family. I'm not asking for the details. I'm just asking you to confirm what I already know."

"You know I would never hurt you, right?" His voice is chocked.

He hisses as I press an antiseptic-soaked round against one of the cuts.

Silence stretches between us as I grab another round and keep dabbing at the cuts.

Finn grabs my hand. "You know that I would never hurt you, don't you, Aves?"

A lump in my throat makes it impossible to form words. I shrug a shoulder and reach for more antiseptic.

Finn lets out a strangled noise, burying his face in his hands.

"When you were in prison, you said that you didn't want to be this person anymore." My voice is soft, but the words are urgent. "You said that you were tired of being your father's pawn but look at where you are."

I can't meet his burning gaze as I motion for him to turn around.

He doesn't, still staring at me. He clears his throat as I reach for another cotton round.

"I also told you that I like the power."

When I don't answer, he takes the pack of cotton rounds and throws them across the room. "Fuck's sake, Ava, talk to me. You're the one who wanted to talk, so we're going to talk."

"Alright." I move away from him, needing the distance to keep a clear head. "What the fuck happened to the man that I've known all these years?"

Finn chuckles and shakes his head, strands of his wet hair falling into his eyes. "You think you knew me? Ava, when are you going to realize that you knew nothing about me?"

"Oh, so you weren't the man who used to bring me half of his snack cake because he knew I didn't eat in the middle of the workday? Not once when you came to clean the infirmary did you ever entertain me on the hard days? Or what about that guard you almost punched because he kept calling me sweet tits? You think I don't know that an inmate *did* attack him later? And I'm not even going back to when we saw each other before..."

Finn smirks and shrugs a shoulder. "That was more than worth the time in the hole I got for it."

I point a finger in his direction. "I knew it was you. You might pretend to be a giant asshole like your brother, and maybe you are, but you never have been when it came to me. So, who the hell are you right now?"

Finn gets up, stalking toward me.

My gaze rakes down his toned body, pussy clenching as water droplets roll down his chest.

Soaked boxers cling to his frame, outlining his hardening cock.

His steps are slow and intentional.

I take a step back for every one he takes forward until I'm pressed against the counter.

The sharp edge of the stone digs into my back as he stops inches from me.

Finn's head dips, taking my earlobe between his teeth in a quick nip. "Who do you want me to be?"

I put my hands on his chest, his skin warm beneath my touch. "Not a man who comes home in the middle of the night covered in blood. I know it's part of your job, but the least you could do is give a woman a warning instead of a heart attack."

He gives me that boyish grin that sends my heart racing a mile a minute. "Would you settle for an orgasm?"

Despite my irritation, I can't stop the smile that creeps over my face. "You're not funny."

"You have to find something to laugh at in this life, Ava. If you don't, you're going to go insane." He traces his fingers along the curve of my hip, leaning in closer. "I was serious about that orgasm, though."

"We're not supposed to go there with each other."

Finn presses his body against mine, his cock pressing into me. "Fuck that. I want you, Ava, and I know you want me too."

One minute, there is air between us, and the next, all the oxygen is sucked from the room.

His lips slide over mine as his hands roam up my body.

His fingers sink into my hair.

The bite of his teeth against my lip has my pussy aching.

I moan into the kiss, my lips parting.

His tongue plunges into my mouth, tangling with mine.

Finn grinds his cock into me as fire surges through my body.

His fingers hook into my waistband.

He pulls the shorts down my body, my pussy wet as he kneels on the ground. His tongue traces a pattern on my inner thigh.

When his lips brush against my clit, my back arches.

He groans, his gaze connecting with mine. "You taste so fucking sweet."

"Don't be a tease."

He sucks on my clit before blowing a cold breath across it.

A shiver rolls down my spine as I sink my fingers into his hair.

I pull him back to my pussy while Finn chuckles, arching one eyebrow.

When I roll my hips closer to him, he pushes my legs apart with his broad shoulders.

He teases my clit, his tongue doing lazy circles while he slips two fingers into me.

My pussy clenches around him as he presses deeper into me.

"Yes." I arch my back more, my pussy pulsating around him. "Just like that."

Finn's fingers thrust faster, rocking against my inner walls.

Tension builds in the base of my spine as he grazes my clit with his teeth.

When he pulls back to look up at me, he crooks his fingers.

My wetness coats his hand as I come hard and fast.

He groans, delight in his eyes as he leans forward and keeps teasing me with his tongue.

My hips rock faster as my legs shake.

Finn sits back on his heels.

His tongue flicks against his bottom lip as his gaze drops to my dripping pussy. "Fuck, I need to be buried inside you."

Heat floods through me, my mind spinning as I pull my shirt over my head and toss it to the side.

His cock springs free as he drops his boxers. "So eager to have me fuck you. I knew you wanted me. How many times have you fucked yourself to the thought of me, Aves?"

I can't lie. Not now. "Too many."

Lust burns hot in his eyes at my admission.

He closes the distance between us, capturing my lips in a fevered kiss.

Finn cups my breasts, brushing his thumbs against my nipples. He teases them until they're stiff and aching.

I press my breasts harder against his hands as the head of his cock brushes against my wet clit.

My breath comes in short bursts. "You're being a tease again."

"There's pleasure in denying yourself something you desperately want, Aves." He pinches my nipples, sending shockwaves through my body.

"There's more pleasure in taking your cock and fucking me with it until I don't know my own name."

He barks out a short laugh, wrapping my hair around his hand.

Finn yanks my head back, forcing me to look up at him.

The tip of his cock presses against my pussy.

He slides himself through my wet folds before entering me in one quick thrust.

His cock stretches me as he rolls his hips and presses himself deeper.

I moan as I hold onto his forearm, my nails digging into his skin.

Finn's muscles flex as he pulls out before slamming into me again.

His grip on my hair keeps my back arched while his other hand falls to my hip.

The imprint of his fingertips is going to still be there in the morning.

The thought of his mark on my body only turns me on more. I'm soaked as he thrusts harder and faster, his cock throbbing.

My pussy pulses around him as he lets go of my hair.

Finn's head drops to my neck, nipping and kissing at the sensitive flesh.

His teeth graze my earlobe. "Come on my cock."

I lock my legs around his waist, rocking my hips in time with his.

He thrusts deeper into me, his cock stiffening.

Finn stops thrusting, leaning against me as he comes.

His orgasm fills me, sending a shudder through my body as I come.

Our movements are lazy, the thrusts slow as we ride out the high.

When my body finally stops shaking, Finn picks me up, letting out a soft hiss.

I try to wriggle away from him. "Put me down. You're going to hurt yourself more."

He smirks and takes me into the bedroom, tossing me onto the bed. "Aves, I've never felt better. Now, shut up and let me get another taste of you."

Against my better judgment, I lean back against the pillow as he crawls up the bed and buries his head between my legs.

I should walk away, but I don't because he's right.

I want him just as much as he wants me.

I just hope I can keep my heart out of this.

11
———

FINN

As I stand in the driveway and look at my home, I consider turning around and going back out for a few more hours.

Ava is going to be buried in whatever paperwork she's managed to get her hands on this time. She's going to be a shell of a human, and I'm not looking forward to it.

For the past week, she's been single-minded in her pursuit of her father's secret life. Almost obsessive. More often than not, she'll be studying whatever she can find from the time she wakes up until the time she goes to bed.

It's not healthy.

But I can't just stand out here. If she looks out the window, then she'll see me and wonder if I'm losing it.

With a sigh, I continue up the driveway to the front door.

The muffled whisper of voices greets me as soon as I enter the house.

I kick off my shoes and glance at Ava and Brooklyn.

They kneel around the coffee table, their heads bent together as they look at the paperwork in front of them.

Ava stabs one finger into the middle of a paper.

Brooklyn takes it from her, a thin line appearing between her eyebrows.

"You're home early." Ava doesn't bother to look up. Instead, she rummages deeper into the pile in front of her.

I tuck my hands in my pockets and wander over to them. "Yeah. Cillian didn't have more work for me today, so I came home. Might have to run back out tonight if Dawson finds something."

She hums and nods, her attention still elsewhere. "I was thinking of lasagna for dinner."

Brooklyn puts the paper back in the pile and looks up. "Hey, Finn. Long time no see. I think maybe twenty-four hours?"

"Something like that." I perch myself on one of the armchairs. "What's going on in here? I thought the two of you were thinking about taking a break today? Coming back to everything with fresh eyes later?"

Ava waves a dismissive hand. "There's no need to worry about that. I found some other things to look at while we're taking a break from Dad's childhood. Did you know that he had arrest records? *I* didn't know that. They were sealed. I can't get much information out of them. Too much is redacted."

My shoulders slump, wondering what else Jeremiah Redford did that's going to break his daughter's heart.

Though I heard some things about him back in Virginia, I didn't think much about it. Whatever he was up to was happening in Tennessee. It didn't touch my life back then.

Maybe I should have paid more attention so I could make Ava's search for the truth easier now.

She wouldn't have those dark bags under her eyes and a half-eaten sandwich on the table beside her.

Part of me wants to sit down and help her.

Although, the little I learned about her father after I went to prison is enough to make even a sane person snap.

I know one thing for certain.

Though I may want to make this search easier for her, I'm not going to be the one to tell her the worst of the things that her father has done.

Keeping those secrets from her may make her hate me, but I would rather have her hate me than drag her down into the dark spiral her father went down.

I lean forward and take one of the arrest reports from her. "Aves, this barely has anything on it. Why don't you take a break, finish that sandwich, and then we can talk about making that lasagna for dinner?"

Her hand taps the table, reaching across the surface until she finds her sandwich. Even as she takes a large bite, her attention remains on the arrest records.

Brooklyn looks at the gold watch on her wrist. "Actually, he's right. It's getting late in the afternoon, and I have to work on a mural for the local rec center."

She grabs her purse from the couch and winks at me.

Without Brooklyn here to help her, Ava might take a breather.

I nod my thanks as she heads for the door.

I should have known better, though.

If anything, Brooklyn leaving only fuels her on. She shuffles the papers before opening a notebook. Ava pulls a pen from behind her ear and writes down a couple notes.

The moment she drops the pen, I snatch the notebook from her and toss it onto the other armchair.

She looks up at me with narrowed eyes. "What the hell did you do that for?"

I stand up and nod to the kitchen. "Come on. Dinner is

going to take nearly an hour to make, and that's before it goes into the oven."

"I'm busy. I can help you in a few minutes, but I need to finish this."

"That's what you've said every night for the last week no matter what time I come home at." I take her hand and pull her to her feet. "Break time, Ava. You're going to burn yourself out if you keep going at the rate you're going."

She snatches her hand from mine. "I need to do this, Finn. I don't expect you to understand."

I roll my eyes and gather up the rest of her things, piling them onto the armchair with her notebook and the arrest record I was looking at. "I understand that you are willing to make yourself sick over this. Tonight and tomorrow, you're taking the day off. I am too."

That stops her in her tracks. A tirade is on the tip of her tongue, but the anger seems to deflate as her eyes widen. "You're going to take a day off?"

"If it can keep you from researching yourself to death, then yes. That's what I'm going to do. We're going hiking in the morning."

Ava looks at the pile of paperwork. "I have things I need to do, Finn."

"And we have a fake engagement to uphold." Throwing the deal back in her face might be the only thing that gets her to listen to me. "If we want to look like a couple, we're going to have to spend some time together."

"We could spend time together while you help me figure out the missing information from my father's arrest records. I'm sure that we can find news articles on the internet about them."

"Ava!" I gesture to the length of her body. "You are barely holding on. You look like you haven't slept in a week, and you're barely eating. This has become an obsession for you. We're taking the day off tomorrow, and that's final."

She crosses her arms and cocks her hip. "You can't tell me what to do."

The defiance shining in her eyes is nothing but a turn on.

I want to throw her over my shoulder and carry her off to the bedroom. She would learn that I could tell her what to do. Hell, she'd love it.

Instead, I stand taller and raise an eyebrow. "Fucking try me, Aves. You're killing yourself over this, and it's only just the beginning. We're in this together until we both get what we want out of Oregon. That means that if I see you trying to fucking self-destruct over a piece-of-shit father, I *am* going to tell you what to do. Now, get your ass away from the table and do literally anything else while I make dinner."

She spins on her heel and heads for the bedroom without a word.

The door slams shut, leaving me standing in the middle of the room.

I growl to myself before heading into the kitchen. "Infuriating woman."

It takes several minutes to find everything I need to make dinner. In the time that we've been here, Ava has rearranged the kitchen twice. Even finding the cheese grater takes more time than it should.

The entire time I boil the noodles and cook the meat sauce, Ava stays locked away. The only noise that fills the house is the shower running.

By the time the lasagna is covered with foil and in the oven, she reappears, her wet hair hanging down her back.

She pads over to the kitchen and pulls out garlic butter and a loaf of bread.

"So, you know how to cook too."

I nod. "Had to learn if I wanted to eat. Dad was never good at it and couldn't see the point in spending money on a cook when he usually wasn't home. Mom used to love it, though. She taught me a few things before she died."

She nods and her shoulders slump. "I'm sorry. You were right. I do need to step away from this for a day or two before I go insane."

"Hiking tomorrow." I lean against the counter as she slices the loaf of bread in half. "In the morning. We're going, and I'm not going to let you back out of it."

Ava's smile is distant as she butters the bread and puts it on a baking pan. "I'm not going to back out of it. I just can't shake the feeling that there is so much to learn, and I'm not going to have enough time to learn it all."

"You'll have more than enough time. I might be able to pull some strings and find out what exactly was redacted."

"You'd do that?" Her eyes are wide.

"I would." That and more, but no use saying that.

Her face lights up as she throws herself at me and wraps me in a tight hug. "Thank you!"

I hug her back, but I let her go before I decide to forget dinner and spend the rest of the night wrapped in her arms. "I'm not promising that I'm going to be able to find what was taken out, but I can try."

"I know. Thank you either way." She hums to herself as she tops the garlic bread with cheese.

Hopefully, she's still in a decent mood when we go hiking in the morning.

Ava eyes the motorcycle in the driveway as the sun creeps over the horizon, bathing the sky in warm orange light. "You want me to get on the back of that? When did you even buy this?"

I dangle the baby blue helmet at her. "Had it dropped off this morning. Dawson brought it by. Now, come on. The helmet is your favorite color."

"How do you even know my favorite color?"

I shrug and shake the helmet. "You usually wore scrubs that were the same color. I assumed."

She purses her lips, holding back a smile as she takes the helmet. "I'm going to look goofy as hell."

I laugh as she pulls the helmet on. The strap dangles beneath her chin as she strikes a pose before leaning over to look at herself in the mirror.

Ava smirks and straightens up, buckling up the helmet. "I told you I was going to look goofy."

"Pretty, too." I grab my own helmet from the handlebars and put it on.

"Why did Dawson bring it over this morning?"

I swing my leg over the seat and push up the kickstand. "Needed a little bit of engine work. He finished it up last night. Wasn't going to pick it up until this weekend but figured you could use a little excitement in your life."

She snorts as she climbs on the motorcycle behind me. "Like I don't have enough of that already. Do you even know how to drive one of these things?"

"Yes." I rev the engine to life as she leans forward and wraps her arms around my waist.

I'm grateful for the leather jacket separating us so I can't feel her body pressed against mine more than I already do.

Ava holds on tight as we leave our house behind and head for one of the trails that leads deep into the forest.

I can't wait to see the look on her face when she catches sight of the giant trees for the first time.

It's a short drive along a winding road.

When we arrive at the trailhead, Ava sits up a little taller. She shifts behind me on the motorcycle as I park. Her thighs squeeze me a little tighter before she gets off and slips off her helmet.

"Wow!"

That soft whisper is more than enough to make taking a day off worth it.

The helmet dangles from her fingers as she tilts her head back. "This is amazing."

Massive redwoods stretch toward the sky, their green leaves blowing in the wind. The sun shines bright overhead as I take both our helmets and store them in the saddlebags.

I take her hand, lacing my fingers through hers as if it's natural.

She looks down at our joined hands before turning her attention back to the forest and doesn't pull away.

Mulch crunches and shifts beneath our feet as we walk onto the trail.

Our hands swing between us while birds chirp all around us.

Ava keeps looking up at the trees. "I can't believe that redwoods get this big. How many people do you think it would take to wrap around that one over there?"

I glance over to the tree she nods at.

The trunk is massive, and the roots sprawl on the right side of the trail. "At least twenty people. Maybe more."

She stops at the base of another one and lets go of my hand. She stretches her arms wide, trying to wrap them around a tree that would take at least ten people. I laugh and pull out my phone, snapping a quick picture of her.

This is something that I'm never going to want to forget. Even when our fake engagement comes to an end.

When she turns back to me, the smile falls from her face. "I never would have been out here to see these trees if I didn't have to hunt down whatever it is my bastard father was hiding from the family."

I take her hand and spin her around under my arm before pulling her to me.

She laughs as I loop one arm over her shoulder. "We're not going to talk about the drama with your family right now. You need a moment to yourself."

"I don't know if that's going to be possible. There's too much going on, and I have a lot that I still need to find out. I've been looking for information for over a week, and I still can't seem to get anywhere."

Other people pass us as I pull her to the side of the trail and cup her face in my hands. "I'm serious, Ava. No more talking about the family drama. Not today. We're going to try to have a good time."

"Finn, I appreciate you getting me out of the house, but I don't know how *not* to think about everything going on. It feels like I can't shut my brain off."

I pull my hands away from her face and take her hand again, leading her deeper into the forest.

Though we're not far from the trail, we're far enough back that we aren't visible. Not unless someone steps off the trail to get a better look at the surrounding forest.

She's about to start protesting when I drop my face to her neck and flick my tongue against her pulse.

She tilts her head back with a soft moan, giving me better access as I suck on the sensitive flesh.

"Someone is going to see us." Her gasp is breathless as I pull her leggings down and spin her around.

I wrap my arm around her torso and pull her back against me. "You seem like you could use a distraction."

She whimpers as I slide one hand down her hip and to her pussy.

I run a finger through her wet folds, groaning softly when her hips rock forward into my touch.

Ava tilts her head back onto my shoulder, reaching behind her to run her fingers through my hair.

I swirl my finger around her clit while nipping at her neck.

Her hips rock forward as I push two fingers into her.

My thumb presses against her clit with every thrust of my fingers.

My hardened cock digs against her ass as she grinds into me.

I graze her earlobe with my teeth.

'Yes." She rolls her hips into me as her hands slide beneath her sweater.

Her hands cup her breasts, her thumbs brushing against her nipples.

I move my fingers slower, teasing her as she plays with the stiffened peaks.

Ava rolls her nipples between her fingers, moaning and writhing.

My inhale is sharp as she pinches her nipples, the soft little noises she makes growing louder.

"Come for me." I pepper kisses up and down her neck, my fingers pressing against the spot I know drives her wild.

Her pussy pulses, clenching my fingers.

Ava's chest heaves up and down as she comes, grinding into my hand until her orgasm subsides.

I step back long enough to pull out my cock, stroking my hand up and down my length.

Ava's gaze drops to my cock, her tongue darting out to lick her full bottom lip.

She drops to her knees in front of me, her hand wrapping around the base of my cock.

I groan, my fingers weaving through the soft strands of her hair as I guide her to me.

Her tongue slides along the head before she takes me in her mouth.

As she hollows her cheeks, she grips the base tighter.

"Fuck yes. Just like that." I pull her hair, rocking my hips in time with the bobbing of her head along my length. "Good girl."

Ava moans, moving her mouth and hand.

My cock throbs as she swallows and takes me deeper.

"Holy shit." My hips move faster as her eyes water. "You look so fucking stunning on your knees for me."

She grips my thigh with her free hand, her nails digging into my skin and sending me over the edge.

I moan as my come fills her mouth.

Ava swallows every drop, licking my length from base to tip before pulling back.

Her little smirk as she stands and fixes her clothing has me wanting to pull her deeper into the woods and bend her over a rock.

"You're right." She looks over her shoulder as she brushes by me and heads back to the trail. "I did need a distraction."

I laugh as I tuck my cock back into my jeans.

She disappears behind the trees as I take a moment to collect myself.

When it comes to Ava, I lose all sense of the careful control I've had over myself for so long.

I'm fucked.

12

AVA

Finn grabs his helmet off the console table and winks at me before heading for the door. "I should be back in a couple hours. Try not to stay up too late reading those things."

I roll my eyes but smile. "I'll be fine. You just go take care of whatever it is you need to deal with, and I'll be right here."

The door shuts behind him with a soft click, and the security system beeps as it engages.

I nestle deeper into the armchair and glance at the stack of journals and photo albums on the side table.

The day after hiking with Finn, my aunt gave me stacks of my father's photos and journals.

The photos were easy to go through. Dad smiling with his friends, cigarettes hanging out of their lips as they leaned against one thing or another. Even in his pictures back then, his smile looks rehearsed.

While the photos were easy to go through, it's taken a few days to work up the nerve to look at the journals. Now that I finally have some time alone, I'm ready to read.

At least, I think I am.

I never thought of my father as the kind of man who would keep a journal. It just doesn't seem like him.

Even though I try hard, I can't imagine my father sitting down to write about his life. I can't see him pouring his heart and soul into the pages of a journal, even though they are sitting right beside me.

As I reach for the first journal, my hand trembles. I snatch my hand back and stare out the window at the backyard.

Wind rustles through the bushes, making the branches dance while the stars shine overhead.

When I look back at the journals, I'm still too nervous to crack them open.

I need a glass of wine for this.

After pouring myself a healthy glass of white wine, I take a big sip.

The sharp edge to my nerves dulls a little as I sit back down.

"Come on, Ava. You can do this."

Nodding, I take the first journal and open it up, flipping to a page in the middle.

That bitch is pregnant. I don't know what to do. She's trying to trap me here in this fucking state. I don't want kids with her. I've never even wanted a future with her. She was just supposed to be a bit of fun before I went.

She came over after school yesterday and told me. I'm going to have to have a paternity test done. The last thing I want is to have to father a baby that isn't even mine.

Although, the last thing I really want to have is a child at seventeen.

This is going to fuck up the rest of my life. I know it is.

When my father finds out, he is going to insist that I do

the right thing and marry the girl. I can't do that, though. She's nice enough, but this baby is just a trick. It's a trap to get me to stay in Portland.

She's never liked that there is an entire life out there waiting for me.

Nobody has.

Everyone thinks that I should stay home and run the family business.

I'll die if I have to spend the rest of my life running a fucking hardware store.

Their insistence is only going to get worse once they find out about the baby. Especially since that bitch is staying here and going to the community college.

She thinks that she's making the right choice but putting her future on hold.

I'm sure that she thinks I'm going to stick around and provide for her.

She even said she thought that I would change my mind about children. She still thinks that I will want to stick around and be a father once I hold the baby for the first time.

I think she's full of shit. There is no way that a baby is going to make me put my entire life on hold. I won't allow it.

I've worked too hard to get into a good university.

I'm going to pack my shit and move across the country. I'm going to become a politician and everyone back home is going to wish that they didn't doubt me. They're going to wish that they had spent more time supporting me instead of telling everyone I was going nowhere in life.

I'll show all of them.

My breath catches in my throat as I read the passage over again. Though I knew that I was born when my dad was eighteen, I assumed that he and my mom were always deeply in love.

Though, relationships are never quite that simple. They were young and clearly having their problems. An unexpected and unwanted pregnancy would be enough to send even the calmest person spiraling.

I flip to another passage, running my finger over his scrawling letters.

How am I going to be a father and a politician?

School starts in a little less than a month. I have to move soon and start university. The baby is going to be born while I'm there.

I'm going to have a little girl.

It seems insane to think that she is going to be here in a matter of months.

I've been spending a lot of time thinking about what she is going to look like. What her personality is going to be. I think about her future and what's going to happen when my baby girl wants to leave the nest.

And I keep thinking about how I never want her to be anything like me.

If she does half the things that I did only a couple weeks ago, I don't know how my heart will survive.

Hell, I don't know how I'm going to survive in the first place.

I don't know what it's like to be a parent or how I'm supposed to be a good one while I'm building a life for us.

I'm probably going to be a horrible parent.

Hopefully, her mother can make up for it.

I didn't think that finding out the gender of the baby would change this much for me.

I'm still going to leave and make a name for myself. Working in politics is the only choice I have now. My little girl deserves the best out of life.

She is going to be the brightest light in my life. She's

never going to know all the horrible shit I've done. I'm going to be better for her.

I scoff and reach for my wine, taking another sip.

It seems like he never did change his true colors.

As I lean over and grab one of the pictures from the stack beside me, another is stuck to it. I separate the pictures and flip them over, finding another story on the back.

First year of university is finally over, and it felt like hell. I don't know why mom insisted on the picture walking out of the airport, but she did.

At least I have someone waiting for me.

Although, the ring in my pocket feels like it's burning a hole through my slacks.

I hope she says yes.

I don't know what I'm going to do if she doesn't. She's perfect for me. It might have taken some time to see that, but I love her.

And then there's my baby girl. Waiting for me to come back home and hug her. Hold her close. Leaving her again at the end of the summer is going to be impossible.

Although, I could get back home and find out that my daughter hates me. She's a baby, but she could still hate me, right?

Who was this person?

This man either writes in journals or whatever scrap of paper he finds. The backs of his pictures are imprinted with stories that have next to nothing to do with the people on the front.

Looking at these pictures and stories, I see a man I never really knew. A man who thought my mom wasn't going to be a permanent fixture in his life. One who fell more in love with her over the course of a year away.

What happened in that year? Would Mom even be willing to tell me about it if I asked?

The thought is fleeting. I have no desire to talk to my mother. I'm not sure that I could trust whatever she tells me either.

I take another sip of wine before continuing through the photos and journals.

Dad was sporadic when he wrote. His perspective on his life is hazy at best. It's as if he's writing like he's sure that he's running out of time. As if he can't possibly get all the words on the page before someone tells him his time has come.

It's a side of my dad that I never knew.

While I was growing up, Dad was calm. Sensible. He thought things out before he said them or wrote them down. Maybe that came with being a politician.

I grab another stack of pictures.

All of them depict my father in university with his friends. Some of the photos have notes to his mom written on the back. Others have stories about his friends.

The night is growing darker as I get to the bottom of the stack. Everything is silent as I pick up the last photo album and spread it open in my lap.

I'm barely past the first page when my phone starts ringing.

I don't bother to check the ID, instead sliding my thumb across the screen while flipping to the next page. "Hey Finn. You going to be out later?"

"Funny." The voice on the other end of the line sends a shiver down my spine. "I really thought that my brother would have had better taste. You would think that he would know better than to go after something that belongs to me."

"I don't belong to you." Venom is in my voice, though my hands are shaking.

This is exactly what I didn't want to happen.

Declan chuckles. "You should sound more excited to hear from me, pet. I told you when you left that I was going to track you down one day. You've had a few years of freedom, but did you really think it was going to last?"

"It's over between us, and it's been over." I stand up and go to the security panel on the wall, making sure that all the doors and windows are still locked. "I'm going to block this number."

"Block it all you want. I'll call back from another one, pet. This little cat and mouse game has been exciting, but now who is going to protect you? Your daddy is dead."

The security system chimes as the front lock beeps. Finn walks in, blood stains on the hem of his light gray shirt.

My eyes widen at the sight of more blood on him, but right now, Declan is the bigger problem.

"You're going to leave me alone." I'm proud when my voice doesn't waver, even though I feel like I'm going to break down. "You're not going to call this number again, and I'm certainly not yours."

His chuckle makes my stomach turn. "You would think that, wouldn't you, pet? It's funny how easily you've forgotten the way we used to be together."

Finn's eyebrows shoot up his forehead.

I don't know if he can hear his brother's voice, but the look on his face is murderous.

"Is Finn there now?" Declan's voice is a purr that promises pain.

It still has me shaking and wishing to be anywhere else.

"No." I shake my head as Finn holds out his hand. "He's not here."

Finn tries to take the phone from me, but I spin out of his way.

Declan blows out a long exhale on the other end of the line. "How many times have I told you not to lie to me, Ava? Put my brother on the phone. Now."

Finn loops one arm around my waist and pulls me to him, plucking the phone from my fingers before letting me go.

I wrap my arms around my torso, trying to hold myself together as Finn lifts the phone to his ear.

"Declan. Why the hell are you calling my fiancée?" Finn leans against the wall, crossing one leg over the other at the ankle.

Declan says something that makes Finn pull the phone away from his ear and take a deep breath.

I shift my weight from one side to the other, wanting to be done with this conversation as soon as possible.

Finn brings the phone back to his ear. "You are *not* going to call her again. If I find out that you did, you're going to have me to answer to."

His tone is dangerous.

A shiver crawls along my spine looking between Finn and the blood on his shirt.

If he is willing to speak to Declan like that, what did he say to the person he made bleed?

Finn ends the call and puts the phone on the console table. "I'm sorry that he was able to get in contact with you. I should have made sure that all his numbers were blocked when I gave you the new phone."

"It's not your fault. He would have just changed his number and tried again."

This isn't the first time that Declan has contacted me over the years, but I've never spoken to him that long before.

Most times, I hear his voice and hang up. And today shouldn't have been any different. I should have just hung up and blocked the number.

I rub my arms, trying to chase away the chill that's running through my body. "I'm sorry that I've put you in a difficult position with your family."

Finn lets out a short laugh and kicks off his boots. "I've never been in anything but a difficult position with them. You didn't put me into anything."

"Still." I move into the living room, going for my glass of wine and draining what's left.

"Still, nothing. I agreed to let you come out here with me, and I'm going to protect you while you're with me. From everyone. Including my brother."

I set the empty glass down on the table. "If that's true, then why are you coming home with blood on your shirt again?"

He glances down at his shirt, searching for a moment before he looks at the hem. "I didn't know I got blood on me. Sorry. Cillian took care of some business. I was there, but I wasn't really involved with it."

"And is that supposed to make me feel better?"

I drop down into the armchair and tilt my head back, sighing. "I'm sorry. I'm lashing out at you even though it's your brother that's upset me."

"Lash out at me all you need to." Finn perches himself on the arm of the chair. "I know that dealing with Declan is a lot. He's never been an easy person to be around."

"I couldn't imagine growing up with him."

Finn shrugs. "It wasn't so bad when Cormac was around. He used to take the brunt of Declan's pissy attitude and turn it right back around on him."

"Cormac was your older brother, right?"

He nods and gets up from the couch. "He is. I'm going to go get cleaned up. Want to watch a movie before bed?"

I nod. "I could use something to get my mind off that call."

He heads for the bedroom as I prop my feet on the edge of the chair and hold my knees to my chest.

Before Finn disappears into the bedroom, he turns around to look at me.

"Aves, I'm serious. I hope you know that. I will do whatever it takes to keep you safe."

As his eyes pierce mine, I start to believe him.

13

FINN

I'm still pissed. It's been days, and I still haven't gotten over the call Ava had with Declan.

I might not know everything that happened during their relationship, but it was clear that she didn't want to talk to him.

Hell, she looked terrified.

Cillian clears his throat, pulling me from thoughts of how I'm going to throttle my brother. Cillian nods to the man tied to the chair.

The man thrashes, trying to free his wrists and spit the gag out.

With a sigh, I stalk toward the man, cracking my knuckles. Even though brute work isn't something that I do much of anymore, I'm willing to do what it takes to get closer to Cillian.

Thing is, the closer I get, the more I struggle with the decision to kill him and allow my father to take his territory.

Cillian is a good leader. His people look up to him. They follow him without question, and I've yet to see anyone step out of line.

I stop nearly a foot in front of the man and tuck my hands in my pockets. "We're all friends here, Murphy. I would hate to see something happen to you because you didn't want to give Mr. O'Reilly the information he needs."

Murphy mumbles something that sounds a lot like *fuck you* against his gag.

Cillian sighs and shakes his head. "Murphy, Finn doesn't want to hurt you, but he's going to if you won't cooperate. What I want to know is simple. I know that you have the answer. So, are you going to do this the easy way or the hard way?"

Murphy thrashes in his seat again, glaring daggers at Cillian.

I reach out and grab the top corner of his seat, tilting him back slightly. "Now, you're going to want to think carefully about your choice. I don't want to break your bones, starting with your fingers. Hate the sound. But I will if I have to."

His hands flex where they're tied to the arms of the chair. His wrists are rubbed raw and blood soaks the ropes.

Dawson chuckles in the corner, shaking his head. "Finn, stop toying with him."

Cillian nods. "It's clear that Murphy has made his choice."

The bright fluorescent lights shine overhead as I shove the chair backward. Murphy collides with the ground, groaning as his head bounces off the white tile.

I move to crouch beside his head. "I was hoping that you were going to tell them everything you know instead of wasting my time. If I come home with blood on my shirt one more time, I'm going to be upsetting a very important person." As I say the words, a niggling in the back of my head lets me know I mean every single one of them.

Murphy screams muffled curses through the gag as I set the chair upright.

"Luckily, I won't get blood on me when I break your fingers."

I grab his index finger and snap it.

The sickening crunch is barely audible as Murphy continues to shout against the gag.

When I look at Cillian, he gives a sharp jerk of his chin.

Murphy tries to move away from me as I grab another finger.

I bend it backward and pull out his gag.

Murphy spits on the ground at my feet. "Fuck you all."

The finger snaps.

He howls with pain as I take another finger and bend it.

The color drains from his face as he swallows hard.

Cillian smirks. "Make this easy on yourself, Murphy. Who the fuck stole my gun shipment?"

Murphy's breath comes in sharp bursts as a dark stain appears on the front of his pants. "Dorian Roach."

Cillian spins on his heel and leaves the room.

The heavy metal door slams shut behind him.

I pull the gun from the holster on my hip.

Murphy's gaze darts to the gun before looking up at me. "Let me go. Please. You don't have to do this. You can let me go, and Cillian never has to know. Both of you. I can make it worth your while. I'll disappear."

The metal mouth of the gun meets his temple.

My finger wraps around the trigger. "*I'd* know. Besides, you made your bed, and now it's time to lie in it."

The gunshot echoes through the room as Murphy's body slumps to the side, remaining seated in the chair due to his bindings.

A thin rivulet of blood trickles down the side of his face.

On the other side of the room, the doors swing open.

The cleaning crew walks in, already dressed in white disposable jumpsuits.

Dawson grins as I tuck the gun back in my holster. "Looks like our job's done here for the day. What do you say we get out of here?"

"I could use a drink." I yawn and scratch my jaw. "I have some beer at home. You could come over and watch the game."

"Not a big football fan, but I am interested in meeting this woman of yours. You don't strike me as the type of man to be engaged. Honestly, you're more like the kind of man I've seen alone for life."

I chuckle and lead the way out of the room and up the stairs.

Machines whir on the factory floor as we step out of the hidden stairway.

Dawson stretches and taps his hands on the doorframe while I hide the door to the factory's basement again.

"Ava is going to be happy to meet you. She thinks that I need to get out and make more friends." I give a one-shouldered shrug, as if Ava doesn't have a clue about what I'm doing. "She thinks that I spend most of my day at work and then go to the gym for a couple hours."

A line appears between Dawson's eyebrows. "What does she think when you have to take off in the middle of the night? I know that's always been hard to hide from girlfriends who aren't in the loop."

"She doesn't ask. I tell her that there's a work emergency, and then I head out."

"Man." Dawson shakes his head as we weave through the factory and out to the parking lot. "What I wouldn't give to have a woman with that much trust in me. The woman I was last with thought that I should allow her to check my phone every few days. She wanted to make sure that I wasn't cheating on her. My girlfriend now is a lot better, but she still gets pissed off about my work. She hates it."

I walk over to my motorcycle and pull the helmet out of the saddlebag. "Ava isn't like that. She's an incredible woman. I have no clue how I got lucky enough to have her in my life, but I did. Hell, I don't know what I would do without her at this point." The truth of my words hits me again, but I push it back. Now is not the time to think about this.

Dawson laughs. "Well, you sound like you're a lovesick fool."

"For Ava? Always." I pull the helmet on, leaving the visor up. "I'll meet you back at the house."

A lump in my throat threatens to choke me, but I swallow it down. I may not be a lovesick fool for her, but that's the game of pretend we're playing. Even if those lines get blurrier by the day.

And she *is* an amazing woman. Better than anyone I've ever met.

Far too good for the likes of me.

He nods and gets into his car, the engine revving as I sling my leg over the bike.

We take off toward my house, the sun shining down.

When we get to the house, Ava's car is in the driveway, and Brooklyn's bicycle is near the front porch.

I sigh and pull the motorcycle in beside her car before killing the engine.

Dawson pulls in behind me as I'm sliding off my helmet.

The car door slams, and he lets out a low whistle. "I didn't know that people were still riding bicycles."

"Ava's friend is over." I climb the steps and push open the front door. "They've been working on tracing a family history on her father's side."

Dawson looks around the entryway as we step inside.

Soft voices filter to us from the living room where the women are bent over yet another journal.

I kick off my boots before padding across the house to Ava.

She looks up with a bright smile as I dip my head to kiss her. Ava nips at my bottom lip as I pull away, amusement bright in her eyes.

"Aves, this is Dawson. Dawson, this is my fiancée, Ava, and her friend, Brooklyn."

Ava gets up and makes her way over to Dawson, pulling him into a tight hug. "It's nice to meet Finn's only friend."

I laugh as she steps away from him. "See, Dawson? What did I tell you?"

Dawson chuckles and looks around the house. "You two still unpacking?"

Sweat beads on the back of my neck as I try to figure out where he is going with the question.

I look around the house, trying to see it through his eyes. It seems like a cute little home that a couple would start off on.

But there are no pictures.

Ava's gaze cuts toward me quickly before she looks away. "Yeah. Moving has been a hell of a time. There's still some pictures packed away in a box. I don't have the time to hang them and neither does Finn."

"We'll be getting new ones anyway." I loop my arm around her waist and pull her to me. "Engagement photos should be here soon, and I'm sure that Ava is going to insist on updating every other picture at the same time too."

Ava blushes and rolls her eyes, giving me a playful swat on the shoulder. "He says that, but he's the one who insisted on the engagement photos. I thought the money would be better spent going on a vacation, but he was sure that we should take pictures to commemorate the moment instead."

"And I was right." I kiss her temple before heading into the kitchen to grab a couple of beers. "I was thinking of ordering in some pizza for dinner."

Dawson follows me into the kitchen and takes one of the beers. "Pizza is good with me if it's good with the women."

Ava nods before kneeling back down beside the table with Brooklyn. Their heads bend together over the journals, and Brooklyn takes more notes on a sheet of paper beside her.

I take a swig of the beer before pulling out my phone and placing the order for pizza.

Dawson leans on the counter beside me, his back to the living room.

He hums to himself for a moment, his gaze darting around the room. "You've got a nice place here. I know that Cillian said things were hard for you, but you seemed to clean up when it came to the housing market."

"Got pretty lucky. I didn't think that we were going to get anything in a good neighborhood." I take another sip of the beer, trying to keep my tone even and natural. "It was a house in foreclosure. We paid off the debts and the interest. Ended up being a lot cheaper than market value. And we were able to close on it soon after our offer was accepted. We've already done a ton to the place. It needed a lot of work, but with a great deal, it was impossible to say no."

He nods and sips his own beer. "My girlfriend and I are looking to move soon. She wants to get out of the city, but with my job, I don't know if I can. She's knows some of what's going on, but she doesn't understand fully. She doesn't like that I have to leave in the middle of the night sometimes. She hates when I have to take trips or go on a run."

"And yet, you want to move in with her soon?" I tip the neck of my bottle toward Ava. "I wouldn't be in this life if I didn't know that she could handle it."

"Nora can handle it, most of the time. She wants the house and the kids, though. I want that too, but I don't know how to make it work when she can't fully accept that part of my life. Hell, most of it I can't even tell her for now."

"It's going to be a lot of uphill battles. And you're going to have to figure out which hill you're willing to die on. It's a careful balance to maintain."

Ava throws her head back and laughs, pointing to something on one of the papers.

I smile. "And it's going to sound stupid when I say it, but it's worth it. All the little fights we have about what I'm doing and where I'm going are worth it in the end because I get to come back home to her." My chest tightens.

Ava turns her attention to me, winking before turning to say something to Brooklyn. The two of them laugh and shake their heads, reaching for the glasses of wine in front of them.

Dawson nods. "I know it is. We have our problems, but Nora's the only woman I want to go through life with."

"Then I'm sure you'll figure out a way to make everything else work."

"How much did you pay for a ring?"

The words open a pit in the bottom of my stomach.

I never bought her a ring. We're supposed to be

engaged, and I never even thought about what would happen when people asked to see her ring.

And how much does a ring even cost?

Another swig of beer is enough to put off answering for a couple seconds.

"A couple thousand or so since we're sinking so much money into the house. Aves doesn't care about fancy either, so I picked the ring I knew would make her the happiest within the budget I had."

Dawson finishes off his beer. "Good to know. Nora *is* the fancy kind. I didn't want to get into the five-figure territory on a ring, but I'm sure that she's going to expect it."

I raise my bottle in his direction. "At least we're paid well for the work we do."

He clinks his bottle against mine. "Amen to that."

A COUPLE OF HOURS LATER, DAWSON LEAVES WHILE the women are still bent over the papers.

Empty pizza boxes sit on the counter and nearly a dozen beers are scattered across the table.

I grab my coat and my keys. "I have to run out for a few minutes. I shouldn't be too long. I'll get the mess cleaned up when I get back."

Ava waves a hand. "Don't worry about the mess. Brooklyn is going to be on her way out shortly and then I'll get it cleaned up."

I cross the room and lean over to kiss the top of her head. "I'll handle it when I get back. Just take the rest of the night to relax. You've had a long day."

Brooklyn looks between the two of us with a soft squeal. "The two of you are too cute for words."

Laughing, I leave and shut the door behind me.

As soon as the door is shut, I slump against it and run my hands down my face.

The line between our fake relationship and the real attraction I have toward Ava is starting to get blurrier than ever.

I breathe out a deep breath and head to a jewelry store not far from our house.

When I walk inside, stones glitter at me from the shelves.

I look around for something that suits Ava.

I've never seen her wear more than a necklace, but I can't remember for the life of me what that looks like.

Sometimes, she wears tiny hoops or stud earrings, but I have no clue whether they're gold or silver.

The picture at the redwoods.

I pull out my phone, hoping that her necklace is visible or that she's wearing earrings in the picture.

Sure enough, there are a pair of gold studs in her ears.

Thank fuck.

A man steps out from behind one of the counters. "Is there anything I can help you find tonight?"

"An engagement ring. Something simple. Understated and beautiful."

The man nods and leads the way over to one of the counters on the far side of the room. He rounds the counter and unlocks the glass door, reaching inside to pull out a tray of gold engagement rings.

"This one is perfect." I point to the ring in the middle of the tray.

There is a small emerald in the middle of the ring, surrounded by filigree that reminds me of vines and leaves.

It's not as simple as I thought it would be, but everything about it screams Ava.

The man nods and talks about sizing for a moment before I pay for the ring. It looks like it should fit on her finger.

Worst-case scenario, I get it resized.

With the ring in my pocket, I head back to the house.

I have no clue what to say to her as I walk past her car. Brooklyn's bike is gone, leaving the two of us alone.

I take a deep breath as I walk into the house.

Ava looks up from the table, soft music playing in the background.

She smiles as she stands, taking her empty wine glass to the kitchen. "Where was the fire?"

"Well, I thought about something while Dawson was here." I pull out the little black box. "I'm sorry that I didn't think about this sooner when I asked you to be my fiancée."

Ava's eyes widen, and she shakes her head. "I didn't think about that either."

Crossing the room feels like crossing the middle of the ocean without a life vest.

I stop in front of her and flick open the box.

She gasps, her hand flying to her mouth as she sets down her wine glass on the counter.

Ava is careful as she lifts the ring out of the box and studies it beneath the shining overhead lights.

"This is stunning, Finn, but it's too much. This is the kind of ring you give the girl you're going to marry."

"I picked it for you, Aves. For the purpose of our little game, you are the woman I'm going to marry. I wanted you to know how much I appreciate it."

I pluck the ring from her fingers and take her left hand.

Her slight smile is laced with a look I can't quite decipher.

There is a tremble to her hand as I put the ring on her finger and give her hand a squeeze.

"There." I bring her hand to my lips and give the back of it a kiss. "Right where it belongs."

As I let go of her hand and walk away, my heart crashes through my chest.

If those lines with Ava were blurry before, they're nearly invisible now.

But I can't go there with her. I promised to protect her while she was with me.

And that includes protecting her from me.

14

AVA

The early morning sun is chasing away a cloud of fog as I take my mug of coffee and my phone out to the backyard.

I drop into one of the loungers and put the mug on the table beside me.

Rays of sunlight catch the stone in the center of the ring.

It's too much.

But it *is* a stunning ring.

Finn was right. It's exactly the kind of ring I would have picked out for myself.

I love the little vines and leaves that frame the emerald stone.

I stop admiring the ring and call Zoe.

The phone rings several times before the call connects. "Hey, Zoe. I got your text about the will reading. I don't doubt that planning it is giving you a headache. How's that going?"

She laughs and shuts something. "It's alright. I mean, it is a lot. The executor of Dad's will is a pain in the ass to track down, and Mom keeps trying to get in contact with me. Billie and Hadley were just visiting too."

"Sounds like a lot to deal with all at once. I wish that I could be there to help you." I reach for the mug of coffee and take a sip. "You haven't talked to Mom at all, have you?"

"No. I have nothing to say to her. The executor said that the will put me in charge of planning a reading. I don't know why Dad thought that we all needed some sort of party to read his will. He wants the reading down and then a big party afterward. Something to celebrate his life."

"Who is the executor anyway?"

She scoffs. "Some asshole named Carter from his office. According to what Carter is willing to tell me, Dad thought it would be better if nobody close to him had to read out where his belongings were going."

I reach up for the necklace, twisting the little diamond heart on the end.

Dad gave it to me when I was in high school.

Even though I know I should take it off now that I know part of who he was, I can't bring myself to do it.

It's the one memory I have of him that isn't tainted with all the other things that he's done to destroy the family.

I drop the heart. "Are you going to be alright in a room with Mom again?"

Christian says something in the background that I don't quite catch.

Zoe's voice is muffled, likely by her hand over the phone as she replies to him.

"I don't know, Aves. I like to think that I've put all that in the past, and that I can see her and not want to lose my shit. I want to believe that, but I don't know if I can. Is it wrong to say that you hate your mother? Because that's how I feel a lot these days, especially dealing with this."

Guilt creeps through me. After everything our father did to Zoe, she shouldn't have to be the one to organize his will reading. She shouldn't have to deal with any of this and still have to dodge our mother.

"I'm sorry that I'm not there to help." I take another sip of coffee as the last of the fog is chased away. "Let me know if there is anything I can do from here, and I'll get it done for you."

Zoe clicks her tongue. "Nope. Nothing I can think of. Just focus on what you need to do, Aves. I promise that I'm good here. Billie and Hadley have helped with as much as they can. Christian is keeping Alessio and Jovan out of my hair. Everything is fine."

"Okay. As long as you're sure."

"I'm sure." The noise in the background gets softer as a door shuts. "Now, tell me. How are you doing out there?"

As much as I want to tell her everything that I've found, she doesn't want to hear it. Zoe has made it clear that she wants as little as possible to do with our parents and their pasts.

I have to respect that, even if I want to spill everything I've found to her.

Instead, I keep it to myself.

"Everything is going well. I spend most of the days I'm not busy with Brooklyn."

"That's the artist, right?" Zoe sighs.

I can picture her right now, running a hand through her hair. Her face is likely pinched with stress that she's trying to let go.

She's desperate to distract herself with my life, asking questions she already knows the answer to.

Our calls may be infrequent, but we spend most of our

days texting on and off. I've even sent her pictures of Brooklyn's work.

If this is how she wants to avoid everything else going on in her life, I'm more than happy to oblige.

I cross one leg over the other and lean back, getting comfortable. "Yeah. She is the artist. I keep thinking that maybe I should learn to paint one day. I'm already pretty good with my hands."

Zoe's laugh is music to my ears. "You're horrible at painting. Great at sewing people up."

"Yeah. You're probably right about that. It looks like painting a masterpiece that someone hangs in a museum is going to be out of the question for a while. What a shame too. I was looking forward to being the next Picasso."

"Funny. And how is everything going with Finn?"

"It's alright. He's been at work for most of the night, so I'm sure that when he walks in, he's going to head straight for bed."

She makes a small noise. "It sounds like you two are a married couple already. You know that, right?"

My cheeks warm. I shrug, even though she can't see it. "I don't know. I came out here with him as friends—if you could call us that—but I don't know. It feels like something is changing between the two of us."

"What kind of change? Good or bad?" Excitement drips from her voice. "You're going to have to tell me all the details. Please tell me that you got your senses together and are sleeping with that fine man. And don't you dare lie to me."

My entire body is an inferno as the sliding door opens behind me, and Finn sticks his head out. "Speak of the devil, and he arrives home."

Zoe groans. "No. You're supposed to be telling me all the dirty details. Tell him to go away."

The corner of Finn's mouth creeps upward. "Does your sister know I can hear her?"

Zoe bursts out laughing. "You always keep the volume on your phone too loud. Turn it down, Aves, then tell me about the dirty details."

Finn smirks and takes a step back into the house. "I'll just let the two of you continue your conversation. Have fun describing the way you milk my cock when you come."

Zoe gasps for air on the other end of the line. Tears are probably running down her face. "He is funny. I like him."

"Yeah, well, that makes one of us right now. I'm going to go in there and wring his neck for making this worse."

"Oh, come on, the man is funny. You have to love a sense of humor." She sighs. Voices grow louder in the background. "I have to get going. We're supposed to be heading out for something to eat."

I grin. "Off the hook for the dirty details."

"Not for long. Next time we're on the phone together, I want to know how everything with that part of your life is going."

"If you say so."

"I do." Sadness enters her voice. "I miss you, Aves. I love you."

"Love you too, Zoe. We'll talk later. Have a good time out."

As soon as the call ends, I take my coffee and head back inside.

Finn is sitting at the kitchen island, his head bent over papers in front of him. He looks up with a smile as I make my way into the room.

"You're in a good mood this morning." I get onto one of

the stools beside him and take a sip of my coffee. "Good night at work?"

"Better than some." He shoves the papers to the side and twists in his seat. His full attention is on me as he takes the coffee from my hand and drains nearly half of it. "You're getting better at making a decent cup of coffee."

"Says the man who spent the last three years of his life incarcerated and drinking shitty coffee."

His eyes light up with his widening smile. "And yet, I still know how to make a better cup of coffee than you."

"Fine. I'll give you that."

He gives a satisfied nod. "How was the call with your sister?"

"It was good. I miss her a lot, though. It feels weird to be nearly a country apart from her. Even when I was in Virgina, I would go home and visit her every couple weeks."

"If you want to go visit her, say the word, and I'll book you a plane ticket."

I shake my head and take my mug back. As I hold the mug between my hands, guilt curls its cold fingers around my throat again.

Though I miss Zoe, I don't want to go home.

For the first time in a long time, I feel free. If I go back home now, I know that I'm going to lose that feeling. I'll start to feel worse for leaving her the second I set foot in Tennessee. I'll start to wonder if I should stay there and make sure that she is alright.

Finn leans closer to me, twirling a strand of my hair around his finger and giving it a light tug. "Where did you just go in that incredibly intelligent mind of yours?"

"Are you always trying to charm people?"

He snorts. "Only you, Aves. Only ever you. Now, tell me what's going on."

I sip the coffee, stalling for a moment. "I feel like shit. I know that I should want to go back home and see my sister, but I don't. I know her husband is looking after her, and I feel like I would only upset her if I went."

"Why would you visiting upset her?"

"Because right now, all I would want to talk about with her is our father. And she absolutely does *not* want to hear about any of that. She wants to cut ties with everything to do with him. The will reading is coming up, and after that, she'll finally be able to."

Finn nods, understanding in his gaze. "And you're being a good big sister and respecting her wishes even though it seems like it's eating you alive inside."

"I feel like I should have protected her more." I swallow hard, trying to get rid of the lump in my throat. "I feel like if I had just known who he was and what he was capable of, then none of this ever would've happened."

"What exactly did he do to her? You said something about selling her to sex traffickers? Am I remembering that correctly?"

If he had slammed a fist into my gut and knocked the wind out of me, it would have been easier to form a sentence.

How do you tell someone what a monster your father is?

"Yeah. He got in with the wrong crowd, I guess. And when it came time to pay, he just sold her. If her husband hadn't been around to save her, I don't know what would've happened." Tears roll down my cheeks as I stare down into my mug of coffee. "I should have been the one to protect her. I should have fought harder against my parents."

Finn loops his arm around me and pulls me into his lap.

The scent of his cologne soothes part of the terror

running through my mind, but it can't chase away the what ifs.

What if Christian had never gotten there in time?

What if she was successfully sold to the traffickers?

What if I never saw my sister again?

Finn kisses my temple, sending butterflies fluttering through my stomach. "There's nothing that you could have done, Aves. Trust me. I know what it's like to have a piece of shit father. You did the best you could for her. You were there to support her in the only way you knew how, and you're still there for her now."

I sniffle, wiping away the tears. "I can't get into all of this right now. Not when I don't have all the answers about my father."

"Alright." His hand drifts up and down my spine. "What do you want to talk about, then?"

"How was your day?"

Finn chuckles and hugs me tighter. "That's really what you want to talk about? It's pretty boring. I spent most of my day with Cillian, learning some of the strings of his business. He wants to pull me deeper into things."

"Are you sure that's a good idea?" I look up at him, trying to figure out what's going on in his head. "You told me that you wanted to get away from that life, and yet, you're getting deeper into it."

"Like I said, I know what it is to have a piece of shit father. He wants me to get deeper with Cillian, so that's what I'm going to do."

"Does he always force you to do things you don't want to?"

Finn shrugs. "I guess you could call it that, though it isn't really forcing. Growing up, the consequence of disobeying him was a beating you never wanted repeated.

After the first time or two, the thought of disobeying him rarely crossed my mind."

Tears spring to my eyes for the broken little boy sitting in the body of a man.

My dad may not have been the best man, but he didn't beat me and Zoe growing up. He pretended he loved us and then only showed his true colors once he was an adult.

Although, I don't know which is worse.

Finn's thumb swipes away a runaway tear. "Don't cry for me, Aves. I knew what life was, and I learned fast. It was easier that way. I didn't have to worry about Dad coming after me as long as I did what was expected of me."

"That's not the way that any child should ever have to live." I move off his lap and head to the fridge, pulling out two bottles of beer. The edges of the caps dig into my hands as I twist them off. "Here's to shitty parents. May we learn enough to be nothing like them."

Finn takes the bottle I hold out to him, raises it high, and touches the neck of my bottle with his. "That's quite the toast."

I shrug and take a sip of the beer. "It seems like something we can bond over."

"That we can." He takes a long gulp of his drink before setting the bottle on the counter. "There were times when he wasn't all bad. Although, it was usually something Declan had done that made him happy. Declan's been the only one that Dad's ever liked."

I snort. "That seems hard to believe."

"They're exactly alike in some ways. Completely different in others. Declan is a little kiss-ass, so he's always more willing to please him than I am." Finn drums his fingers on the counter. "It's funny, they stop hitting you once you get big enough to fight back."

"You got into fights with your father?" I lean against the counter, trying to picture a life in which I would ever raise a hand to one of my parents.

Finn's shoulder dips, the corner of his mouth curling. "He wanted to test his luck."

"And where did that get him?"

"Internal bleeding."

A chill runs down my spine at the reminder of who the man in front of me really is.

Though he's never been anything but kind to me, he's still a killer.

I'd be a fool to let all the good things overshadow all the horrible things he's done.

And yet, the man I see right in front of me is no monster. He's someone I could very easily fall for.

I guess you could call me a fool.

15

FINN

The house is dark as I walk inside late at night, rolling my shoulders back and trying to relieve some of the stiffness.

My spine cracks as I flick on the hallway light and kick off my shoes.

Water splashes somewhere in the house, followed by a soft moan.

My cock jerks as another moan plays like a sinful melody through the house.

I wander down the hall, Ava's siren song calling to me.

The bathroom door is open wide as she tilts her head back and closes her eyes.

Her long hair hangs over the edge of the tube, the scent of vanilla wafting from the lit candles that line the counter.

The soft glow in the room only highlights the way her hand moves beneath the water.

She circles her fingers around her clit, her other hand massaging her breast.

Two fingers slide into her pussy while she rolls her nipple between her fingers.

I lean against the doorframe, unzipping my jeans to relieve my aching cock.

Her stiff nipples point toward the ceiling as she arches her back and moves her slender fingers faster in her pussy.

"Finn." My name falls from her full lips as she switches to teasing the other nipple.

"Aves, if you keep that up, I'm going to have to show you how much better my tongue is than your fingers."

Her eyes fly open and water splashes over the side of the tub. She keeps moving her fingers deeper into her pussy, a sultry smile spreading.

"Maybe that's exactly what I want." Her gaze drops to the obvious bulge in my pants. Her eyes flick back up, burning with lust. "Your clothing looks dirty. You should probably take it off."

Fuck.

Ava's never been shy about demanding what she wants, but when she looks at me like that, I'm powerless to resist. Even if I wanted to—which I don't—I couldn't deny her anything.

I pull my shirt over my head and toss it to the side. The rest of my clothing hits the ground, and my cock springs free.

I grip the base, sliding my hand up to the tip.

Ava watches me, moaning as I roll my thumb over the head of my cock. "Fuck, that's hot."

"Dirty girl." I continue to stroke my cock in time with the thrusting of her fingers. "Should have known that you were going to like watching me fuck my fist."

She nods, her head tilting back again. "I'm so close."

"Eyes on me, Aves." I stop stroking until her gaze snaps back to me. "Make yourself fucking come for me."

Ava pinches her nipple hard before switching to the

other and repeating the process. She pulls her fingers out of her pussy, circling them around her clit.

"Finn."

She comes, her body tensing before it releases.

I stop stroking, stalking toward the bathtub. "Do you want my cock, Aves?"

"Yes."

She moves forward, leaving me enough room to slip behind her.

I get into the water, groaning when she keeps her back to me and straddles my thighs.

The head of my cock brushes against her slick folds.

Ava braces her hands on the sides of the tub as she keeps herself hovering above me.

I run my hands along the curves of her waist as she rolls her hips, taking just the tip of my cock.

"You're being a tease." My thumbs flick across her nipples.

Her body jerks as she rolls her hips, sinking further down onto me.

Her pussy squeezes my cock as I cup her breasts.

She gasps as I lift my hips, pressing my cock deeper into her. "I'm not being a tease."

"Oh? What do you call grinding your dripping wet pussy against my cock, then?"

Ava looks over her shoulder and smirks at me. "A good time."

I grab her hips and pull her all the way down onto me, groaning when she rolls her hips.

Her back presses against my chest as she leans back and rocks her hips.

Her little gasp as I suck on the sensitive skin at the base of her neck only makes me harder.

Water sloshes around us as I drive my cock harder into her.

Ava reaches behind her, holding onto my shoulders. She rolls her body, moaning as I press deeper inside her.

Her pussy pulsates around me as my hands return to her breasts.

"That's it, Aves. Ride my cock like the dirty little slut we both know you are."

Her nails dig into my skin, her pussy clenching harder. "Fuck, Finn. Yes."

She pushes her breasts harder into my hands as I pinch her nipples, pulling them away from her body.

Ava writhes against me, her moans growing louder.

Her gasp when I release her nipples has my cock throbbing.

I reach around her hips, dipping my hand down to the apex between her thighs.

When I pinch her clit, her hips buck.

I chuckle, thrusting to meet the rocking of her hips while I toy with her clit.

My fingers move faster, keeping time with the movement of her hips.

Ava throws her head back, her thighs squeezing hard against mine.

She comes hard, rolling her hips and drawing out her orgasm.

I keep thrusting until I come, my cock stiffening before I empty myself in her.

She gets up, nearly losing her footing as she gets out of the bathtub.

I reach out and steady her, keeping her hand locked with mine until she's safe on the bathmat.

I get out and turn on the shower. "Looks like we could both use a little washing up."

Ava smirks and lowers herself to her knees in front of me.

My cock hardens again as she cups my balls.

She squeezes them as she takes the head of my cock into her mouth.

"Fuck, Aves, if you do that, I'm not going to last long enough to fuck you in the shower."

She looks up at me from beneath dark lashes and hollows her cheeks.

My cock presses against the back of her throat as she squeezes my balls again.

I weave my fingers through her hair, pulling it back from her face.

She moans as I rock my hips forward.

Ava takes my cock deeper, her head bobbing down my length with every thrust.

My hips move faster as her hand leaves my balls to grip the base of my cock. She slides her hand in time with her mouth, swallowing me as much as she can before her eyes start to water.

I pull her hair, guiding her head faster. "I'm going to come, and I want you to swallow every last drop I give you like a good little slut."

Ava sucks me harder, sending me over the edge.

She drinks up everything I give her, taking her time to lick my cock from base to tip when she's done.

"So." She stands up with a wicked smile and steps into the steaming shower. "Still got enough energy for another round?"

I groan and follow her into the shower, knowing that we're going to be in there until the water runs cold.

Ava sits on the couch a couple of hours later, our thick duvet wrapped around her shoulders. She stretches her legs out, her feet kicked up on the coffee table in front of her while I take a seat in one of the armchairs.

I don't know how to broach the conversation I need to have with her.

How do you tell someone that because of the shit you're getting into, they need to know how to protect themselves?

I promised that I would protect her while we're here, but that call with Declan a while ago only proved that I can't protect her from everything.

It's been eating away at me ever since.

Ava grabs the remote and turns on the television, flicking through the list of movies and shows. "What do you want to watch tonight? There's a show about people finding their lost families. Or tracing back their family histories. Those are both pretty interesting shows."

"Actually, I need to talk to you about something." The words on my tongue are like trying to juggle a mouthful of hot coals.

She sets the remote to the side, twisting to face me. "What's going on?"

Guilt wracks through me, tearing at my conscience.

I should be able to protect her. I shouldn't have to tell her that I might not be able to hold up my end of the bargain.

I lace my fingers together, leaning forward to brace my forearms on my knees. "There are some things going on with Cillian and his men. I'm not going to tell you everything, but you should know that I'm starting to make his enemies my own. Tonight was a rough night, and I think that sooner or later, someone is going to be coming after me."

Her lips press together, but she nods, waiting for me to continue. Those piercing eyes seem to stare right through me, cutting through the layers that I use to protect myself and heading straight to my soul.

When she looks at me like that, I feel even worse.

Ava arches an eyebrow, the message clear.

Start talking.

"Tonight, before I got home, I had to go on a run that didn't end well. A couple men were killed, and I'm sure that there is going to be someone coming after me. And if they're coming after me, they might be coming after you, and I need you to know how to defend yourself." I take a deep breath. "So, I want to teach you to shoot."

The corner of her mouth twitches. "I already know how to shoot."

My mouth hangs open.

But why am I so surprised? I should have known that someone would've made sure that she could handle herself.

Her father was the Head of State. He wouldn't have left her entirely defenseless.

Although, knowing what to do if someone breaks through a security team is different than knowing what to do against a member of a rival mafia.

But she sounds confident in her abilities.

She's hinted at her brother-in-law having connections. Hell, she pulled out enough weapons to stock a small armory when we moved out here. She said that he was the one who got them for her.

Who the hell is her brother-in-law?

I clear my throat, wishing the heat in my cheeks would dissipate. "I'd like to see you shoot. I don't know how much you know or how confident you are in shooting someone that's coming at you."

That little smirk turns into a short laugh. "I appreciate that you worried about me being the target of whoever you pissed off, but I can take care of myself."

"This isn't just about being able to take care of yourself. This is about killing a person to save your own life if you have to. Are you able to do that?"

Ava's glare turns cold as she nods. "I can. If it means my life or someone else's, I'm going to save my own life. You don't need to worry about that. My brother-in-law has drilled it into my head more than enough."

I sit back and run my hand along my jaw. "I have to ask. Who the fuck is your brother-in-law?"

It's a question that I should have asked her when she pulled out all those weapons. It's also a question that I'm not sure she's going to answer.

Ava pulls the duvet tighter around her, sinking down into the cushions and getting comfortable. "Does that matter?"

"Yes. You keep saying cryptic shit about how he taught you this or he gave you that. If whoever your brother-in-law is will cause another problem for me, then I need to know."

"Christian Herrera."

Fuck.

If I thought I was playing with fire by having her here before, I've thrown myself into an inferno now.

I nod, trying to process that information.

Though I'm on good terms with Christian, if anything happens to Ava, I'm sure I'll shoot to the top of his shit list.

"Alright. Well, then you probably do know how to shoot."

Ava giggles and rolls her eyes. "I know you promised to

protect me—and I appreciate it—but if I have to, I can protect myself."

"Are you keeping a gun with you at all times?"

She jerks her chin in the direction of the large purse she carries when she goes out. "There's one in there all the time, and there's another hidden in my car."

Knowing that she doesn't go out into the world defenseless makes me feel a bit better.

I stand up from the chair and move into the kitchen as Ava grabs the remote again.

"Cillian and his wife are going to be coming for dinner next week. He wants to meet you. Says that it's important to him to get to know all the people who are close to his personal business."

"Okay. I'll figure out something good to make."

My phone buzzes on the counter, my father's number lighting up the screen.

I groan and grab the phone, already heading to the door to go outside. "I've got to take this call, Aves, but after that, we can watch whatever you want."

She waves one hand without looking at me, the engagement ring on that finger glistening beneath the dim glow of the lamplight.

What would it feel like if what ring represented were real?

I shake the thought from my head and step outside, sliding my thumb across the screen.

I don't have time to think about alternate realities when I already have more than enough to fill my plate in this one.

"Hello, Dad."

He scoffs. "Took you long enough to answer the fucking phone, Finnigan. How are things going there? How much longer do you think it will be before you can make your move?"

This is the call I've been dreading. I know that, sooner or later, Dad is going to start pushing harder for me to kill Cillian and take control.

The only problem is that I don't know if I can do it anymore. If I even want to.

After seeing how Cillian runs his organization, I don't know if I want to turn against him. His people are content. There are no random beatings. I don't get sent to kill people who pissed him off—only those who wronged him.

It's an easier life. One that doesn't weigh as heavily on me.

I clear my throat and sit down in one of the patio loungers. "Everything is fine. He's not a trusting man. I'm in his inner circle, but he usually sends another man with me. It should only be a couple more weeks before he trusts me on my own."

"Stop wasting time." The call ends, leaving me alone in the dark night.

If Dad ever finds out that I'm lying to him right now, he will kill me.

The truth is that I've been going out on my own for the last few days.

Cillian allows me to be near him without any other members of the mob around. He trusts me.

And I don't know if I can continue to plot against him, even if it means my own death in the end.

16

AVA

"Are you going to be good with finishing this off?" Brooklyn stirs the sauce bubbling on the stove one last time, the scent of garlic and oregano filling the room.

I chop the sun-dried tomato into small chunks and nod. "I should be. I just have to throw this into the sauce and let it simmer for a few more minutes. They're not supposed to be here for another half hour."

"Then I'm going to head out now." She grabs her purse from the dining table and slings it over her shoulder. "Try not to burn the garlic bread and everything should be fine."

"Thank you for the help, Brooklyn. I was in a massive panic when I called you."

She laughs as I put down the knife and toss the tomatoes in the sauce.

I follow her to the door, wishing that she could stay and make dinner with Finn's boss a little easier.

"I'm glad that I don't have a fiancé who wants to bring their boss to dinner. That sounds like hell."

"It does." I shrug and open the door for her as she slides into her sneakers. "But everything is going to be fine. Finn says that they're nice people. I've just been up most of the last two nights worrying about what to give them."

"Well, that carrot cake I brought over is always a favorite at the café. As long as you give them a huge slice of that, I'm sure they'll fall in love with you."

"I hope so."

Brooklyn heads out, picking up her bicycle from where she leaned it against the porch railing. "Are we still looking at your father's yearbooks this weekend?"

"Yeah. My aunt was going to finish digging them out tonight and then she's going to drop them by here tomorrow night before she heads out of town for the weekend."

"Are you sure that Finn is going to be alright with that?" Her eyebrow arches. "You know he never seems very impressed when I'm over to look through your dad's things with you."

I wave a dismissal hand. "That's just Finn. He's got a lot on his plate right now."

Her eyebrows climb a little higher. "Are you sure? Is everything alright? I hate to be the thing that comes between the two of you when he looks at you like you hung the moon."

My cheeks warm as I roll my eyes. "That is not how he looks at me. And the relationship is good. He really is just stressed with work. He also thinks that chasing down ghosts is going to upset me."

"As long as you're sure."

"I'm sure. Come over on Sunday, and we'll go through the yearbooks together. We might be able to find some juicy high school drama."

She chuckles, her shoulders relaxing as she nods. "Alright. I'll be over Sunday. There better be drama, though."

"There will be."

I'm sure of it. After reading my dad's journals, I'm sure that there was more going on in his life than I've found so far. Aunt Courtney has been able to fill in some of the gaps, but there is a lot that even she doesn't know.

I want to find it this weekend.

Brooklyn straddles her bike and puts her bag in the basket on the front. "Have a good dinner."

"Have a safe ride home."

She takes off into the night, leaving me to fight with my own mind about how tonight will go.

This dinner needs to be good.

Cillian and his wife are going to be sitting across the table and watching how Finn and I interact with each other. If we don't seem like enough of a couple to them, are they going to say something about it?

I'm supposed to be his fiancée, though I still don't know why. All I know is that it's important to whatever he's doing here, and whatever he's doing here clearly has something to do with Cillian.

After exhaling slowly and trying to shake the nervous trembles from my hands, I head back inside.

Finn whistles as he walks into the kitchen, his hands in his pockets. "It smells good in here. What's that?"

He wanders over to the stove and pulls open a drawer beside it, taking out a spoon.

"Sun-dried tomato pasta. It's got some lemon, garlic, and white wine in the sauce. I've still got to chop the basil that goes in it too, but Brooklyn said it's delicious."

Finn grins and spoons up some of the sauce and tries it. "Brooklyn is right. That is delicious."

He tosses the spoon in the sink while I grab the basil from the fridge and toss it onto the cutting board. Finn bumps me out of the way with his hip and grabs the basil, plucking off leaves and putting them into a neat little pile.

I stand to the side, stirring the sauce as he rolls the leaves and cuts them into thin ribbons.

I watch him for a couple of seconds. The serene smile on his face, the relaxed stance he doesn't wear often. "You really enjoy cooking, don't you?"

I glance at the clock, reaching up to toy with my necklace.

The little diamond heart twists in my fingers as I go through the mental list of all I need to have ready for tonight.

"I do." He smiles. "Reminds me of the good times I had in the kitchen with my mom."

Finn he puts the basil in the pot. "She would have liked you if she met you. She would have thought that you were good for the Byrne boys. Those would have been her exact words too."

My cheeks warm as I roll my eyes. "I doubt I'm that good for you. I wanted to come out here and deceive people with you."

He chuckles and leans a little closer to me, his mouth ghosting over mine. "That just proves you have what it takes to not get crushed by this life."

The doorbell rings, cutting him off as I reach for the box of pasta.

He goes to answer the door while I dump the pasta into the pot of boiling water.

Voices come from the front hall, soft and growing louder as they get closer.

I wipe my sweaty palms on my slacks before smoothing down my sleeveless satin blouse.

Finn walks into the room with two people trailing behind him.

The man is tall and broad, with dark red hair and bright green eyes. His jaw could be cut from polished stone, if not for the scar marring it.

The woman offers me a soft smile, tucking her short chocolate-colored hair behind her ear. "Hello."

I paste on my warmest smile and head over to greet them. "It's nice to meet you."

Finn smiles and loops his arm around my waist, pulling me against his side. "Aves, this is Cillian and Becca. Cillian, Becca, this is Ava."

Cillian returns the smile. "It smells delicious in here, Ava."

"Thank you." I press a quick kiss to Finn's jaw before heading back to the stove. I grab the pan with the chicken and pour it into the sauce before stirring the pasta. "Everything should be ready in just a few moments. There's a couple bottles of wine on the table there and some beer and soda in the fridge. Feel free to help yourselves to whatever you like."

Becca comes over to help me, sliding on oven mitts as the timer starts beeping. "I hate just sitting down and watching everyone else do the work."

I step to the side, allowing her to pull out the garlic bread. "Thanks. I have to admit, I like cooking, but with nursing, I barely have any time for it."

She nods and puts the tray on a trivet. Her gaze is bright, the warm smile still in place. It falters when she glances down. "Beautiful necklace."

"Thanks. My dad gave it to me." I turn off the stove as the pasta finishes cooking. "If this tastes awful, I've got the number for the local pizza place on speed dial."

She chuckles and makes a show of sniffing the air. "It smells amazing in here. I'm sure it's going to be delicious."

I wish I had her confidence as I dish up the food, trying to make it look as nice as possible.

Becca helps me bring it to the table, taking the seat beside her husband and putting their bowls down.

Finn pours me a glass of wine as I take my seat. "Thanks for the dinner, Aves."

"You're welcome." I take a sip of wine before tasting the pasta.

Flavors explode on my tongue, the basil and garlic blending with the cream perfectly.

Cillian nods after his first forkful. "This is spectacular."

Becca takes another bite before sipping her wine. The smile she gives me is hesitant but honest and open.

This might be going better than I thought it would. Which is good.

Finn needs to make a good impression with his boss.

I'm going to owe Brooklyn a massive thank you for this recipe.

Finn shovels food into his mouth, stopping every now and then to say something about the business to Cillian.

I barely hear it. I'm too busy trying to focus on not spilling pasta down the front of my shirt.

I can almost feel Becca's gaze on me a few times, but she doesn't say anything.

One of those times, I catch her eyes, and she just smiles. I take a sip of my wine and she does the same, drinking it quickly before turning her attention back to her food.

Does this mean this dinner is going horribly? What if she decides to go home and tell Cillian to cut ties with Finn?

I don't know what that would mean for Finn, especially

after all that he has already done for Cillian.

Finn may not tell me everything, but I know enough to know that if he isn't careful, he's going to land himself back in jail. Or worse.

Cillian is the first to finish, putting his fork to the side. "So, Ava, how are you liking Portland? Finn tells me that you're not working right now because you're looking into some family history."

I nod and twirl more of the pasta around my fork. If I don't keep my hands busy, my heart is going to race until it feels like I'm about to explode. "I never thought that I would love living somewhere it rains constantly, but Portland has really changed my mind about that."

"I imagine it would." Cillian leans back in his chair, draping his arm over the back of Becca's. "How's the search for the family history going?"

I shrug one shoulder, the corner of my mouth turning upward. "It's interesting. It turns out that there's a lot I don't know about my family."

Becca stands up with a polite smile. "Excuse me for a moment. Where is your washroom?"

Finn points down the hallway. "Just down there. First door. You can't miss it."

Cillian's eyes are glued to his wife's back as she hurries away from the table.

Her heels click against the floor until she disappears into the bathroom.

I glance at Finn, wondering what that was about, but he and Cillian are already talking about business again.

After a moment, I shake it off and join in the conversation, hoping that this night ends soon.

I can't bear the thought of being the reason something terrible happens to Finn.

17

FINN

Rain pours down on the windshield of Dawson's car as he pulls into my driveway.

I reach into the backseat and grab the bag of groceries we stopped for on the way home.

Dawson drums his fingers on the wheel as I flip up my hood. "Cillian is giving us a couple days to relax after that Dorian Roach debacle. One less Roach infesting our town, I guess."

"Funny. But thank fuck. I could use a nap. He was at my house for dinner Thursday night and things haven't slowed down at all since then."

"I'm sure Ava is going to be happy to see you for more than a couple hours at a time."

I roll my eyes as the rain pounds down. "I'm sure that she will be if she can tear herself away from her father's yearbooks. Her aunt dropped them off last Friday and as far as I know, she's spent most of Sunday pouring through them with her friend. Probably today too."

"You don't sound like you're a fan of that."

"Ava is brilliant, but she's got an attachment to a piece of shit father that has her exhausting herself to try and figure out what was going on in his life. I want her to slow down and actually get some sleep for once, but she seems to want literally anything else."

Dawson snorts. "I know what that's like. My girlfriend is the kind to throw herself into things and not come up for a breath. Sometimes, you just have to put an end to things yourself."

I turn his words over in my head.

Ava is going to work herself to the bone trying to figure out who her father really was. Brooklyn isn't stepping in to stop her either.

But at least she is watching her when I can't.

Dawson nods to the house. "You better get in there before she starts to think you're not coming home."

I open the door and step out into the rain, hurrying up the steps.

As soon as my feet hit the porch, Dawson pulls out of the driveway.

A couple of days without having to go on a job will be nice. I finally get to sit back and spend some time with Ava.

It will be nice to spend time with the one person I don't have to lie to.

Ava looks up as I kick off my wet shoes and coat. "Hey, I didn't think that you were going to be home so soon. You're never going to believe what I found out today."

The stack of yearbooks sits in the corner of the coffee table. One is spread open in front of her and Brooklyn, pictures of people circled in bright red.

I head into the kitchen and put the groceries away. "Oh yeah?"

"Yeah." She taps the book. "This man right here is a bookie, and this other one is a known drug dealer."

A pit opens in the bottom of my stomach. Her tone suggests that it's just the beginning of what her father could be involved in. I'm hoping that she hasn't dug any deeper than that yet.

I walk over to her and take a seat on the couch while she and Brooklyn kneel on the floor.

Brooklyn offers me a tight smile. She doesn't look any happier than I feel with Ava's obsession.

Ava shifts to show me the pictures. "I thought that these men looked familiar, but I couldn't quite place why. So, I started looking through some pictures of my dad at different events. These two men appear in the background a couple different times."

I sigh and rake my hand through my hair, knowing where this is leading. Though I may have only been in Tennessee for a few years, I recognize the men in the pictures.

If her father was associated with them, the trouble goes deeper than she thinks.

Although, I doubt that it gets much worse than trying to sell his own daughter to sex traffickers. Did he try to do the same with Ava? What if he had? What if he had succeeded?

If he was still alive today, I would kill him myself.

Ava stands up, dark bags under her distant gaze. "I need something to drink. There's still another few yearbooks to go through from his time in university, and I have no clue what I'm going to find in there."

She wanders into the kitchen while Brooklyn looks over her shoulder at me.

I lean closer to her, making sure Ava can't hear me. "This is insane. I'm going to take her out and try to snap her out of this. At least for a couple hours. She's going to get hurt if this keeps going on."

Brooklyn nods. "It's sweet that you want to protect her from hurting her heart. I'll make an excuse to get out of here in a few minutes. She's been going like this all day. She told me last night that she was up in the middle of the night to sort through them before I got here."

I feel sick thinking about Ava sitting up all night and trying to find clues about her father's past.

Ava comes back as I lean into the cushions and stretch my legs out. She sits on the ground and leans back against the couch, her shoulder pressing into my knee.

Ava sets her drink on the table and pulls one of the yearbooks into her lap. "If he has ties to a bookie, do you think that there could be a tie to the sex traffickers there?"

I tap out a beat in the air with my foot, trying to figure out what to say to her. The last thing I want to do is send her down another spiral. Not when she's barely sleeping.

Brooklyn clears her throat and gets up, grabbing her purse. "I've got to get going. My ride is supposed to be here in a minute or two."

Ava's eyebrows pull together, a thin line appearing. "I thought you were going to stay for dinner tonight?"

Brooklyn shakes her head. "No. I got a message from my mother, and she needs some help at home with my uncle. He's not doing so well these days."

Ava's frown fades. "Okay. Let me know if you need anything. I can come over and help."

"Will do. See you later." Brooklyn races for the door, shutting it softly behind her.

Ava buries her nose back in the yearbook as I glance at the stack.

There is no way that this is healthy. She's going to make

herself sick if she keeps trying to figure out the connections her father has.

It's too much for one day, and it's time she took a break.

I stand up and take the stack of yearbooks, moving them to the dining table.

Ava gives me a dirty look. "Why are you moving those? I wasn't done with them yet. It's going to take a couple hours to finish going through all the information there."

Shaking my head, I go over and take the yearbook she has in her hands. "Nope. We're done with this for tonight. You need to take a break."

Ava gets to her feet and plants her hands on her hips. "I don't need to take a break, Finn, and quite frankly, it's none of your business."

I scoff and stride over to her. "It *is* my damn business, Ava. I told you that I was going to protect you."

"And what are you protecting me from right now?"

"Yourself." I take her chin between my fingers and tilt her head until she's looking at me. "Ava, you've barely slept, and I know for a fact you aren't sleeping much any other night."

"Are you asking me to stop after you said that you would help me?"

"No. I'm telling you that tonight, and probably tomorrow, we are going to be taking a break. I have a couple days where I don't have to work, and we're not going to talk about what's going on with your search at all."

She jerks back. "I don't have time to take a break, Finn."

"Why not?" I cross my arms, looking down at her. "What is the rush? We're in Portland until we both get what we want out of our deal."

Ava throws her hands up in the air. "I don't even know what it is you want out of the deal!"

"It's safer if you don't."

She rolls her eyes. "I don't know why you think that I don't know what it is that goes on in your life. I dated your brother for years when I was younger. He might have been a colossal asshole at times, but he didn't hide shit from me."

"And how is that working out for you now?" I pinch the bridge of my nose as she recoils like she's been slapped. "I'm sorry, Aves, but I'm not going to stand here and argue with you about this. I've told you enough to keep you safe while not keeping you ignorant."

"To you, that's enough, but what if it's not to me?"

"Ava, enough. I saw the look on your face when you were on the phone with my brother. That is more than enough to convince me to protect you as much as possible, even from yourself. We're taking a break from the yearbooks and the arguments. If you want to keep arguing with me tomorrow, then you can, but tonight, we're going out."

"And what if I don't want to go out?"

I point down the hall. "Go get changed. We're going out on a date, and you're going to have a good time."

"I really do need to work more on going through those yearbooks. I want to note all the comments Dad made throughout them and see if they can be connected to somebody else. It's going to take time, Finn. I need that time."

"You have all the time in the world."

"No. I don't. I feel like time is running out, and the closer I get to figuring out exactly who he was, the farther away the information gets."

I gesture to the stack of yearbooks. "It will all still be waiting here tomorrow, when our date is over."

She sighs, her shoulders slumping forward. "Finn, we don't need to go out on a date. This entire thing between us is fake."

I step closer to her, invading her space.

She takes a step back, her eyes widening as I follow.

Her ass hits the dining table, stopping her in her tracks.

I plant my hands on the table on either side of her and lean in.

"Aves, this stopped being fake for me weeks ago."

18

AVA

My heart crashes through my chest as Finn looms over me.

He keeps me pinned against the table, that piercing stare searching mine.

I swallow the lump in my throat and shake my head. "You don't mean that."

Finn dips his head toward mine, kissing the racing pulse point on my neck. "You know I mean it, Aves. Your heart is racing."

I don't know what to think. Though he's been sweet to me, I didn't think we would ever get to a point where we were confessing our feelings to each other.

Hell, I didn't think that he would have any feelings to confess.

Finn kisses my fluttering pulse again before pulling back. "Ava, I want to take you on a real date. No more of this pretend bullshit. Go get changed into something comfortable."

"Where are we going?"

His smile lights up the room.

Though I can't find the words to tell him how I feel about him right now, accepting the date seems like enough for him.

Finn is a good man. He's not going to hurt me the way his brother did.

Nobody could compare to that level of hurt.

But Finn is still a man with a commitment to the mob. He goes to work every day, and I never know if it's going to be the last day I see him.

I wouldn't recover if he was killed. I know I wouldn't.

Over the last few weeks, I've been the fool who has allowed another Byrne boy to worm his way into my heart. I've allowed him to get close and see me fall apart while I go on a wild goose chase.

I've given him the power to hurt me like I swore I would never give anyone ever again.

Yet, he hasn't taken advantage of that power once.

Hopefully, letting this Byrne boy in won't break my heart.

Finn pushes off the table, taking a few steps back. "Go get changed, Ava. As much as I may like the little sundress, it's not going to be practical for the fair."

Excitement surges through me. "We're going to the fair? I haven't been to one in years."

He laughs and nods, giving me a gentle nudge toward the bedroom. "If you keep taking this long to go get ready, the fair is going to leave town before we even get there."

I hurry down the hall, disappearing into the bedroom to get changed. I pull out a pair of black leggings and a lilac crop top, swapping them for my dress quickly.

As soon as I have a pair of high-tops on, I head back out into the living room.

Finn grabs the black and white flannel from where I

tossed it on the armchair earlier today. "You're going to want this. It's cold out, and it might rain before we get home."

I take the flannel and slide it on, stuffing my phone and wallet into one of the pockets.

Finn takes my hand, lacing his fingers through mine.

My heart skips a beat as we leave the house, grabbing the motorcycle helmets on the way by.

We stop beside the motorcycle, and Finn takes my helmet.

His touch is soft as he puts it on me before snapping the buckle beneath my chin. He does the same, putting his visor down and getting onto the motorcycle.

He nudges the kickstand with his foot before starting the motorcycle. It roars to life as I climb on behind him.

I'm too aware of every inch of my body pressed against his as he drives us to the fair.

My hands press against his toned stomach, and my thighs bracket his. As I press closer to him on a sharp turn, my core aches.

I need him.

Finn reaches down and puts his hand on my thigh, squeezing it as we enter the parking lot.

Bright and colorful lights ignite the night. Cheery music plays, and the scent of funnel cakes wafts through the air.

My mouth waters at the delicious smell while Finn parks the motorcycle.

We get off, and Finn takes the helmets, stashing them in the saddlebags.

I'm bouncing on my toes beside him, already eyeing one of the rides that locks you in a cage and flips you upside down.

Finn takes my hand again, his palm rough and warm. "What do you want to do first?"

"That." I point at the ride flipping people upside down. "And then I want to go on that one that spins you in a circle backward. And then there's that other one that spins really fast and kind of looks like an eggbeater."

Finn tugs me closer as we walk over to the ticket booth.

I don't miss the way women look at him. A group giggles as he passes, whispering things to their friends and nodding to him.

The entire time, Finn just pulls me closer, letting go of my hand to wrap his arm around my waist. He kisses my temple as we join the back of the line, waiting our turn to get wristbands.

When it's finally our turn, he pays for the wristbands while I get mine put on. As soon as we're both ready, we walk through the gates into the fair.

Children are screaming and running while tired adults walk behind them, carrying cotton candy and cheap prizes. Teenagers sneak sips of something from a brown paper bag before heading for another ride.

As I look up at Finn, I can't help but notice how out of place he seems in all this.

He catches me watching him as we head for the first ride. "Why are you staring at me?"

"This doesn't seem like the kind of date you would like. We can go somewhere else if you like."

"I like spending time with you, and you seem like the kind of person who likes fairs."

Though it may not be the most romantic thing anyone has ever said to me, my heart still skips a beat.

His fingers brush against the bare skin on my ribs.

A shiver rolls through my body.

Finn's fingers drift a little higher, sliding beneath the hem of my shirt and grazing against my lace bra.

I nudge him. "If you keep doing that, then we're not going to make it on any of the rides."

Finn gives me a wicked smile as we approach the front of the line. "You can get on whatever ride you'd like."

I burst out laughing as the worker nods for us to get in one of the cages.

Finn smirks, his hand moving to my lower back as he waits for me to climb in.

I take a seat on the metal bench, and he sits beside me.

The bar above is pulled down and locked into place.

The worker shuts the door to the cage and slides the bolt into place before starting the ride.

We move slow at first, going in a circle without the cage being flipped over.

Finn's hand leaves the bar and lands on my thigh as we start the second circle.

I glance down at it before looking up at him. 'What do you think you're doing?"

His fingers drift to my inner thigh, brushing against the thin fabric at my core. "Nothing."

He presses a little harder, rubbing my clit through the layers.

My hips rock as the cage flips upside down.

I moan as Finn slides his hand into my leggings and thong.

He circles my clit as the cage continues flipping.

As the ride moves faster, so do his fingers.

I moan as he presses them deeper into my pussy.

"Fuck, Aves, you're already soaked. There is no way you're going to make it through the night without wanting to go on the best ride here."

His little smirk is nearly as teasing as his touch.

Finn's fingers keep rocking into me as my pussy clamps down around them. His thumb presses against my clit as he drives his fingers deeper into me.

I moan as he turns his head and captures my mouth in a kiss.

As my legs start to shake, his tongue tangles with mine.

His fingers move faster, pressing against the spot that drives me wild.

Finn nips at my bottom lip as I come, chuckling to himself.

I roll my hips, riding his fingers until the waves of pleasure come to an end.

He pulls out his fingers and holds them out to me.

"Taste yourself."

My pulse races as I lean forward and take his fingers into my mouth.

I take my time licking my juices from them as the ride slows, flicking my tongue and sucking the same way I've done to his cock before.

Sure enough, when I pull away and look down, his cock is hard and pressing against the front of his pants.

"Looks like you've got a problem there."

Finn tucks his hand into his pocket, adjusting himself quickly. "You just wait until I get you alone. I'm pretty sure I saw a funhouse here."

The ride comes to a stop, and our cage opens moments after Finn takes his hand back out of his pocket.

He gets off the ride first, smacking my ass as I pass him.

I press my thighs together as the pulse starts in my pussy.

As much as I want to go on other rides, right now, I need him.

Finn walks off the ride's platform with me, leaning down to press his lips to the shell of my ear. "You look like you're thinking of one other ride you desperately want to get on."

"And whose fault is that?" I look at him over my shoulder as we step onto the grass. "Where's the damn funhouse?"

He laughs and loops his arm around my shoulders, his fingertips brushing against my pebbled nipple.

Finn keeps up the teasing touches as we navigate our way across the fairgrounds and over to the funhouse.

By the time we step into the first dark hallway, my entire body feels like it's about to combust.

The neon lights shine bright as Finn takes my hand and pulls me through the twisting hallways.

Other people are screaming and laughing as we head deeper into the funhouse.

He stops when he finds a small closet hidden behind one of the neon blue mountains. With a smirk, he opens the door and drags me inside with him.

The closet is barely big enough for the two of us, but I can still drop to my knees in front of him and unzip his pants.

"You're going to have to be quiet." His eyes burn with lust as I pull out his cock and run my thumb over the tip, catching the drop of moisture. "The music is loud, but you're louder when my cock is buried in your tight little pussy."

"Guess you better fuck my mouth to shut me up, then."

His fingers slide into my hair, and he pulls it back from my face.

He uses his grip on my hair to tilt my head back.

As he pushes his cock into my mouth, I stroke the base of it.

"Fuck, what a good little slut you are."

I flick my tongue over the head of his cock before dragging it along the underside.

He groans, his head dropping back but his gaze still on me.

I hollow my cheeks and swallow his cock, trying to take him deeper when the head hits the back of my throat.

I moan as I bob my head, trying to take all of him.

Finn groans, his hips thrusting forward.

"Fuck yes, Aves, take it all."

My hand cups his balls, squeezing them hard as I breathe through my nose and take his cock as deep as I can.

Finn holds my hair tighter, keeping me in place as his hips piston faster.

My eyes water as my pussy aches.

He groans, his cock throbbing in my mouth.

Just when I think he is going to come, he pulls out and tugs me to my feet. Finn grabs my chin and hauls my face to his for a searing kiss.

Our tongues tangle as he smacks my ass hard.

My pussy clenches as he drags my leggings down my legs before spinning me around and pushing me up against the wall.

His hands run over my ass, smacking one cheek and then the other.

I arch my back, pressing my breasts harder into the wall and giving him more access.

Finn's fingers slip into my pussy while he grabs one wrist and then the other. He pins them above my head, keeping them locked in his grip while his fingers pound into me.

My pussy is soaked, wetness dripping down my thighs as his fingers move faster.

I bite down on a moan as he pulls his fingers out and slams his cock into me.

I push my ass back, widening my stance to take more of his cock.

He groans, his free hand finding my clit.

My pussy pulsates around his cock with each thrust, sending me closer to the edge. "Fuck yes, Finn. More. Please. I want to come on your cock. I want you to come in me."

He groans, his chest pressing against my back as he takes my earlobe between his teeth. "You're going to be dripping my come while we go on all those rides later. Is that what you want?"

"Yes."

"Beg for it."

I thrust my hips back to meet him as he drives into me harder. "Please. Please fill me with your come."

Finn groans, both hands flying to my hips as he rams his cock into my pussy harder.

His cock stiffens as my orgasm crashes through me.

My pussy milks his cock as he comes, his thrusts slowing until we are both spent.

When he pulls out, I take my time pulling my leggings back up, his low growl only turning me on more.

"Aves, if you keep doing that shit, we're going to spend the rest of our date locked in this tiny ass closet."

I comb my fingers through my hair, smoothing it down. "And that would be bad because…?"

He laughs and tucks his cock away before pushing open the door and stepping back out into the funhouse.

Thankfully, there is nobody in front of the mountains as we step around them and continue through the funhouse.

Clowns laugh and taunt children while neon spirals dance on the walls. A hall of mirrors has Finn moving closer to me, dipping his head to kiss my shoulder.

"I should have fucked you in here." His tone is husky as he nips at my pulse.

My cheeks burn bright as we leave the funhouse and head for another ride.

Finn keeps his arm around me, or his hand twined with mine as we move from ride to ride.

Though it is new territory for us, it feels right.

And that's what scares me the most.

There's more than just a physical attraction between us. If the last few weeks have shown me anything, it's that.

Finn is easy to be around. He challenges me and makes me laugh.

There isn't another person I would come home to at night.

Right now, it's easy to picture that this is just another date night for us.

We'd be going to our home, knowing that nothing would ever change between us. We'd fall into bed together and talk about the day we finally got married and had kids.

We would plan a future together.

If it weren't for who Finn's brother is, that could be our reality.

When Finn smiles down at me as we get on another ride, it sends my mind spiraling.

This is a great night, but that's all it can ever be, no matter how much I think I'm falling for him.

19

FINN

Ava moves around the kitchen like a little hurricane. She moves pots and pans, pulling a roast out of the oven and setting it on the stovetop to rest.

She glares at me over her shoulder as I pull down a bottle of wine. "I wish that you would have told me about this dinner sooner. They're going to think that I don't have my shit together."

"Well, I was a little distracted." I take down five wine glasses as well, carrying them and the bottle over to the table. "Between fucking you at the fair the other night and fucking you in the backyard last night, I barely have time to think."

She scowls at me, but the corner of her mouth twitches. "You're impossible. It's not my fault that you can't seem to keep your damn dick in your pants."

I laugh and raise an eyebrow. "As I seem to recall, you're the one who dropped to your knees and pulled my cock out."

Ava grabs a dish towel and tosses it at my head.

I duck and the towel sails by, landing on the floor.

With an irritated huff, she turns back to the stove and stirs the gravy.

I finish setting the table before wandering back over to her and wrapping my arms around her waist. "Everything is going to be fine. Cillian couldn't stop singing your praises after the last time you made him dinner. I'm sure that he's going to love this too. Besides, Dawson is coming with Cillian and Becca. Even if everyone hates the food, he'll keep them too distracted to notice."

She swats my bicep before wriggling her way out of my embrace. "That's not helpful, Finn. I'm here to try and help you make a good impression with these people, and you just want to stand here and make jokes."

"Aves, everything is going to be perfect. You're a great cook."

Ava pokes at the potatoes surrounding the roast. "Do you think these are crispy enough? There's nothing worse than horrible roasted potatoes."

I lean over and look at the potatoes. My stomach growls as I nod. "Those look like the best roasted potatoes ever."

The doorbell rings before she can start worrying about the next thing.

I kiss her temple before heading to the door and pulling it open.

Dawson walks into the house like he owns it, a tray of desserts in his arms.

Becca and Cillian follow with a bottle of wine.

I hold my hand out for the wine. "I can take that, Becca."

She smiles and passes me the bottle before sliding off her coat and heels. 'Where is Ava?"

"In the kitchen. She's made a roast that's had me

drooling for hours. I was going to try to sneak some of it away when she wasn't looking before you showed up."

Becca laughs and hurries into the kitchen. A couple moments later, she and Ava are talking about nursing.

Cillian nods to me, leaving his shoes and coat in the entryway as he follows me to the living room. "We need to have a chat about the upcoming gun run. I have a deal with Christian Herrera in Tennessee. His men are going to be here in a couple days, and once they get here, I need you to get the guns and transport them to our warehouse."

I put the bottle of wine on the dining table, and Dawson drops the desserts beside them.

We both head back into the living room, taking the empty armchairs.

Cillian jerks his chin at Dawson. "You're going to be waiting at the warehouse for the shipment. This one has to be kept quiet. The only people to know are those within the inner circles."

My eyebrows knit together. "Didn't you just get a shipment from someone up in Canada a couple days ago?"

"Yes." Cillian glances over at his wife and Ava before leaning forward. "There's some problems brewing with the Russians. I'm hoping to diffuse the tensions, but I want us to be prepared if I can't."

Dawson rolls his eyes. "I told Joey that stealing from them was a bad idea."

I cross my arms, the corner of my mouth tugging upward. "Well, I dealt with Joey. He won't be causing any more problems."

A loud crash and laughter cut off our conversation.

I glance over my shoulder as Ava leans into Becca. The pair of them are nearly in tears as I get up and head into the kitchen to see what just broke.

. . .

Ava looks up at me with wide eyes, her laughter dying on her lips.

Becca nudges the roast on the floor with her foot, and Ava loses it again.

Ava shakes her head and points at the shards of glass from the roasting pan. "I told you a roast was a bad fucking idea. I'm never making a damn roast again."

I crouch down and grab the roast, tossing it into the sink. "You're going to hurt your feet if you step in any of the glass. Hop up on the counter while I get this cleaned."

Ava tries to hop on the counter twice, but both times she is laughing too hard to hold herself steady while pulling herself up.

Becca laughs with her, and the pair of them seem to send the other into a fit of giggles each time someone gets control.

I grab Ava by the waist and lift her onto the counter as her laughter stops. "At least you don't have to worry about if the potatoes are soggy or not anymore."

Ava's eyes widen, her smile stretching from one side of her face to the other. "I hate roasts."

Chuckling, I get the broom and sweep up the glass. "I can see that. I didn't think you hated them to the point of throwing them on the ground."

Cillian comes over with a rag to start mopping up the spilled pan drippings while Dawson grabs the pizza menu from the fridge.

Becca sits on the counter, her legs dangling. "It's my fault. I thought that dumping the pan drippings into the gravy would give it the flavor Ava wanted. Then I dropped the pan."

"Because I nudged her."

Cillian tosses the dirty rag into the sink and moves to stand between Becca's legs, his hands drifting up her thighs.

Ava's gaze cuts to them, her smile faltering slightly. "Pizza is a good dinner too."

Becca nods and cups Cillian's face, kissing the tip of his nose. "We've never met a pizza that we didn't like."

Within a few minutes, Dawson has the pizza and beer ordered and everyone is sitting in the living room with some show about dating in private pods on television. I lean back in the chair, my hand on Ava's hip as she perches on the arm beside me.

Becca leans into Cillian's side, her gaze on Ava instead of the show.

I wasn't sure what to think when I brought Becca and Cillian over for the first time. I certainly hadn't been expecting it to go as well as it did.

But the women hit it off, spending most of the night talking to each other.

Tonight, they seem to be closer than ever.

Ava leans over, her hip shifting against my hand as she whispers something in Becca's ear. The pair of them exchange a look before settling back into their seats.

My phone starts ringing, the shrill tone cutting through the sound of the show.

With a sigh, I get up and go outside, pulling the phone from my pocket. The number flashing across the screen sends dread straight to the pit of my stomach.

I slide my thumb across the screen and hold the phone to my ear. "Christian. How did you get this number?"

Christian chuckles. "I have my connections. Thought I would check up on you. Make sure that you're still out of Tennessee."

"I am." I sit down on one of the loungers and look up at the clouds drifting in front of the moon. 'Things are going well. I've been working again. Think I might like to stay where I am for the foreseeable future. No desire to return to Tennessee."

"Or Virginia?"

"I have zero plans of returning to Virginia."

Christian hums. "Interesting. I know your family is close. So is mine. I don't know what I would do if one of them decided that they weren't coming back home."

I swallow hard, wondering what it is he thinks he knows to be calling me. Does he know that his sister-in-law is with me? Does he think that I'm going to ruin her life?

I've been doing my best to give her everything that she could ever want, but there is a little voice in my mind that tells me it's still not enough. *I*'m not enough.

This call could be to warn me away from her. To threaten me to walk away and leave her in Portland before Christian tracks me down.

But from the calls I've overheard with her sister, she doesn't give much information about what's going on in her personal life.

Her sister knows that she's here with me, but I don't think she knows who I am.

Christian would be able to put the pieces of the puzzle together, though.

I don't want to lie to him, not after all he has done for me, but I will if I have to.

"How is your family?" It's a safe enough question to ask, and one that might reveal what he knows.

Christian clears his throat. "They're good, but that's not why I was calling. We've had a couple problems here, and I wanted to make sure that they had nothing to do with you."

"I haven't been in Tennessee since the day I was released. I saw my chance and got the hell out of there." I chuckle, trying to lighten the mood slightly. "I can assure you that whatever is happening there isn't me."

"What about your father or brother? They've always been power-hungry and stupid."

"That they are, but as far as I know, they're focusing on Virginia."

There is a long pause, and something closes in the background of the call. Floorboards squeak.

It's easy to picture Christian pacing across the floor, deciding whether or not to trust me.

The last thing I need is to make another enemy.

Christian hums again. "You've been useful today, Finn. I hope it remains that way if I ever have a reason to call you again."

The call ends, and I can finally release the breath I've been holding since I answered the phone.

Christian is nothing if not an intimidating man. Between him and the other powerful men he associates with, I would be buried in the blink of an eye if he thought there was something going on between me and his sister-in-law.

I've escaped his wrath this time, but I know the lie will come back to haunt me.

20

AVA

Aunt Courtney smiles as Lola races down the driveway to me, her tail going a mile a minute. The dopey doggy smile is all I see as she hops up on her back legs and plants her paws on my shoulder.

Lola licks my cheek, her entire body swaying with her wagging tail.

I rub her fuzzy head, laughing as she gets down and trots away.

The big dog finds a stick and carries it off to a shady spot beneath a large tree.

Aunt Courtney sits on the porch steps as I cross the yard. "It's good to see you. It feels like it's been forever. How was that dinner with your fiancé's boss the other night?"

I grin and turn one of the lawn chairs to face her before dropping down. "Managed to drop the roast on the floor. We ended up getting pizza instead. His boss's wife is really nice. Becca."

Aunt Courtney sits a little stiffer, reaching for the glass of water beside her. "Becca?"

My eyebrows pull together as I kick my feet up on one of the steps. "Yeah. Do you know her?"

"Maybe. What's her husband's name?"

"Cillian."

Aunt Courtney's hand trembles as she brings the glass of water to her lips. She takes a long sip, avoiding meeting my gaze. When she puts the glass down, she takes her time staring at Lola.

My pulse races, the hair on the back of my neck standing. "Aunt Courtney, do you know them?"

"I knew Becca once upon a time. Back when we were in high school. She was my friend for a little while, until your father started dating her."

"Did it end badly?"

She shrugs, picking at her nails. "I don't know, honestly. He never told me what really happened between the two of them, and she didn't like to talk about it either. Our friendship changed a lot after she was with your father."

"Should I ask her about him? I keep running into dead ends. He talks about someone he dated in high school and university, which would be my mom. It seems like they had a lot of falling outs in the relationship."

Aunt Courtney clears her throat. Her hands drop to her lap, and she takes a deep breath. "I really shouldn't be the one to tell you this, but I doubt anyone else is ever going to."

My stomach twists in tight knots as my feet drop to the ground, and I sit forward. "What are you talking about?"

"Your dad didn't date your mom in high school. He never even met her until he went to college."

"That's impossible. That would mean... No. I've seen pictures of me with my mom as a baby."

The oxygen is sucked out of the atmosphere as I lean forward. None of this makes sense.

I've got dozens of pictures of me with Mom while I was growing up.

But have you seen any picture with of you two at the hospital?

I used to ask Mom about it when I was younger. Back then, she said that she was so excited to hold me that she didn't think about getting a picture taken.

She would tell me that I was perfect. That she had been so wrapped up in staring at my little face that no other thoughts occurred to her.

Except now my aunt is telling me my father didn't meet the woman claiming to be my mother until after I was already on the way. Maybe even after I was already born.

It was all a lie. My whole life is a lie.

Aunt Courtney gives me a sad smile. "She was around because she was friends with your father. He would come down for long weekends to visit you. He would bring her with him."

"My mother's not my mother?"

The earth falls out from beneath my feet. Bile rises in my throat as I put my head between my knees and try not to throw up.

I look up at Aunt Courtney, my vision blurring as tears gather. "This isn't possible. This has to be some sick joke. I know that he wasn't a good man, but he wouldn't spend my entire life lying to me about who my mother was."

I remember feeling like I wasn't love. Like I didn't belong. An outcast.

Zoe had admitted more than once that she did too.

This entire time my whole life has been a lie.

My dad and the woman I've called mother made sure that I would never find out the truth.

Was Dad plotting this from the beginning?

Is that why he brought Mom home on school breaks, even when they weren't dating yet?

Aunt Courtney clears her throat. "I know this is a shock, but your dad did love you. Very much. He might not have wanted you at first—what teenager would want a child—but once you were here, you could see the love in his eyes every time he looked at you."

Even though I knew that my father's journals were unreliable and frantic, I didn't think that he would leave out something as big as my mom not being my birth mom.

A thousand different words are on the tip of my tongue, but they all disappear the moment I open my mouth.

My jaw snaps shut, the world still spinning around me.

After a moment, I sit back and stare up at the sky. The shock gives way to a numbness that consumes me.

When I look back at Aunt Courtney, she looks like her heart is breaking.

She shouldn't have to be the one to tell me the truth about my life. My mom or dad should have told me.

But why keep it a secret?

Maybe my birth mom decided that she didn't want me?

Aunt Courtney blinks back tears. "I wish that someone else would have told you. Nadia used to come back here with him on every trip. Both of them loved you."

"Do you think they were planning to make me look like hers from the beginning?" I have to force the words out. My voice sounds strangled as Lola trots back and dumps her stick in my lap.

I toss the stick for her, watching her chase after it as Aunt Courtney picks at a loose thread in her jeans.

She shakes her head. "No. I don't think that they were planning it. I think that they all got along, and then at some point, your father started loving Nadia far more than he ever did Becca."

"Becca? As in O'Reilly?"

"I'm sorry. I don't think…"

"Please, Aunt Courtney. I need to know who I am."

Her bottom lip wavers and her shoulders sag.

She nods. "She used to be Becca Hammer back then, but yes."

"Becca's my mom…" I'm shaking me head. My world is so far off its axis that I'm about to drown.

My aunt touches my hand.

I look at her. "Dad's ex-girlfriend is married to one of the most dangerous men in Oregon."

She nods.

"My fiancé's boss."

"Yes."

"And you're sure Becca O'Reilly is the woman who gave birth to me?" I cross my arms, trying to hold myself together so I don't fall apart.

I've spent evenings with the woman, and she never once mentioned that she was my mother. She smiled and laughed, treating me like a friend.

Does she know who I am? Does she even care?

My mouth goes dry, and my body is numb as I start to analyze every interaction with Becca I've had.

Nothing would have given her away as the woman who gave birth to me.

I choke back the tears, gasping for air. I can't seem to get a deep enough breath, even as I link my hands behind my head and stretch my elbows out wide to open my chest.

This is all too much. I never thought that coming to Portland would lead me to a mother I didn't even know I had to find.

I take another moment to gather myself before looking at my aunt. "Will you go with me to see her? I don't think that I can do this on my own."

Aunt Courtney nods. "Give me a minute to get Lola settled and grab my keys."

She whistles to Lola and takes her inside, the screen door swinging shut behind them.

I run my hands down my face, taking deep breaths and trying not to freak out more than I already have.

Becca O'Reilly is my mother.

Is that why my mother never showed me love? Because I'm not hers?

And why wasn't my birth mother a part of my life?

Has she been spending time with me, knowing that I'm her daughter, and not saying anything?

Aunt Courtney walks down the steps with her keys dangling from her fingers. All the color is drained from her face as she unlocks the doors to her little blue car.

The numbness continues to spread as I push myself up from the chair and head to the car.

The drive to Becca's house is long, but it doesn't give me any time to clear my head. There are too many thoughts to just focus on one.

I'm furious at my father to lying to me throughout my life. He had years to tell me that I had another mother out there—one who might love me and miss me—but he didn't.

Instead, he raised me with a woman who barely looked at me, no matter how much everyone claimed she loved me. No matter how she herself claimed that for a little while when I was younger.

Did Becca care about me? Had she ever?

Whose choice was it to have me be raised away from her?

As we pull up to the massive house, my heart leaps into my throat.

I should have thought more about what I was going to say when I got here. I can't just march in there and ask her why she didn't love me.

Though I might be angry, I'm not a petulant child. I can be angry and civil at the same time.

Becca steps onto the front porch as we're getting out of the car. Her hands are tucked into the pockets of her cream linen slacks. Her dark gaze focuses on me, the corner of her mouth twitching.

Aunt Courtney gives her a thin smile. "I probably should have called or something before we came over, but Ava is looking for answers that I can't give her."

It's only now, standing in front of Becca, that I realize the resemblance between the two of us.

We have the same dark eyes and hair. The same mouth.

I should've seen it before, but I didn't know that it was something I should've been looking for.

Becca nods. "We have some things to talk about. Come inside. We can talk in the living room. I'll get everybody a glass of wine. We're going to need it to start digging up the past."

I follow her into the massive white house, large windows letting in light from every angle.

She leads the way into a beige living room with dark accents.

Everything looks classy and timeless.

Stepping into Becca's home is like stepping into another life that could've been mine.

Becca pours three glasses of wine, and we take a seat on the couches.

I sit opposite her, the glass coffee table keeping us a few feet apart.

She looks down at the necklace I'm wearing.

"That used to be mine." Becca takes a sip of her wine before putting the glass down on the table. "Back in high school. Your father gave it to me when we first started dating."

Butterflies beat against the inside of my stomach. "So, it's true, then. You gave birth to me."

She winces and nods. "Yes. I did."

Aunt Courtney leans back in her seat, crossing one leg over the other. She said on the way over that she was going to stay out of the conversation unless I needed her.

I appreciate her being here for emotional support.

My hand trembles as I raise the wine glass to my lips and take a sip.

The wine does little to chase away my nerves, but it gives me something to do while I try to gather my thoughts.

I put the glass down. "Why did I not know about you?"

Becca wrings her hands together. "I thought about getting in contact with you over the years. I even tried. Every time Jeremiah came back to town, we would talk about the day that I got to be with you again. He said that it would be soon. Soon never came."

"You let him take me." My knee bounces up and down. "He wrote in his journals that you were excited to have me, and he didn't seem to want me."

"No. He didn't want to have a baby. He was angry with me for a good portion of the pregnancy. We stayed together while he was in his first year. Our relationship ended after. Nadia made our relationship difficult, even if the two of them didn't get together until he was in his last year of university."

That much, I do believe.

My mother is stellar at making lives more difficult. She wants things her way and doesn't care much for anyone else's opinion.

My next sip of wine only makes me feel more nauseous. "Why weren't you there? How were they able to take me from you in the first place?"

Becca runs her hand through her hair, her gaze distant. "I was in a rough spot at that point. Jeremiah told me that he was going to propose to Nadia and that they would be living in Tennessee after they both graduated. He said that he wanted to take you with him for a year. I said no way. I wouldn't allow it."

"But it happened."

She clears her throat, blinking back tears. "It did. You were about two and a half. Your father told me that he had moved in with some friends. Nadia was one of them. He kept promising that he was going to look after you and just wanted a year with you. I agreed, thinking that I would be able to visit. I was barely keeping my head above water, and I knew his family was paying his way."

She shakes her head and looks down at her hands. "And I liked Nadia. I thought that you would be safe with them. He was always supposed to bring you back to me at the end of that year, but he never did."

Aunt Courtney reaches out and takes my hand, giving it a hard squeeze.

The edges of my vision dance with the tears I'm holding back. Anger and confusion are at war in my mind, each fighting for dominance.

I take a ragged breath. "When did you realize I was your daughter?"

Guilt flashes across her face. "When I saw you wearing

the necklace. I gave that to Jeremiah on the day he took you. He promised me that he would tell you about me. As the years went on, it became clear that he never would, and I had to make a choice."

My mind is swirling with questions, but before any is formed, Cillian and Finn walk in, laughing about something.

Finn glances over at me, his laughter drying. "Aves, is everything alright? You look like you've seen a ghost."

I stare at Becca, rolling my bottom lip into my mouth. The sharp pain from biting down on it keeps me from crying. "I can't do this. I-I need to go home."

Aunt Courtney gets to her feet. "Come on, kiddo, I'll take you."

Finn shakes his head. "No. I've got this."

I look at all of them as I get to my feet and back toward the door. "I-I need to be on my own right now. This entire day has been a lot to process, and I just need some time. It's all too much."

Before Finn can argue with me, I spin on my heel and take off.

I hurry down the front steps, my heart hammering in my chest.

Finn calls for me, but his words are muffled as if he's shouting at me from the end of a long tunnel.

As soon as I'm in the driveway, I head for the road.

I just need to get away for a while. Get some distance.

As my legs start to hurt, running turns to walking.

And I walk.

I wish I could walk until everything that's tangled up in my mind straightened itself out.

Finn falls into step with me within a couple minutes. "Do you want to talk about it?"

I stop and turn to look at him. The concern in his eyes has the floodgates opening.

I point in the direction we came from. "She's my mom, Finn. Becca O'Reilly gave birth to me and then stepped out of my life when I was a toddler. Becca said that I was about two and a half when Dad took me and started raising me. Nadia was there too, as his friend. I don't even remember Becca. I always thought that my mom was my mom. She just didn't love me. Nobody told me any different."

Finn's mouth drops open. "I've heard some twisted shit, but that takes the cake. I have half a mind to get on a fucking plane right now and go speak to your mother."

I sniffle as tears track down my cheeks. "As much as yelling at someone would make me feel better, I just want to go home."

He loops his arms around me, pulling me into a tight hug.

I hold onto him, my tears soaking his shirt.

Finn kisses the top of my head. "We're going to go home, and I'm going to get you one of those hot baths you like going and then we're going to watch one of those sappy movies you like so much."

"I don't think that I can handle a sappy movie right now."

"Then we'll watch something filled with blood and guts. Whatever you want to do." He rubs my back as I clutch his shirt in my hands. "You're not going to go through this alone, Aves, I'm here for you."

21

FINN

AVA SITS ON THE COUCH WITH A BLANKET WRAPPED around her shoulders like she has for the last four days. She pours over her father's journals, looking for any clue that might have told her about her birth mother sooner.

When we came out to Portland together, the last thing I was expecting was to find out that my boss's wife is Ava's mom.

I perch on the arm of the couch as Ava scribbles more notes on a scrap piece of paper. "Aves, don't you think that it's time to get out of the house for a little bit? Maybe get some fresh air."

"Windows are open." She doesn't bother to look up as she flips to the next page in the journal.

"And it's dark outside. You were sitting here when I left this morning and you've still been here since I got back. Which means that you haven't gotten off this couch all day. The windows being open all day isn't enough."

She finally looks up at me, her gaze cutting through me. "I have too much that I need to figure out. Nothing I knew is the truth. Nobody in my fucking life other than my sister has told me the truth."

I reach out and take the journal from her. "We're getting out of the house. I have a job to do, and I'm not going to let you spend another eight hours spiraling about your family."

"Wouldn't you be losing your mind if you were in this position too?" Her tone is sharp as she shoves the blanket off her shoulders and crosses her arms. "Finn, my entire life has been upended."

"And you're going to make yourself sick if all you do is sit here and worry about what you might've missed that would've told you about your past sooner." I put the journal on one of the side tables and stand up. "Let's go. We're taking a break."

"Not happening."

I arch an eyebrow before lunging.

She yelps as I pick her up and toss her over my shoulder.

I chuckle as she smacks my ass. "Aves, I told you that we were going to get out of here for a little bit. I'm worried about you, and I'm not going to keep leaving you alone to get lost in your own head."

"Put me down. I don't need a babysitter. I need to figure out who the hell I am."

"You know who you are. Having a different mother than you thought you did doesn't change that." I carry her through the house and out to the car. I hold her as I open the door before putting her into the passenger seat.

She scowls at me. "I don't have a damn clue where I come from, though. There's this entire other person who should have been in my life. And how do I know that she's telling the truth? If she really wanted to be part of my life, why didn't she fight harder?"

"You'd have to talk to her about that."

I close the door and round the front of the car, sliding into the driver's seat beside her.

Ava squeezes her eyes shut, rubbing them with the heel of her hands.

"Finn, I don't know what to do about any of this. I know that I said I wanted to find out what my father was hiding, but I didn't think it would be this. I didn't think that there was going to be an entire person that I should have known about. Or that I was going to have an aunt that I never got to know growing up."

I turn on the car and back out of the driveway. "You're doing the best you can with everything that's happened. It's okay to take a break and step away from it all for a couple days."

She sighs. "I know. Logically, I know that, but my head keeps telling me that there has to be more I don't know. I want there to be a good reason for why he kept my family from me."

"You may never get a good reason for that."

I glance at her from the corner of my eyes, watching the tears slip down her cheeks. Each one ripping my chest in half.

She wipes them away and glares at the road in front of us.

Ava sniffles and tosses her head back. "If this damn crying would stop, that'd be even better. Distract me with something, please. What are we doing tonight?"

Drumming my fingers on the wheel, I look for the right words to tell her that I have to kill someone. "You know what I used to do for my father?"

She swallows, her throat bobbing. "Yeah."

"Well, I do the same thing for Cillian on occasion."

Ava looks out the window, her hair falling like a curtain between the two of us. She's silent for a moment before her laughter fills the car. "That's what you thought would get my mind off everything going wrong in my life?"

I shrug and turn onto the highway, heading for the warehouse where my target should be tonight. "You'd at least know that there's somebody out there having a worse day than you."

She scoffs, but she can't hide the slow smile creeping across her face. "That's horrible."

I put my hand on her thigh, squeezing it gently. "You're the one who smiled. So, who really is the horrible one here? Not me."

Ava traces a pattern on the back of my hand with the tip of her finger as I get off the highway and drive down a dark back road.

I follow the road until it opens up to the rear entrance of the warehouse district.

As I turn down another street, I cut the headlights.

Ava squeezes my hand before sitting back and watching the buildings pass us by.

I stop a few buildings away from the one I need to be in.

I turn to face Ava, reaching into the glovebox and pulling out a gun and silencer. "You're going to stay here. I'm going to go get the job done. You'll see a white truck coming back around that corner. If it's not me driving, you get in the driver's seat, and you speed out of here like a bat out of hell."

Ava shakes her head. "I'm not going to leave you here if things start going sideways."

"Yes, you are. If I'm not coming around the corner in a

white truck in ten minutes, get out of here and don't look back. Call Cillian. Tell him that the job went wrong, and he'll handle the rest."

I pull out another gun and hand it to her.

Ava sighs and checks the chamber and the magazine. She keeps the gun on her lap as she glances at the warehouse.

As I get out of the car, she shifts into the driver's seat.

I lean down in the doorframe, giving her a quick kiss. "I mean it, Ava. Ten minutes, then you get the hell out of here."

I kiss her again, deeper, before shutting the door. When I point down at the button, she locks the doors.

Once I'm sure she's safe, I creep through the shadows toward the warehouse.

People are speaking in one of the other buildings as I round a corner and see an open door.

I glance inside. Neither of the men standing near massive crates is armed. They don't look up from their phones as I pass by the door, sticking to the shadows.

My pulse races as I near the warehouse my target is in.

Dim lights shine from the frosted windows, casting shadows on the ground.

I stick close to the building, keeping my head down and my face hidden from the cameras.

As I enter the warehouse, I'm careful not to make a sound. I move behind a stack of shipping containers. After making sure that the safety on my gun is off, I head toward the back where my target should be working in his office.

There are no other people as I weave around the shipping containers.

I stop when I get to the back.

The target's office door is wide open. He sits behind his desk, white bricks of heroin stacked in front of him.

The wall behind him is glass, and in the shadows, Ava sits in the waiting car.

I enter the office and shut the door, twisting the lock. The man looks up, all color draining from his face as I aim the gun at his forehead.

"Hell, Roger, you've been a very bad boy." I smirk as I approach the desk. I tap one of the stacks of heroin. "Stealing was a very bad idea."

"I didn't want to do it. I had to do it. I need the money. Please."

With a sigh, I walk around the desk and press the gun against his head, tsking. "Roger, you should know better."

Tears stream down his face and a dark stain spreads across the front of his beige slacks. "Please. I have a wife and kids."

Roger is still sobbing when I pull the trigger.

His body slumps in his chair, his eyes still wide.

I tuck the gun into the holster on my hip before grabbing the back of the chair and pulling Roger to the door. His body shifts slightly in the chair, his head tilting to the side and that vacant expression looking up at me.

After opening the door, I tug him through the warehouse and out to the white truck that's waiting on the other side of the building.

I lift the body up and toss it into the back of the truck. As soon as I have a tarp pulled over him, I pull out my phone and send a message to Cillian.

Now that the job is done, his cleaning crew is going to go in and wipe the building. They'll take back his stolen heroin and make sure that there is no trace of me anywhere in the building.

Although, there wouldn't be a trace to begin with.

I'm good at my job. I stay in the shadows and keep my back turned to the cameras.

I spent the last week staking out this warehouse just so I would know where to hide when the time came to kill Roger.

The cleaning crew arrives as I'm getting into the truck.

I nod to them before getting in.

While Cillian may have a cleaning crew, I prefer to dispose of the bodies on my own. I can't trust that someone in his crew won't slip up and leave evidence behind.

I drive over to the car where Ava is.

She looks up at me, one eyebrow raising.

I don't know how much of what just happened she saw through that window. While I'm hoping it was minimal, this is also the part of my life that she's going to have to be okay with.

As I park the truck and get out, she rolls down the window.

I lean down, resting my arm against the car. "Get in the truck. We have to get rid of the body."

Her eyes narrow, and her lips press together. "You're just going to leave your car here?"

"One of the members of the cleaning crew knows where it's parked. The plan always has been that one of them was going to drive it home while I handle this. Now, come on."

Ava rolls up the window and gets out of the car. She doesn't look at the tarp-covered body in the bed of the truck before climbing in.

I get back in the truck and start it up, heading for the highway.

Stars hang bright in the sky as I leave the city and head into the country.

Ava says nothing, reading a book on her phone while I drive.

She should be more bothered by what's going on. For someone who hasn't been raised in the mob, she is eerily calm about it all.

I don't stop driving until we reach a marina nearly two hours outside Portland. Ava slides her phone away as we drive down to the pier where a boat is docked and waiting.

"Aves, go get on the boat." I park the truck and get out.

Waves lap at the docks, the boat rocking in the window.

Ava gets out and crosses her arms. "Finn, what are you doing?"

"Getting rid of a problem for Cillian, I thought that was obvious." I wrap the tarp tighter around the body, tying it in place with some rope.

"Yes, it is, but I was more concerned with why you thought this would be a good way to get my mind off everything." She follows me to the boat, climbing on and settling in one of the seats. "It seems like you're trying to scare me away."

"You know, you're too calm right now." I toss the body onto the boat beside her.

Ava winces and flinches away from the body. "I'm not okay with being here, Finn, but it's not the worst thing I've ever seen either."

My pulse jumps as I untie the boat from the dock and toss the ropes inside.

Ava gets up and winds them around the cleats while I push the boat away from the dock and jump in.

I take my place behind the wheel, starting up the boat while keeping the lights off. "It's not?"

She shakes her head. "I dated your brother, Finn. I've seen a lot worse. And to be honest, I think you only brought me tonight to scare me off. I don't think this was about distracting me from my father, even if you say it is."

My knuckles turn white as I grip the wheel.

She's right about that, even if I didn't know that's what I was doing when I told her to come with me. There was a subconscious choice made to try and push her away from me.

Because I'm not the kind of man she should be with. She deserves far better.

Ava sits down again as spray from the harbor cascades around us. "You're trying to be something you're not, Finn. For whatever reason, you think that scaring me is going to make me run for the hills. After all the shit that's happened in my life, you should have thought twice about that."

"We're in too deep." My voice is tight. "You have to see that."

She nods. "I do, but I'm still not going anywhere. And to be quite honest, I'm tired of other people trying to control decisions that should be mine. I'm in this with you."

I sigh and shake my head. "It isn't as simple as that. This was mild compared to some of the things I've had to do."

Ava stands and strides over to me. She stands beside me, her arms crossed until I stop the boat and turn to face her.

"You're more than a killer, Finn. You used to say that you wanted to step out from beneath your father's thumb, and I believe that you can do that. You just have to try. You deserve better too."

Shaking my head, I start the boat again. "Ava, this is the life we're trapped in. If it was my choice, this is not the life that I would give you."

"That's bullshit, and you know it is, Finn. If I didn't want to be here, I would have broken our agreement and left, but I'm not doing that."

"Why?"

The corner of her mouth twitches. "Because, Finnigan Byrne, I think you need me just as much as I need you."

As she helps me dump the body over the edge of the boat almost an hour later, I think she might be right.

There is a large part of me that needs her, even though I know I will never be the man she deserves.

But boy, how I wish I could be.

22

AVA

Zoe squeals as she runs through Aunt Courtney's front yard and straight into my arms.

I laugh, stumbling backward as I try to keep the both of us upright.

She laughs as we rock, hugging me tighter before pulling away.

A visit with my sister is just what I need right now.

I called her the day after helping Finn dispose of a body, wanting to hear her voice, needing her close to me. Two seconds after she picked up, she told me that the first chance she got, she was getting on a plane out here.

Now, three days later, Zoe is finally here.

Tears flood my eyes as I hold my baby sister tighter.

I didn't think that being away from her this long would be as hard as it is. "I've missed you so much. I can't believe that you came all the way out here to see me."

"I needed to get away from planning that damn will reading." She shakes her head as we walk through the front yard and into Aunt Courtney's house. "I swear, the man had more stipulations for a will reading than a normal person. He wanted it to be some grand event, as if it isn't just going to tear open all the old wounds."

"Is Mom at least leaving you alone?" I crouch down to hug Lola as she comes barreling into my arms. Her tail thuds against the wall as I pet her fuzzy head. "She doesn't have the number for my new phone, so I haven't spoken to her at all."

Zoe shakes her head as I stand, and we head into the kitchen. "No. As per Dad's instructions, she gets the final say on everything."

"Which means that she's using this as an opportunity to be a pain in your ass and try and worm her way back into your life?"

Zoe laughs as she goes to help Aunt Courtney carry the food for dinner over to the table. "You've got that right. We're speaking minimally, and it's only because I have to. Any time she brings up something other than the will reading, the conversation is done."

"I'm glad that you still have boundaries with her."

Zoe nods. "There is no way that she is going to be shoving her way back into my life. Not that Christian would ever let her, even if I didn't want to keep her out. You should see how he's handling this entire thing."

"I doubt that he's happy about it at all." Smiling, I grab a bottle of wine and some glasses. "It's good to have you here, Zoe. I didn't know if you were going to be able to come with everything else you have going on."

Aunt Courtney smiles as she puts the tray of roast beef down and comes to hug me. "I'm so glad that you were able to bring Zoe out here. I was really hoping I would get to meet her."

I pull out of the hug, and the three of us sit down to eat. "How have things been going here?"

Zoe plucks a couple of pieces of the roast beef from the tray and puts them onto her plate. "Everything here is good. We've been getting to know each other for the last couple hours."

I spoon some mashed potatoes onto my plate and drown them with gravy. "That's good. I would have been here sooner, but I had to finish packing away Dad's things."

Zoe's gaze flickers to mine.

There's still a lot we have to talk about, but I don't want to get into it in front of Aunt Courtney. Zoe deserves to have the truth come from me when we're alone and have time to talk about it.

Aunt Courtney starts rambling about some work she's doing in the garden while I slip Lola pieces of beef beneath the table.

For the first time in a long time, it feels like I'm sitting down to have a normal family dinner. I doubt that it's ever going to happen again, or at least any time soon, so I savor the moment while I can.

Once the plates are cleared from the table and the dishes are washed, me and Zoe head out and get into my car, both of us lost to our own worlds as I drive out to a lookout for sunset. Soft music plays through the car, filling the silence so I don't have to.

When we reach the lookout, I back the car up toward the railing before turning it off.

We get out and sit on the trunk, leaning back against the window to look up at the sky.

Streaks of pink and orange start to overtake the blue.

Zoe sighs. "How bad is it?"

"Here?" I shrug before linking my hands together behind my head. "It's really not that bad. I like it. Takes some time getting used to the rain."

She laughs, rolling her eyes. "You know that's not what I meant. How bad is whatever you found out about Dad?"

"I know Dad tried to sell you to sex traffickers, but how bad was it really?" My voice is strained as I look at her, tears already making my eyes burn. "I need to know, Zoe. Please."

Zoe's jaw flexes as she stares up at the sky. "It wasn't good. He wasn't just selling me, he was selling my virginity to the highest bidder. First to Christian, then to the traffickers, when things with them became worse than he expected. I don't think he ever counted on Christian coming for me."

I know how much she was willing to sacrifice, making no waves when Dad told her she had to marry Christian. I'm so glad he loves her to death.

"But the worst part was seeing him there. For a second, I thought he had come to save me. To take me away from that cell, from that nightmare."

She shakes her head and I grab her hand in both of mine. I have no idea how painful her memories are, but I can at least remind her she is no longer there.

"I'm so sorry."

She smiles as tears track down her face, her eyes turning to me. "It's not your fault." She pats my hand with her free one before turning back to stare at the horizon.

"He just looked at me like... like I was something to be pitied. Not like his daughter. And when the other guy came, all he cared about was whether the debt was paid."

Her eyes close and her chin touches her chest.

Whatever she is remembering, it's bad. I squeeze her hands.

"When the guy said no, he..." she took a deep breath as my lungs stopped working altogether. This was it, her secret. "He offered you to them to."

My mind just fills with white noise. No thoughts at all.

My sister's body starts shaking and heart-wrenching sobs rip from her. "I'm sorry. I couldn't tell you. You loved him. I couldn't do that to you. It crushed me. How could I crush you? It wasn't fair."

"It's okay." I hold her as tight as I can. I don't know if I'll ever be okay again, but this is not her fault. "I'm sorry for pushing you so hard."

She shakes her head. "No. You were right to. I should have told you. I didn't want to ruin your memory of him, though. And I was so scared. And how could I just come home and tell you that?" She is shaking her head as if trying to erase all her thoughts, all her memories. Of that time. Of our dad.

Her words cut through me, a knife driven straight through my heart. Tears stream down my cheeks as I struggle to get in a full breath of air.

Our own father tried to sell both of us to sex traffickers. He cared for the two of us so little that he was willing to get rid of us. We were like prized cattle, nothing more. And our mother just stood by and allowed it all to happen.

My stomach ties itself into knots just thinking about what could have become of my life.

Our parents never really loved us. We were pawns in their game. Something that they could use when the right time came.

This is worse than I thought.

I was almost sold to sex traffickers.

The thought circles over and over in my head. Endless thoughts of what could have happened to me follow them, all blending together as bile rises in my throat.

I slide off the car and race to the bushes, pulling my hair

back just in time as I throw up. I heave, but nothing else comes up.

Zoe looks up as I come back, holding out a bottle of water she must have taken from the car while I was throwing up. "Feel better?"

"Not even a little bit, but that puts together the final pieces of the puzzle. It felt like there was something I was still missing, and I knew that there were things you weren't telling me."

Zoe shakes her head, her eyes pleading for understanding. "What was the point? You didn't have to go through all of that. You never needed to know that he would have sold you too if he hadn't been killed in the process."

"I owe Christian an even bigger thank you than I ever thought I did."

"He wouldn't accept it anyway." Zoe smiles and takes my hand, lacing her fingers through mine. "What else did you find out? You said that you had some big news."

"Well, I'm done digging for the truth about our father now. I don't think there's anything else to find and to be honest, if there is, I don't want to know. I know what kind of man he is now. Especially after he kept me from my mother all these years."

Zoe shoots up. "What do you mean, *kept you from your mother*? We were all right there."

I swallow hard, more tears rolling down my cheeks. I wipe them away, trying to find the words to explain everything to Zoe.

My tongue feels like lead in my mouth.

How do you tell your sister that you have another mom? How do you explain that everything you thought you knew growing up was tainted with lies?

"Zoe, I'm only your half-sister. I have a different mom.

Dad tricked her into letting her take me, thinking it would be for a short while when he and Mom moved to Tennessee. They claimed they were going to give me a better life. Then they kept her from me and lied about it."

Zoe's mouth drops open as I sit up and run my hands through my hair. She sighs and pulls her knees to her chest as the sky grows darker.

Pinks give way to dusky purples, the first stars twinkling against the evening backdrop. A warm breeze ruffles the leaves on trees while the sun continues its descent.

I pick at a loose thread, snapping it off and letting the breeze take it from my fingers. "I didn't know how to tell you over the phone. It seemed like the kind of news that needed to be shared face-to-face."

Zoe lunges for me, her arms wrapping tight around me. "You know that this doesn't change anything, right? You're still my sister, and you always will be. It doesn't matter who your mother is."

"I know. We're sisters, and we always have been. It just makes the past make a little more sense. It always felt like Mom held something against me, and now I know what it is."

"Do you know who your mother is? Are you planning on staying here now that you've gotten everything you need out of the trip?"

I nod. "I know who she is, and I am going to stay here. I like it in Portland. It's not as hot, and the rain is nice. And the redwoods. Holy shit. Before you leave, I have to take you to see them."

I'm ready to quit searching for more information on my father and accept that he is never going to be the man I hoped he was.

I'm staying for Finn. I promised him that I would stay

until he got what he wanted out of Oregon. Though, even if he already had, I don't know if I could leave him.

Zoe grins and leans against me as the sky turns a midnight blue. "I miss having you around, Ava, but you seem happier out here. Lighter. It's as if none of the problems in the world can touch you."

She's right. Sitting on the back of a car, watching the sunset in Oregon, I finally feel like I'm free from the past.

Now, all I have to figure out is what I want for my future.

As that thought crosses my mind, the memory of Finn's smile and the way he makes me feel crosses my mind.

23

FINN

Dawson hums along with the song on the radio as he speeds down the highway. "I didn't think that you were going to come on the run with us. Didn't you say you had family in town this week?"

I shrug and lean back in the seat, crossing my arms and closing my eyes.

It's a long drive to the border, and I need all the rest I can get. "We do. Ava's sister has been here for almost a week already. Staying with Ava's aunt. Ava wanted to go out with her tonight. I think her brother-in-law flew in this morning too, so the three of them are off having fun."

"Which means that you get to spend the entire night driving to the British Colombia border with me and back. How exciting."

I chuckle and stretch my legs out as far as I can. "Her brother-in-law is an intimidating man. The less time I have to spend around him, the better."

At least it's just Christian who flew out. If he had brought Alessio and Jovan with him, I would have been worried that they were coming out here to see me.

If he had brought his right-hand, Ruben, with him, I would have been running for the hills.

Instead, Christian nodded to me when I dropped Ava off at her aunt's house this morning. He didn't approach the car or say a single word, but the nod was friendly enough.

Dawson laughs. "I know the feeling. My future in-laws are terrifying. I would never see them if I had a say in the matter. Unfortunately, I don't."

My eyes open as the car jerks hard to the side. "What the hell?"

Dawson glances in the mirror. "There was something in the middle of the road."

"Do you think we're about to be in some deep shit?" I pull my gun out of the glovebox.

"Yeah."

Three black SUVs race out from around a corner up ahead. They speed toward us, no signs of slowing down.

My heart pounds as I roll down the window and lean out, aiming at one of the front tires.

The gunshot cracks through the air, followed by the sound of a tire bursting. The SUV I shot loses control, hitting the rim hard. It's moving too fast to stay upright, flipping onto its side.

Dawson throws the car into reverse, backing up and spinning us around before taking off.

He swerves around whatever was in the middle of the road, but seconds later, the sound of spikes popping tires fills the car.

He slams his hand against the wheel. "Fuck!"

I fling the door open and get out of the car, ducking behind it and using it as a shield.

Dawson does the same on the other side as the two remaining SUVs get closer.

Nobody was supposed to know about this drop. Cillian would've been the only one, other than me and Dawson. He said that he wanted this to go off without a hitch. He was sure that we were the only ones who could get this done.

Did he find out about the plan my father has?

I don't have time to worry about that right now. I fire at one of the other vehicles, but the bullet buries into the hood instead of one of the tires or the person driving the SUV.

The SUVs stop in front of us, four men pouring out of each one. They use the SUVs as shields, firing off shot after shot.

My heart hammers in my chest as I pop around the side of my door just long enough to shoot one of the men.

Another bullet grazes my arm in the process, pain searing through my bicep.

Dawson takes out two of the men in the time that it takes me to kill another one. Four down, four to go, but I've lost sight of them.

To the left of us is a massive cliff that leads down to the frigid water below, but there is a forest to the right.

Dawson creeps around the front of the car to join me. "We're going to steal one of the SUVs and get the run done. You're going to be the one to do it. Grab the money from the back and make a run for it. I'll cover you and then clean up here."

I nod and slide around the door and into the car long enough to grab the bag of money.

Dawson kills another one of the men while I sling the bag over my shoulder.

He groans as a bullet lodges into his thigh. "Fuck, that hurt. Get out of here, Finn."

I shoot another man as he runs toward us, blood

spreading across his white shirt as his body falls to the ground.

One of the men runs back to the SUVs.

I follow behind him, grabbing him by his collar and hauling him out of the vehicle.

He groans as I throw him to the ground and stand above him, my gun pointed at his head.

He grins and spits at me.

My finger curls around the trigger and a second later, he's dead.

I get in the SUV and slam the doors shut before gunning the engine to life.

I'm going to make the drop, and then I'm going to talk to Cillian about what the hell this was.

Cillian is sitting behind the desk in his home office when I walk in late the next evening.

Becca gives me a small smile and gets up from her chair.

She clasps her hands together as she looks at me. "How is Ava doing?"

"She just needs a little more time. I'm sure that she'll come around eventually, but the last couple weeks have been a lot for her to process."

Becca looks at me like she's expecting me to say more.

I keep my mouth shut.

She might be Cillian's wife, but my loyalties lie with Ava.

The sooner Becca learns that, the better.

Becca nods and leaves the room, her head hung low.

Cillian looks up from his paperwork, leaning back in his chair. "You know, I was wondering how long it was going to take you to walk in here. Especially after I got a visit from Christian Herrera."

I stand taller, focusing on not reacting to his words. "Alright."

"Close the door." He waits until the door is closed before crossing his arms. "Want to tell me why Christian would ask me to keep an eye on you and make sure that you're okay?"

"Only if you want to tell me why you sent several men after me and Dawson."

He smirks. "When I get a visit from the former cartel leader in Tennessee, I tend to pay attention. If you have connections to Christian Herrera that I don't know about, it makes me wonder what else you've been hiding, Finn."

Right now, I could tell him everything and risk leaving his office in a body bag. Although, if he's talking to Christian and already knows the truth about everything, then lying to him would only result in said body bag.

I link my hands together behind my back, looking down at him. "My name is Finnigan Byrne, and I was sent here to kill you."

Cillian leans forward, his smirk dropping. "Well, now that you're finally willing to tell me the truth about yourself, why don't you sit down and tell me everything?"

Though it's a question, his tone makes it clear that my only option is to start talking.

"I was sent here by my father to kill you. He and the rest of the Byrne mob are still in Virginia, but they are expecting me to kill you in the next couple days so they can take control of Oregon."

Cillian's folded arms land on the table. "And what exactly are you going to do? You've had many chances to kill me already over the course of the last couple months. And yet you didn't."

"I like Oregon, and I hate my father."

"And that should tell me all I need to know?" He shakes his head and jerks his chin at the seat across the desk from him. "Sit down and tell me what the plan is."

I take a seat, perching on the edge of the chair.

Even though it doesn't seem like I'm going to leave this conversation in a body bag, I'm still on edge.

"Ava is the most important person in my life. She is the only person who has ever believed that I can be something more than my father's pawn. I owe her a better life than the one I'm currently giving her. I don't want us to be tied to my father for the rest of our lives."

Cillian leans back in his chair again. "I can offer you that better life, but I have to know that you're going to be loyal to me. The fact that you haven't killed me and told me the truth is a start, but you have lied to me about who you are for months."

I relax a little, shifting back in the seat. "Ask me anything. I'll tell you whatever I can."

The corner of his mouth twitches as I try to make myself comfortable. It's going to be a long night, but it's worth it if it means getting a better life ready for me and Ava.

The sun is just starting to creep over the horizon and filter through the windows as I walk into my bedroom the next morning.

Ava sits up in bed, a book in her hand. She puts it to the

side as I drop into the bed beside her and lean back against the pillows.

She leans over and kisses me. "You've had a long couple of days."

"Is that your way of saying that you missed me?" I take her hand and lace my fingers with hers. "It *has* been a long couple of days. We were attacked while we were out on a run. I had to get a couple stitches in my arm after a bullet grazed it, but nothing too bad."

Her eyes widen, and her mouth drops open. "What the hell, Finn? That's the kind of thing you tell me about as soon as it happens. You don't come home after being gone for two days and just casually announce it like that."

I laugh and kiss the back of her hand. "I'm fine, Ava. I just had a lot to deal with. What happened while I was gone?"

"Christian and Zoe went back home. The will reading is getting closer, which means that I'm going to have to start looking at going back to Tennessee soon for that."

"I don't know if I'm going to be able to go with you." My thumb drifts over the back of her hand. "I have a lot coming up in the next couple weeks."

Even though I'm not going to tell Ava that, I promised Christian that I wouldn't set foot in Tennessee. She doesn't need to know that I made that promise to Christian, or that he's the one who made sure people didn't kill me in prison.

Ava shrugs. "You don't have to go with me. I can go on my own."

"Do you really think that's a good idea after that call you got from Declan?"

She leans into my shoulder, her eyes closing. "I don't want to fight about this right now. How about we have a nap and then I can yell at you about getting shot when we get up?"

I laugh and shift down the bed, pulling her with me.

She yawns and curls into my side as we get beneath the covers.

To my surprise, I'm looking forward to waking up next to her later. I want to hear her give me hell for getting shot.

She does it because she cares about me.

I'm starting to think that it might not be a bad thing.

Maybe the pair of us do deserve to be happy.

24

AVA

Finn glowers at me as he pulls the car over to the side of the road. "This is a bad idea, Ava. I don't know how many times I have to tell you that."

"And how many times do I have to tell you that it's perfectly fine?" I cross my arms and arch an eyebrow. "Everything is going to be okay. Camila and Ruben are picking me up on Christian's private plane. Do you really think Christian's sister would come get me if it wasn't safe?"

I know that he is worried about me going to Tennessee without him, but we've been arguing about it for the past week. If he doesn't think that I'll be safe with Camila, the leader of the damn cartel in Tennessee, then I doubt he'll ever trust anyone to keep me safe.

On one hand, knowing that he cares that much about me makes my heart skip a beat. On the other hand, I need him to loosen up a little.

I'm already terrified of being back in Tennessee and having memories of my father come flooding back. I don't know what's going to happen at the will reading.

Even though I thought I was done looking for answers

where my father is concerned, this will reading is the last chance for him to tell me the truth about my birth mother.

I've been up for nights thinking about it.

He might have written me a letter, telling me everything. He could have an entire collection of journals that would give me some insight into why he kept everything from me.

I should just let the hope go and write my father off completely, but there is a little girl in me who wants to believe her father had a good reason for everything.

Finn sighs and rubs the stubble on his jaw. "It isn't safe, Aves. I saw how scared you were after you got off the phone with Declan. And then learning your father tried to sell you to sex traffickers in Tennessee. How the hell can I believe that you're going to be safe there if I can't be with you?"

I cup his jaw, my thumb running over his cheek. "I'm going to be fine, Finn. You don't have to worry about me. I can handle myself, and Christian will make sure nothing happens."

His eyes narrow. "I know Christian can keep you safe, but I don't like it. I don't like that we're going to be nearly a country apart, and if something happens to you, I won't be there."

"You could still come with me. There's plenty of room on the plane, and Christian won't mind having one more person in his house. Not if Zoe tells him not to mind."

He laughs and turns his head to kiss my palm. "No. I know that everything is going to be fine. You know how to protect yourself. I just worry about whatever the fascination Declan has with you is."

I shrug, guilt clawing at me. If I told him the truth about my relationship with Declan now, Finn would never let me get on the plane. "I don't know. It's been over between the two of us for years. I'm going to be with Camila and Ruben the entire way to Tennessee and someone is always going to be with me while I'm there."

Finn nods and signals to get back on the road. "I know."

"You're welcome to come."

He shakes his head as we continue down the highway to the private airport. "Getting involved with your family right now isn't a good idea. I'm sure that they're nice enough people, but I'm not the kind of man who is going to be able to support a mourning family."

"I doubt that they're going to be mourning after everything my dad did to us."

Finn gives me a flat look. "Aves, you think I haven't seen you cry a couple times this week? Even if he was the scum of your earth, you still have good memories of him. It's okay to mourn those."

I swallow the lump in my throat and shake my head. "I shouldn't be shedding tears for a man like him. Not one."

"If my father died next week, I might cry." Finn puts his free hand on my thigh, giving it a light squeeze. "Don't bottle away all your feelings, Aves. It's only going to hurt more in the long run."

He's right, even though I don't want to hear it.

I know that I'm going to go to Tennessee, and a thousand different emotions are going to come flooding back. There are likely still more tears to come for a man who would've screwed over his entire family to make his life better.

I close my eyes and take a deep breath. When I look over at Finn, he's already glancing at me.

He doesn't say anything, his hand drifting up and down my thigh, sending heat rushing through my body.

"If you keep doing that, then we're going to have to

pull the car over, and we're never going to get to the airport." I put my hand over his as it starts creeping higher.

Laughing, I pull his hand off my thigh. "Damn it, Finn. I mean it."

"Can't blame a man for trying to keep you home with him." He smirks and makes a show of putting both hands on the wheel. "I'm still worried about you, Aves. My father knows about you. Going to Tennessee is like walking straight into the lion's den."

"He's in Virginia, and Camila is making sure that he doesn't cross into her territory. You don't have to worry about that. My family is going to be able to keep me safe."

Finn groans. "I hate that you're so set on going which makes me a massive asshole. I just want you to be safe, Ava. The last thing I want is to get a call from your sister saying that my father got to you."

"Why do you think he's going to come after me?"

Finn's been worried about his father for the last week.

While I know there is reason to worry, especially with Declan, I don't think his father wants much to do with me.

Finn drums his fingers on the wheel. The muscle in his jaw clenches. "I'm working out some business with Cillian that would upset my father. If he finds out, he'll want to do something to hurt me. Taking you is pretty much the only thing that would do that."

My heart skips a beat as I lean over and kiss his cheek. "You don't have to worry. I can pretty much promise you right now that Camila is going to make sure one of her men is with me all the time. She's not going to let anyone get to me, especially once I tell her what's going on with your father."

Finn turns off the highway and onto the road that leads

to the airport. "I know. It's not going to stop me from worrying about you the entire time you're gone."

"I'll call you, and we'll text. Hell, you're probably going to get irritated with how much I text when I'm away from people."

He laughs and follows the signs that lead to the hangars. "I doubt that."

Finn stops in front of the hangar at the very end.

A sleek white plane sits outside, the metal shining beneath the bright sun.

Camila and Ruben sit on the stairs that lead up to the plane, lounging in the sun.

I grin as I get out of the car. I've missed the two of them more than I thought I would. "I can't believe you decided to come all the way to Portland to see little old me."

Camila laughs and races down the steps. "I've missed you so damn much! Club nights haven't been the same without you."

Ruben follows after her. "I didn't think that I would see the day when you lived somewhere it rained all the time."

I smile and hug both of them. "I know. I didn't think that I would love it here as much as I do."

Finn hangs back, hovering near the car as he gets my bags out.

Ruben goes to help him while Camila wiggles her eyebrows at me.

My cheeks are on fire. "Why are you giving me that look?"

"Because the man you ran away with is fine as hell." Camila loops her arm through mine, pulling me away from the men. "You look like you're half in love with the man already."

Butterflies beat against my stomach. "There's something

there. I really do like him, and being away from him for the next few days is probably going to be hell, but everything is going to be fine."

"Is it? He's a Byrne. Which is something you conveniently left out on the phone."

I shrug. "I didn't think it mattered much. He's nothing like his father or brother. Finn is a good man, and he's been nothing but kind to me since we came out here. Although, there's a problem."

"What do you mean?" Camila stops at the bottom of the stairs. "What do I need to know?"

"His father might be coming after me. Apparently, Finn is going to be doing something that pisses him off. It's enough to give Finn reason to think that his father might try to get to me."

Camila purses her lips and nods. "Alright. I'll make sure that you have someone with you at all times."

I bump my hip into hers. "So, you and Ruben? When did that happen? When I left Tennessee the two of you were still dancing around each other and pretending that you weren't sleeping together."

Camila's face is bright red as Ruben and Finn come over.

Ruben coughs as Finn starts laughing.

Smirking, I take my bag from Finn.

Ruben climbs the stairs to the plane with my other bag. "And on that note, it's time to get going."

I grin as Camila scurries up the stairs after him, leaving me outside with Finn.

Finn sighs and moves closer to me, reaching out to twirl a strand of my hair around his finger. He gives it a light tug.

"Aves, I'm going to miss you like crazy." He swallows hard, dropping my hair and taking my hand instead. He pulls me to him and hugs me tight. "Do everything you can to stay safe. And if you don't feel safe, you call me, and I'll be on the next plane out there."

"I'll miss you too, but everything is going to be okay." I loop my arms around his waist and hug him back. "I know what I'm doing and if nothing else, I have to be there for Zoe."

He sighs. "I hope you get what you want out of this trip. Stay safe, Aves."

When Finn kisses me, I want to stay.

The urge to call my sister and tell her that I'm not coming bubbles to the surface.

I want to stay with him and forget about everything that has to do with my father, but there's still a small chance he could be the man I remember.

The chance of getting an explanation for everything is worth more than staying home and being content with letting my father go.

Finn pulls back from the kiss, hugging me again before letting me go. "You better get going before the plane takes off without you."

Laughing, I shift my bag higher up on my shoulder. "I'll call you as soon as I land and let you know that I'm there."

Finn nods, tucking his hands in his pockets and taking a step back.

I climb the stairs and disappear into the plane, hoping that I'm making the right choice.

My heart pounds as the door to the plane shuts. The engine starts as I store my bag in one of the cabinets and take a seat.

Camila sits across from me, crossing one leg over the other. "So, are you sure about going home? Zoe caught me up on a lot of what has been happening, and I can tell you that if it was my father, I wouldn't want to be there."

"I feel like I have to." I sigh and run my hand through my hair, looking out the window to see Finn still standing beside the car. "I want to talk about literally anything else. I need a distraction."

Ruben appears from one of the rooms in the back with a bottle of whiskey. He sits down in the seat beside Camila. "I heard that somebody was looking for a distraction."

At that moment, I'm grateful that the two of them flew out here to get me. If I had to fly alone, I was going to spend the entire trip thinking about my father and everything that he'd done to destroy our family.

With Camila and Ruben here, it's a little easier to breathe, even though I wish Finn was with me.

I have no clue what I'm going to be walking into when I get back to Tennessee, but there is no turning back now.

25

FINN

It's been two days without Ava, and I'm losing my mind.

I never thought that I would hate coming home to an empty house.

For most of my adult life, I loved going home and being alone. There was nobody I had to answer to. It was the one place where I got to be alone with my thoughts.

Now, I'm missing Ava like crazy and spending most of my time with Cillian. He's been keeping me busy since we spoke about my father.

Today is no exception.

I'm sitting in his backyard beneath the sun, running through several of his accounting books.

He's got me putting all the numbers from his legitimate businesses into a new bookkeeping program.

Cillian comes into the backyard with his hands tucked into his pockets. "How's it going out here?"

"I've got most of the numbers from the last three years put into the program. There's still four more years to input, though." I put the binder to the side and look up at the sky, blinking to get rid of some of the ache in my eyes.

Cillian nods and sits down in the chair beside me. "Well, I've given a lot of thought to the situation with you and your father over the last week. I understand that you do not want to follow through with his plan, and I would like to give you a solution to leaving your family behind."

I don't know what to say. There is going to be a catch to his offer, I can hear it in his voice.

"Finn, I can't have you being a risk to my people. If you really do want the better life that you say you do, then I need you to denounce your father. You will have to cut all contact with him, and if I ever hear of you being in communication with him, I will kill you."

"And what would that look like for me after denouncing him?"

Cillian shrugs. "I have an opening as my right hand. Dawson is going to be working in another state to expand our territory, and I need someone to take his place. If you will denounce your father, I would be willing to extend that position to you."

My stomach plummets to my feet.

I promised myself that I would do whatever it took to keep Ava safe. I've wanted to stop being my father's pawn for years.

Now that there is a way to do that, I'm not sure.

All I've ever done is work for my father.

I've been a killer, going out and disposing of people who crossed him, who so much as pissed him off or looked at him funny. I've never been the man who has been in charge of other people.

Being my father's son got me a certain level of respect

and responsibility, but being Cillian's right hand would take that to a new level. I would have to get my shit together in a way that I never have before.

It's a big step, but it's one that would offer me security. I wouldn't have to walk out the door every single day, leaving Ava wondering if I'm going to come home.

My risk of going to prison would go down.

I could build a life for me and Ava.

We would be able to settle down here if that's what she wanted.

There would be a future for us, and it terrifies me to think about that because of how much that is what I want too.

I nod and pull the books and laptop closer to me again. "I need some time to think about it. I do want to cut the ties to the Byrne mob and move on with my life, but there are a lot of different moving pieces to consider."

Cillian stands and nods. "I can understand that. Take a day to consider the offer and let me know by tomorrow what your decision is. Although, Becca wanted me to let you know that if the decision you make gets her daughter hurt, she will be the one to put the bullet in your brain."

"With all due respect, your wife needs to earn the privilege to call Ava her daughter." The words are disrespectful at best, but Becca already knows my loyalty is to Ava before all else.

Cillian stares at me for a moment before nodding, turning on his heels and striding back into the house.

The glass door slides shut behind him, leaving me alone in the sun to dig through the paperwork.

I sigh and lean back in the chair, running my hands down my face.

Though I know that I should jump on the chance at a new life, I don't know if I can.

Right now, all I want to do is go home and talk about it with Ava, but it doesn't feel like the kind of thing I can talk to her on the phone about. This would be a monumental shift in my life, and it would involve her too.

I have to talk to her.

I should have gotten on the damn plane with her.

Christian and the others could have dealt with me being in Tennessee to support her.

I felt it when she got on that plane and didn't look back.

Though we have been talking over the last couple days, it's been brief. Messages sent here and there are short.

She needed me to be there with her. She told me that I was welcome to come, and I should have seen it for what it was.

I know that she's been struggling with everything surrounding her family.

We're pretending to be engaged, but I haven't been the kind of partner she needs right now.

And I wasn't lying when I told her it stopped being fake between us weeks ago. We may not be properly engaged yet, but everything else is feeling more real by the day.

She is the only person I want to be with, and I'm doing a damn good job of trying to push her away.

Things are going to change when she gets back. I'm going to make sure she knows exactly what she means to me.

Dawson comes around the corner of the house with another stack of files in his arms. "There you are. Cillian wanted me to give these to you too. He also said that we should get out of here early and have a good time tonight."

"And why would we be having a good time tonight?" I take the folders from him and drop them beside the others.

"Because I'm tired, and you're moping around because Ava isn't home." He stoops down and grabs all the folders, shutting the laptop as he stands. "Come on, let's get going."

"Where are we going?" I stand and grab the laptop, following him into the house.

"To a bar downtown. You can sit on a stool and be miserable all you want there."

"I'm not miserable."

Dawson scoffs as we head through the house and out to his car. "Sure, you're not. Drop your shit in the car, we can come back for your motorcycle in the morning."

I put the laptop in the backseat, and he stacks all the paperwork on top.

As soon as the door shuts, effectively cutting off my workday, the first thing I want to do is go home and see Ava even though she isn't home right now and won't be for a few more days.

Dawson cranks the music as we get in the car, the pounding bass rattling the windows.

Trees blur by, becoming more spread out the closer we get to town. By the time we're downtown, there are fewer trees and far more buildings.

Dawson stops in front of a little bar and parks the car in one of the open spaces.

It's still too early in the day for most people, and it shows as we walk inside the bar. There is country music playing, the crooning voice blaring through the speakers near the stage.

Old photographs cover the wall above the bar, where a single man sits talking to the bartender.

Dawson makes his way over, sitting down on one of the cracked leather stools.

I take a seat beside him, thinking that he might be right.

If I had gone home, I would be sitting on the couch, drinking a beer, and beating myself up for not going with Ava.

At least this is a social way to drink and try to get out of my head for a little bit. I could use a couple of hours watching drunk people's chaos.

If I'm lucky, it might be enough to take my mind off Ava for a little while.

The bartender greets us with a bright grin. "Hey, what can I get for you?"

Dawson puts down the drink menu he was perusing. "Whatever craft beer you have on tap."

I glance at the menu before nodding. "Same."

The bartender spins to pour the beers from the tap behind her. She hums along with the song playing while she fills the glasses.

She puts the beers in front of us. "If the two of you need anything else, just shout. I'll be at the other end of the bar with Morty."

Dawson drums his fingers on the bar in time with the song.

I take a small sip of the beer, my nose wrinkling.

I shift the drink away from me. "This tastes like licking a pine tree."

Dawson laughs and sips his own beer. "You're right, but it's not that bad."

"I have better beer at home."

"And nothing else to do there but mope." Dawson's smirk has me itching to leave the bar as fast as I can. "Why are you so bothered by her being away in the first place?"

"I make a lot of enemies. I can't exactly protect her when she is away." I take another sip of the beer, regretting it as soon as pine explodes on my tongue. "And she said that I could come with her. At the time, I thought it was just something she was saying but with everything she's going through, it feels like I should be there with her."

Dawson bops his head with the beat of the music. "You're both adults. She asked you to go, and you didn't. She seems like the kind of woman who would tell you if that was a problem for her."

Even if there are real feelings at the center of our relationship—I can admit to myself I am head over heels for her—would she still want me around her family?

We haven't talked about what happens when this is all over. I can't ask her to stay if she wants to leave, and there is no way I can go back home with her.

I sigh and rake my fingers through my hair. "Maybe you're right about that. Ava isn't exactly one to dance around things."

"Not in the time that I've known her at least. Just call her later, tell her that you miss her. And, if you really want the time off, I'm sure that Cillian would be more than willing to let you fly out to her for a couple days."

"I know he would." I drag my finger through the condensation in my glass, tracing frosty patterns. "But there's a lot of work to do. I'll call Ava and get through the paperwork and see where things stand then."

Dawson rolls his eyes and downs the rest of his beer. "If you're going to be nothing but miserable when she's gone, I suggest traveling with her next time."

I doubt there's going to be a next time.

While I know that Ava has her problems at home, she has her problems here too.

After everything that's happened since she started digging into her father, I wouldn't blame her for staying away.

All I can do is hope that she chooses to come back to me.

26

AVA

Only my parents would want to make a massive affair out of a will reading.

The executor of the will, Carter, stands at the front of my father's old desk while the sounds of a party flow through the house.

He clears his throat, the paper trembling in his grasp as he looks down at my mother.

She crosses her arms and leans back in her chair, the train of her dramatic black evening gown pooling at her feet.

Zoe reaches across the space between us and takes my hand. She squeezes it tight as Carter puts his glasses on.

My heart pounds in my chest as we sit in the dark office.

Stars dance in the sky outside, but everything about this night feels wrong.

I should be at home with Finn, dancing in the kitchen as we make dinner together. I should be talking to Becca and finding out more about why she let my dad take me.

She and I could be building a bond right now.

Although, the thought of another family letting me down is almost too much to bear.

Carter lifts the will higher, squinting against the dim light in the room. Yet another one of Dad's requirements for his will reading.

"Ah yes, here we go." Carter hums to himself for a moment as he moves closer to the lamp. "My dear family, if you are reading this, then it means I am gone. To my daughters, Ava and Zoe, I leave the heirloom jewelry I have given them up until the point of my death. To my wife, I leave the estate and everything in it. She may do with our former life as she sees fit."

Carter reads more lines about how much our father loved us, but all I can think about is how fake those lines are.

If he truly loved me, he would have left me with some kind of explanation for why he ripped me away from my family when I was young. He would have told me why he and my mom pretended that I was theirs.

Dad would've never kept Becca away from my life. He wouldn't have tried to sell me and Zoe to sex traffickers.

Hell, the biggest lie my father ever told is that he loved us.

Mom shoots up out of her chair as soon as Carter is done. "Let me see that will. He did not leave thousands of dollars in jewelry to the pair of them. Not when they've turned their backs on this family. I won't allow it."

Carter hands the will to her, sighing as she reads through it. "Mrs. Redford, the will is quite clear. Your husband has left your daughters the inheritance, and that's all there is to it. You could try to contest the will in court, but I would advise you now that it will not go the way you wish it does."

Mom scowls. "I don't care what the damn will says. The pieces he gave them should be returned to me and put in my collection. His own daughters abandoned him. They deserted him. The jewelry is mine."

I get up from the chair and stride to the door. There's no reason to stick around and hear the woman I thought was my mother hurl insults at the poor man.

If she's going to be furious about a necklace, she is more than welcome to be.

Zoe follows behind me, looping her arm through mine as we head down the hall. "I'm sorry the will reading didn't go the way you thought it would. I wanted to believe that he was going to leave you an explanation for why he did everything he did."

I shrug and tug her toward the ballroom. "If we're being honest, I was hoping for the explanation, but I knew it was unlikely. When had Dad ever owned up to anything that everyone else thought was a mistake?"

Zoe gives my arm a gentle squeeze. "At least you have Oregon to go back to. I know you're missing Finn."

A sharp pain stabs through my chest at the mention of him. "I am. I thought that he would come out here with me, though. I could have used him today."

"Did you ask him to come with you?"

"No. I told him that he was welcome to come if he wanted."

Zoe arches and eyebrow, shaking her head as a small smile plays at the corner of her mouth. "You might be my older sister, but sometimes, I think you really are clueless."

I scoff and lean against a little alcove in the wall, not wanting to go into the ballroom quite yet. "I'm not clueless. I know he's a busy man, and I gave him the option to turn me down if he didn't want to come."

"Yeah, but you didn't tell him that you needed him here." Zoe leans beside me, her deep blue dress glittering beneath the shining light overhead. "He's a man, Ava. You have to make it as obvious as possible sometimes. Especially if he's grown up in the mob."

"You know about that, do you?" My sheepish grin makes her laugh.

"Of course I do. Did you really think that Christian wasn't going to tell me?" She nudges me with her shoulder. "I have no room to talk, given who I'm married to."

"I don't know what I was thinking. I guess out of all the things that I notice about him, that seems to be the least important." I toy with the curled end of my hair. "Although, there is the problem with his family. He's Declan's brother, and even though I'm falling for Finn, I can't seem to forget that fact. It's always in the back of my mind, complicating things."

Zoe smiles at two women who pass by and join the rest of the party in the other room. "What's your biggest worry about it right now?"

"I keep thinking that I don't want to end up subservient to a man like Mom did, but it's expected in the mob. I'm supposed to listen to my husband and not speak back. I have to follow his orders without question."

Zoe shrugs one shoulder. "I don't know about that. Demanding, yes, but from what I hear from Christian, Cillian's mob operates a lot like Camila's cartel. People are given respect, and they are not treated as property."

I suck my bottom lip into my mouth before releasing it on an exhale. "Finn may be demanding, but it gets more complicated than that. My birth mother is his boss's wife."

"Your life just keeps getting more and more interesting." Zoe loops her arm around my waist for a tight hug. "Everything is going to be fine. You're not the same woman you were all those years ago, and Finn is not his brother."

"I just don't know if I can do another dangerous life."

"You came home to what you thought was a safe one and look at where that got you." Zoe pushes off the wall and takes a step out of the alcove. "It's possible to love a dangerous man and hold onto the person you are."

My chest aches as I think about that possibility.

I know I could be happy with Finn, but I don't know how long that would last. Declan would come sniffing around eventually.

When that day comes, can I ask Finn to turn against his family? Do I even want to? Is that fair of me?

He's never wanted to be like them, but can he be a different man?

I join Zoe, looping my arm through hers and turning back to the ballroom. "What do you say we go get in there and get this over with?"

Zoe tilts her head back and groans. "I still don't know why Dad wanted a massive party to celebrate his will reading."

"Add that to the list of things about him that we can't possibly begin to explain."

Zoe pushes open the doors to the ballroom, fancy dresses swirling by as a string quartet plays at the front of the room. "Let's get this ridiculous show over with."

By the time I escape the ballroom and shake off the last of the well-wishers, all I want to do is go back to Oregon and crawl into bed beside Finn.

I'm missing him more than I ever thought I would.

As soon as I'm in my room and out of the burgundy gown, I grab my phone and call him.

The line rings for so long that I nearly give up.

"Hey, Aves." Finn's voice is warm and friendly, making me more homesick than ever.

I fall back onto the plush white duvet on my bed. "Hey, Finn."

"I haven't heard much from you. How are things going in Tennessee?" What sounds like a cupboard slams shut in the background.

"Everything is weird. I don't know. I thought that coming back here would feel like coming back home, but it doesn't. I want to be out of here as soon as possible. I think I might get on a plane and come back tomorrow."

"You don't want to stay until the end of the week like you planned?"

I stare at the ceiling, the outline of glow in the dark stars still on the white paint, even though the stars have been gone for years. "No. My mother is on a rampage. She claims that the jewelry that was left to me and Zoe should be hers because me and Zoe abandoned our father. She seems to forget that he tried to sell us."

"Come home whenever you want. It's been quiet around here without you." He sighs as bottles rattle in the background. "I have no clue what the hell to make for dinner."

"I'm sure you'll figure it out. I froze a couple servings of beef stew. You could heat that up."

He's quiet for a couple seconds before there is a dull thud. "You're right. Stew for dinner it is. When you get back, we have a lot to talk about."

My heart skips a beat, and the phone almost falls to the bed.

I scramble to keep my grip, holding it to my ear. "We can talk about it now."

"No." He slams what sounds like the microwave door shut. "It's really something that we should talk about in person. With you gone, I've been doing a lot of thinking."

"Alright. Well, I think I'll book a plane ticket, and I should land tomorrow night, if I can find one for then. I'll send you the details from whatever flight I end up getting."

"I've got a run to go on, so I'm not sure what time I'll be home in the evening." The microwave beeps and he hums to himself. "Dinner is ready. I'll let you go now, but I'll see you tomorrow."

"See you tomorrow."

The silence stretches between us for a few seconds before the call ends.

I toss the phone to the bed, butterflies erupting in my stomach.

What does Finn want to talk about?

Maybe he's starting to fall for me, just like I've fallen for him. He could want to talk about committing ourselves fully to a relationship.

On the other hand, what he wants to talk about could have nothing to do with me. There could be something going on with his end of our deal.

I might get to stay in Oregon with Finn longer.

And what if with me being away he's decided he's better off? What if he wants to end the whole thing?

That can't be it, can it?

For me, our relationship stopped being fake a while ago. He said once he felt the same way.

But it still feels like there are things left unsaid between the two of us.

27

FINN

All I can think about as I drive back into Oregon is going home tonight and finding Ava waiting for me. It's been a long few days without her.

There are still several hours before she gets home, but it's all I've been able to think about all day.

I never thought that having her away from me would be this hard.

The entire time she's been gone, it's felt like there is a vital piece of me missing.

Tonight, I get that piece back, and it's the most excitement I've felt in a long time.

Dawson spent most of the run to the Montana border and back teasing me about it.

The teasing only ended when I left him in Idaho to handle some more of Cillian's business.

For the last couple of hours, the drive has been quiet, giving me time to think about where things stand with Ava.

Right now, we're in limbo.

This fake engagement isn't fake anymore.

She knows that, but we still haven't progressed any further than that.

When I get home, we need to talk.

She needs to know how I feel and then she can decide on what she wants to do going forward.

I'm hoping that she feels the same way and wants to be with me.

I can tell her about taking the deal with Cillian. She's going to be thrilled that I'm leaving my family behind.

I feel good about it too.

With Ava by my side, this is going to be the start of something new for both of us.

I need this, and so does she.

There won't be any more looking over our shoulders and waiting for my brother or father to tear our happiness away. There is going to be a full and happy life to look forward to.

I get to work for a man who values the people beneath him.

Cillian is a good man, and he's going to make sure that Ava is taken care of if anything ever happens to me.

This is everything that I've ever wanted and so much more.

We're going to be able to build a future together.

The life that I used to spend time dreaming about in prison is finally within my grasp.

I drum my fingers against the wheel as I pull into a gas station a few miles from home.

The bright lights shining from the gas station make the stars look dull in the sky.

My phone rings as I get back in the car.

With a sigh, I grab it, hoping that it isn't Cillian calling me to come back to the warehouse.

I slide my thumb across the screen and connect the phone to the car's stereo system. "Hello."

"Finnigan, interesting that you would answer." Dad's chuckle is dark and dangerous, reminding me of how he used to laugh when I was young, and he was about to hit me.

I need to pretend that everything is alright. If he thinks that there's even a chance I've turned against him, I'm fucked.

"Why's it interesting that I would answer?" I turn down a side street as headlights appear in my mirror.

Is he having me followed?

I wouldn't put it past him to have a car tailing me, especially if he's about to attack.

Dad clicks his tongue. "I know that you're turning against me, boyo. Did you think that I wouldn't find out?"

I scoff, my knuckles turning white on the wheel. "What would make you ever think that I was turning against you? I wouldn't do that. I'm loyal to our family. I always have been. I just got out of jail for being loyal to the damn family."

Though I did just serve three years on a charge that wasn't mine, it's not going to matter to him.

He's only going to see what I'm doing right now. And while he's right, I need to know how much he knows.

It's the only way that I might be able to turn this back in my favor.

Dad sighs and something slams in the background. "Here's the thing, Finnigan. I don't believe that you wouldn't turn against me. You may have been loyal, but you've always been sneaky and idealistic."

The greatest accusation he could ever make against me. Idealism.

I shift in my seat, rolling my shoulders back and trying to release some of the tension in my body.

He's always thought that treating people with respect instead of property is beneath him.

"And idealism is wrong?" I glance in the mirror, the car still trailing behind me. As I take another corner, the car keeps going straight, and I relax a little.

Dad might not be following me right now, but that doesn't mean that he hasn't had me followed before. For all I know, there's been someone following me in Oregon the entire time I've been here.

"Finnigan, I know you've made a deal with Cillian O'Reilly. Did you think that it wouldn't get back to me?"

My heart plummets as I take another turn, weaving through traffic. "I don't know what deal you're talking about."

"Funny." Dad slams something else, glass shattering with whatever he's done. "I'm tired of this game. You turned against me, and we both know it. You will die for your betrayal."

I swallow hard, stopping at a red light. "And you think that killing me is going to be the answer to your problems? You would kill your own son?"

"I will. This is the last time you betray me, Finnigan."

Declan shouts something in the background before static comes down the line. "Little brother, what the fuck do you think you're doing out in Oregon?"

Bile rises in my throat. "I don't know what you're talking about, Declan. Put Dad back on the line. He and I aren't done talking."

"You know exactly what I'm talking about. Ava may not be with me right now, but she is mine. She'll always be mine and one day, I'm going to force her back home where she belongs."

At this moment, there's nothing I want to do more than fly to the other side of the country and drive a knife through my brother's chest.

I keep tight reins on my anger, even though I could break the steering wheel in half right now. "You're going to stay the fuck away from her, Declan. She wants nothing to do with you. She's mine."

Declan's laugh is manic. "You're doing this to piss me off, and it's not going to end well for you, Finnigan. I think it's time I take back Ava and show her what a real man is. She might've had fun playing with you, but that's over now."

"If you put a hand on her, I will kill you." There's no way that I'm going to let him get close to Ava.

She's mine.

Declan scoffs. "You've stolen what's mine, Finnigan, and for that, you're going to pay. Everything you love in the world is going to be destroyed. And hell, if going after the one person you seem to care about gets you to respect Dad and finally bend to his will, then that's what it takes."

A sickening feeling in the pit of my stomach tells me that I need to get home as soon as possible. If Declan and my father are already in Oregon, then Ava is in danger.

I promised her that I was going to do everything I could to protect her.

I'll be damned if my brother ever gets his hands on the woman I love again.

Gritting my teeth, I press the accelerator down, zipping through traffic. "You touch her, and the last thing I'm going to do is work for Dad again. I'll spend the rest of my life making sure that the pair of you pay for whatever you think you're going to do to Ava."

"I don't *think* I'm going to do anything to her. I *know* I am. She might be on a plane in a couple hours, but I'll be coming for her soon. Don't you worry."

"You're going to stay the fuck away from her! Declan, I swear to God. Set a fucking foot near her, and it'll be the last move you ever make."

"Oh, would you look at that. She just got to the airport. Funnily enough, I have a ticket for that same flight, and my car just arrived. Dad's going to miss me, don't you think? At least he has one son who respects him."

"Get on that fucking plane with her, and I'll kill you the second you step off in Oregon."

"Calm down, baby brother, I'm just kidding. Taking her now would be too easy. I want you to suffer. I want you to be looking over your shoulder constantly, wondering if this is the moment I take what's mine."

My sharp inhale is enough to have him laughing.

The call ends as a shiver runs down my spine.

I drive faster, needing to get to the house. Ava's plane should be taking off in less than an hour and when it lands, her aunt is picking her up from the airport.

Their drive back from the airport should give me enough time to sweep the house and make sure that there's nothing hidden.

Including my family.

There are too many places they could be hiding in Oregon and not enough time to search them all.

Although, they may not be in Oregon either. They could be back home in Virginia, hoping that I rush back home to kill them, leaving Ava open in Oregon.

Dad could have people planted around the state, ready to attack at any moment.

Declan could be lying about not being at the airport with Ava. He could be there and waiting until they get on the plane to confront her.

Declan's always loved playing mind games. He wants to keep me spiraling and wondering what's going on.

Until I figure out what his plan is and where he is, Oregon isn't safe.

Declan wants me to spend time looking over my shoulder. He knows that I'm not going to relax until I find him and make sure that he never hurts Ava.

His threats are more than enough to send my blood boiling.

Brother or not, he is a dead man when I get my hands on him.

If I'm going to do everything I can to protect Ava, I'm going to have to take drastic measures.

I dial her number, already regretting the choice I'm about to make.

She's going to hate me. I just hope her hatred will keep her safe.

28

AVA

Zoe's car drives away, leaving me standing at the window beside my gate in the airport.

My heart aches watching her car disappear around the corner.

Heading back to Oregon is what's right for me, but being away from her is going to break my heart.

I know that going back to Finn is what I need to do. I've missed him too much to stay away.

I move away from the window and pick one of the hard plastic seats on the other side of the room to settle into.

My phone vibrates in my pocket. As I pull it out, Finn's name flashes across the screen, and my heart soars.

In a matter of hours, I'm going to be back home with him. For better or worse, I'll know if we are done or if I'm going to get to settle down and start building a life with him.

"Hey." I smile and cross one leg over the other. "I didn't think that I was going to hear from you before I got on the plane. Aren't you supposed to be driving back from Montana right now?"

"Nearly home, actually. Drive went faster than

expected, even with having to drop off Dawson in Idaho for another run."

He sighs, car horns honking in the background of the call. "That's not why I wanted to talk to you now, though."

"I thought you wanted to wait until I got home. It should only be a couple hours until I'm there and then we can talk in person. There's a lot that I've been thinking about too.

"Ava, we need to talk about us."

My heart skips a beat as I shift in my seat. "I know we do, but you're right. Waiting until I'm back really is for the best."

"That's why I'm calling. I decided it's best for us if you don't come back." His tone is sharp, and the words cut through me.

My stomach lurches as I sit forward. "What?"

I didn't hear him right. I couldn't have.

Why wouldn't he want me to come home? I knew this was a possibility, but I don't think I ever really believed it.

Finn clears his throat. "I don't want you back. Our deal is done."

"Excuse me?" My heart races, slamming against my chest.

I wipe my sweaty palm on my jeans. "What are you talking about, Finn? You told me that this stopped being just a deal to you, and now you're telling me not to come home and that the deal is done? What happened between last night and this afternoon?"

"I woke up, Ava."

Ava, not Aves.

My heart tears itself into pieces as I bite back tears. "You woke up?"

"I did. I thought that pretending that there was something between us would make the deal easier. I thought that you would be more willing to do what I wanted, and you were. I don't need you anymore, though."

"You don't *need* me? You were using me."

"And you were using me. Let's not forget that. We had a deal in place and both of us made good on our ends. But now it's done. You shouldn't make this more complicated than it needs to be."

"Who the hell am I talking to right now?" I hate the way my voice breaks. "The Finn I know isn't like this. Right now, you sound like your brother."

Finn's chuckle is dark. "Oh? You're just now realizing that? We were raised by the same man. Of course, I'm like him. You should have known that from the beginning."

The air is knocked from my lungs as I lean back and try to take deep breaths. This is all crashing down around me.

I don't know how we got to this place when everything seemed like it was fine.

We were happy together. We were going on dates and spending our nights talking.

It seemed like a real relationship and yet, it was all a lie.

"You were nothing to me, Ava." He spits the words out like they're poison in his mouth. "Nothing. Do you hear me? I used you and played with your emotions to get you to do what I wanted. There was nothing between us, and there never will be anything between us."

"How the hell can you say that after everything that happened between us?" My blood boils as my heart breaks.

I'm torn between wanting to rip his head off and seeking the nearest pillow to bury my face into for a good cry.

Something must have happened in the time that I've been away.

This isn't the Finn I know.

Unless he's been hiding who he really is all along. He could be more like Declan than I ever thought he was.

Finn sighs, his irritation clear. "Look, Ava, I don't know how much clearer I can be. I'm over this game. You mean nothing to me, and I don't want you here. Stay where there are people who care about you. I'll ship your things."

"Finn, this doesn't make any sense." The words are strangled as I get up and pace over to the window.

"It makes perfect sense. We had a deal and now it's done. We're both free of each other."

"And what if that isn't what I want?"

"Doesn't matter. This is done. Have a nice life."

The call ends, nothing but silence in my ear.

I take a shuddering breath, trying to hold the tears back.

There's no containing them. Hot tears track down my cheeks as the plane waits on the tarmac.

I wipe at the tears, tilting my head back to focus on the bright lights.

It takes a few minutes to gather the nerve to call Zoe and tell her everything, but I do.

My hands tremble as I hold myself together with one arm and lean against the window.

I clear my throat seconds before the call connects. "Zoe, can you turn around and come pick me up? I'm not going home."

Zoe's sharp inhale is followed by the clicking of a turn signal in the background. "I'm coming back. What happened? Do I need to send Christian back to Oregon to deal with it for you?"

"No!" I take a deep breath as it becomes harder to breathe. "Sorry, I didn't mean to shout, but right now, I'm tired of having men make decisions for me. Finn called and told me that it was over, and I don't know what to do, but I don't want Christian to go sort him out."

"Honey, you were falling for each other, what the hell happened?" Zoe's voice is soft and reassuring. For just a moment, it tricks me into thinking that everything might be alright.

At least, it does until my mind reminds me that my life is tearing apart at the seams.

I push off the window and head for the escalator that leads back out into the main part of the airport. "I don't know. He just said that we got our ends of the deal, and that we were done. He doesn't want to see me. He said that he was going to ship my things back to me."

"The deal?"

"I was pretending to be engaged to him. He needed it for work, and I needed someone to take me to Oregon and get me in contact with people who might know our father if needed."

"Aves."

"I know." I run my hand through my hair, holding back more tears as they threaten to fall. "I should have kept my distance from him, but he was everything I wanted, Zoe. Even the bad parts. I don't know what the hell I'm supposed to do now."

"Look, I'm still on my way to come get you, but I think it's the wrong move."

I step off the escalator at the bottom, dodging a woman with a cart stacked high with luggage. "I don't. He told me that I was nothing to him. I fell for him. I thought he was falling for me. It turns out that I was wrong."

Zoe blows out a long breath. "Don't bite my head off, but I think that you should go home."

"Why the hell would I go back there when he told me

that there was nothing going on between the two of us?" My voice is strangled, and strangers give me odd looks before continuing through the airport.

"This came out of nowhere. From what you've said about him, I find it hard to believe that he isn't in love with you, even if he isn't willing to admit it to either of you yet. And I see the way you light up when you talk about him. Hell, when I dropped you off a little while ago, you were bouncing up and down, ready to go home and see him."

"That was before I got his call."

"Which sounds like it was a pretty weird call." She groans as a car starts honking in the background. "Looks like there's been an accident up ahead. It's going to take a while to get back to you. But I really think you should think about getting on that plane."

"I'm already outside and waiting for you." I heft my carry-on higher up my shoulder. "I don't know what I would even say to him if I did go back."

"How about what the fuck, promptly followed by telling him how you feel? The worst that he can do is say the same things."

"I don't know if I can hear that a second time."

Zoe sighs. "I want you to be happy, Aves, and if this man makes you happy, then you owe it to yourself to try and make this work. You don't want to have the weight of how you feel sitting on your heart for months."

"And what if he still doesn't want me?" The lump in my throat feels impossible to speak around. "Zoe, getting on that plane is asking for him to break my heart more than he already has. I don't know how I can do this."

"You're the strongest person I've ever met. Get on that plane, tell him everything that you're feeling, and if he still doesn't want you, then I'll borrow the plane from Camila and come to get you."

"You promise?"

"I'm always going to be there for you, Aves. You'll regret this if you don't go."

She's right. I know that she is.

The man on the phone was Finn, but it wasn't. The things he said to me were things that Finn would never say.

Even though he doesn't love me the way I love him, I have to go back and find out what's wrong and why he's pushing me away.

Losing him is going to destroy me, but I have to try.

I swallow hard and turn around, striding back onto the escalator. "I'm going to go back through security in a few minutes, but I'll send you a message when the plane lands. Thank you, Zoe. I love you."

"I love you too, Aves. Go get your man."

The call ends, and I slip the phone back into my pocket. As I step off the escalator, I take a moment to compose myself.

Maybe getting on the plane is a mistake. It's not too late to call Zoe back and change my mind.

No. I need to talk to Finn.

Before I can join the line for security, someone steps in front of me, cutting me off.

My heart stops in my chest as Declan grins down at me.

His dark eyes are as lifeless as ever, but the gun hidden in his waistband tears a hole through me.

Declan reaches out and tucks a strand of hair behind my ear. "Hello, Ava. It's been a long time. I think you and I are long overdue for a little chat about what my woman has been doing sneaking around with my brother."

"I'm *not* your woman."

His hand locks around my wrist as I try to take a step back, the other slipping into my pocket and taking my phone. "You're going to come with me, or I'm going to have the person currently following Finnigan run him off the road. Your choice."

My spine stiffens.

He might not love me, but I still love Finn. I can't be the reason he is hurt. I wouldn't be able to live with myself. However short that life might be now that Declan is here.

I nod.

Declan links his fingers with mine like we're a couple in love while he holds me captive as we go back downstairs and leave the airport. His grip is punishing, making my hand ache more with each passing second.

Declan tows me across the parking lot to a waiting van. He throws open the sliding door before glancing down at me. "Get in."

"What the hell do you think you're doing with me? I left you years ago. I got the fuck out of Virginia. And I want nothing to do with you."

He grabs my bicep and shoves me toward the van.

I stumble, catching my balance just before I fall.

Declan jerks his chin at the empty van floor.

"Get the fuck in, Ava. I don't want to kill you right now, but I will if I have to."

It's the *right now* that sends a shiver down my spine.

I get in the van, shifting until I'm sitting back against the opposite door.

Declan reaches in and takes my bag before slamming the door shut.

The moment he's gone, I scramble to the handle, trying to yank it open.

The front door opens, and he gets inside. "Child locks

are engaged. You may as well sit back and enjoy the ride, Ava. It's going to be a long one."

He doesn't say another word as he leaves the airport behind us.

The road to wherever he is taking me is long and winding. I'm thrown around the back of the van, bruises blossoming on my skin.

Declan finally stops in front of an abandoned apartment building. He gets out and opens the sliding door. "Get out. We're here."

I do as he says, my body aching. "I don't understand why you're doing this."

"Because you're mine." He leers at me, his hand wrapping around my bicep. There are going to be imprints of his fingers there tomorrow morning.

"I'm not yours. I left you."

"And then you went to go fuck around with my brother. How do you think that makes me look?"

"No worse than you already looked."

Declan spins and slams the back of his hand against my face.

My head whips to the side, a metallic taste filling my mouth.

I spit blood onto the ground before glaring up at him.

"Good to see things haven't changed, Declan. You're always going to be a weak man who beats women, aren't you?"

The answer is another slap that has stars dancing across my vision.

"You bitch. I'm going to teach you how to behave yourself one way or another."

I chuckle and spit more blood onto the ground. "Finn is going to kill you for putting your hands on me."

Declan shakes his head, his grin sinister as he leads me through a door hanging off its hinges. "You have no clue who my brother is. It's going to be so nice to watch him kill the woman he loves. You really thought that you could run from me? Well, I hope you had your fun, because now you get to die."

I snort, stumbling again when he shoves me toward a room on the right. "You've got to be kidding me. You think that your brother loves me? Being with him was just for show."

Declan hauls me over to a pole in the middle of the room before jamming his fingers into my pressure point.

I drop to the ground, and he laughs, crouching to grab the rope beside me.

He kicks my leg, forcing me backward.

My spine hits a metal pole, and Declan takes his time securing me to it.

When he's done, he crouches beside me, his face inches from mine. "You can't possibly expect me to buy that load of shit."

"You have for months. Finn doesn't love me. Only you would be stupid enough to believe that. It was all pretend. Everything. He doesn't give a shit about me."

Declan stands and heads for the door. "You're going to regret lying to me. Before Finn kills you, I'm going to have some fun with your punishment."

Blood rushes in my ears as Declan leaves the room.

There is nothing but a broken window and a thin stream of sunlight to keep me company.

My breathing quickens as I struggle against the ropes. They are tied too tight to escape.

Nobody knows where I am right now.

Zoe thinks that I'm on a plane to Oregon, and Finn

thinks that I'm with Zoe. Neither of them is going to come looking for me for hours.

If Finn comes looking for me at all.

I take a deep breath, trying to remain calm.

Is this why he made that call? To keep this from happening? Or was he serious and Declan having me is just a coincidence? A relief for Finn that he no longer needs to deal with me?

This morning, I would have said that Finn would come for me the moment he knew I was missing.

Now, I'm not so sure.

29

FINN

Becca glares at me as she clears away the bottles scattered across my kitchen. "You're a mess. You told Ava that things were over yesterday, and it already looks like you've gone through half a liquor store."

I groan and toss my arm over my eyes, trying to block out the sun.

Becca's disappointed sigh follows. "Finn, get up and get yourself together. You have nobody to blame but yourself."

I move my arm enough to glare at her. "You think I don't know what I did? Believe me, I'm well aware of the things I had to say to protect her. It's better this way."

Cillian shakes his head and grabs my arm, hauling me up from the couch. "You know, I didn't think that I would have to come here and scrape my right-hand man off the ground. How is this better for either of you? Get over yourself. If you didn't want to be with her, then you don't get to drink yourself into a stupor."

Becca snorts and tosses another bottle into the bag at her feet. "Don't know why you broke up with her in the first place. Protecting her is a bullshit excuse. I can promise you right now that you're not going to meet a better woman."

I groan, wobbling on my feet. "I know that. Of course, I know that. She was the best thing to ever fucking happen to me, which is why I had to let her go."

Becca storms across the kitchen and grabs me by the front of the shirt.

Cillian takes a step back, eyeing his wife.

Though Becca seems like a nice and calm woman most of the time, I would be stupid to forget that she's the wife of a man who runs a mob.

She could probably kill me and dispose of the evidence before her husband ever knew she was up to something.

I sway as she tightens her grip on my shirt. "What do you want me to do, Becca? You don't know her. If I tell her that my father is threatening her, then she isn't going to leave. She's as stubborn as a damn mule."

I could have told Ava the truth, but it wouldn't have done any good.

If she was standing in front of me, and I had to tell her to her face that she meant nothing to me, I would break. Telling her over the phone might have been cold, but I need her to hate me.

Ava hating me is the best solution. She won't stay in Oregon, and my father wouldn't dare crossing into Tennessee. Not if it meant pissing off Christian and his friends.

I glance down at her hands. "Let go of me. You know that I'm doing the best that I can right now. Ava comes first. I didn't call Cillian and tell him that I needed a day just for the two of you to show up here and berate me."

Becca shakes me a little, her eyebrows pulling together. "That's exactly what you need right now. It's time to stop being a little boy who is scared of his father and start acting like a man. My daughter is in trouble."

"She's not in trouble right now. That's why I broke up with her." I fight back the lump in my throat that threatens to choke me anytime I think of Ava. "She's in Tennessee. It's safe. She has Christian and Camila to protect her. Christian's friends. They have the manpower to stand up to my father if he comes sniffing around. I have nothing to protect her."

Becca scoffs at me. "You need to pull your head out of your ass right now."

Cillian nods and crosses his arms. "We're a family now, Finn. You're part of the O'Reilly clan, and we keep each other safe. Now, get in a cold shower and then we're going to figure out what to do about your father."

Becca lets go of me and takes a step back. "I'll kill you myself if you let anything happen to my daughter. Every wound that comes to her is one I'm going to replicate on you if you don't bring her back."

For a woman who didn't bother with her daughter for most of her life, Becca seems to care a lot.

I know better than to say anything about it.

Cillian would break my jaw in an instant if I dared to snap at his wife.

"Fine." I lumber down the hall toward the bathroom. "I'll go get showered, but there is nothing we can do about my father. He's always going to hold Ava over my head."

I disappear into the bedroom, stripping out of my clothing.

Before I can step into my bathroom, the phone on my nightstand starts ringing.

With a groan, I grab the phone.

My dad's number is on the screen, making me want to

throw the phone across the room and watch the entire thing shatter into a thousand little pieces.

Instead, I slide my thumb across the screen and let out a deep breath. "Hello, Dad."

"You know, I thought I made myself clear the last time we spoke."

"If this is about Ava, you have no reason to go after her. She meant nothing to me, and I meant nothing to her. She's back with her family where she belongs."

His chuckle has me bristling.

The last of the haze from the alcohol fades as I root through my drawers, looking for fresh clothing.

Something isn't right with him. He's too calm.

"Finnigan, I'm disappointed in you. You're a spineless bastard. I've known that since you were young. This is an entirely new level. Instead of facing me yourself, you tried to hide your woman with the cartel."

"I didn't hide anything." My entire body sizzles with the white-hot anger that flows through me. "She means nothing to me. Do what you want, I don't care about her."

Dad sighs. "I thought that you were smarter than that, Finnigan. I know how much that woman means to you. I've seen the pictures of you wrapped around her little finger. I taught you better than that, which is why I'm going to make you a deal."

The world around me comes into sharp focus as time slows down.

Two things become clear in this instant.

Dad has taken Ava.

He's going to kill her.

I spring into action, desperate to get to her before anything bad can happen.

Although, if my father really does have her, then bad things have happened, even if the worst is yet to come.

I have to play his game. I need him to confirm that he has her before I get on a plane. I need to know where he's keeping her if he does have her.

"What kind of deal?" I haul on the clothing as fast as I can.

My stomach twists into a tight knot as the silence on the phone stretches.

I reach into the top of the closet and take down the box with my fake passport and a new unmarked gun.

I slip the gun into my waistband and tuck the passport into my back pocket.

If I have to fly out to Virginia and deal with this in person, then that's what I'm going to do.

Anything to keep Ava safe.

Dad hums to himself. "You want to live. You've never been one to give up and roll over. Which means that you're willing to do what it takes to survive. And if that's true, then you're going to have no problem killing your little bitch."

"Like fuck!" My blood boils as I yank on one boot and then the other.

"Now, Finnigan, that isn't the answer I'm looking for." Dad laughs, a deeper laugh joining him in the background.

Declan.

"You should've known that there would be consequences for trying to betray me. Killing your little love will set us back on track, and you need to be the one to do it."

I exhale slowly. If I want to protect Ava, I need to play this smart. I've done everything I can to keep her out of this mess, but it seems like my father is going after her either way.

This is my fault. She never would've been put at risk if I hadn't agreed to bring her to Oregon.

I should've picked someone else to play pretend with. Someone who didn't make my heart race every time they stepped into the room.

Swallowing hard, I try to sound natural. "Well, unfortunately, Ava no longer lives in Oregon. And like I've already said several times before, there was nothing between us."

"I'm already showing you great kindness in being willing to forget all that you've done, and yet you're still trying to test me." Dad's tone is low and dangerous. "I am not a man to be tested, Finnigan. If you want to live, you're going to kill Ava. Consider this practice."

"If you fucking touch her, I will kill you." I storm out of the room and head back into the living room.

Cillian looks up, his eyebrows furrowing.

"I swear to all that is fucking holy, I will kill you if you so much as look at her. Leave her out of this."

Becca's hands fly to her mouth as I snatch my car keys from the coffee table.

Cillian pulls out his phone, his words flying out too quick to pay attention to while my dad laughs in my ear.

Dad's laughter dies. "Do you really think that I would be stupid enough to call you without having your little whore in my possession? You don't want to know how easy it was to take her from that airport, Finnigan. She went without a fight. If I didn't know better, I would say that she loves you."

My heart slams against my chest as I clench the keys tight in my grasp. "Where is she?"

"Tennessee. A bit of a drive from the airport. It really is a shame that it's going to take you so long to get to her." Dad is no doubt wearing a smirk right now. "I'll send you the address. Hopefully, she's still alive when you get here. Declan is frothing at the mouth to punish her for all she's done to him."

The call goes dead as I rush for the door.

Cillian moves fast, stepping in my way and planting his hand on my chest. "What the hell is going on, Finn?"

Tears stream down Becca's face. "Is Ava alright?"

"My father and brother have her somewhere in Tennessee." I glare at Cillian, ready to throw him out of my way if I have to. "I need to get on an airplane now, but I need your help. I don't know what I'm walking into when I get there. I'm not supposed to be in Tennessee. I'll call Christian on the way to the airport, but I may not be able to get to Ava in time."

Becca shakes her head. "That's not an option. You're going to rescue her, and you're going to bring her back here where she belongs."

I move past both of them. "I'm going to do everything in my power. If things go bad, you need to kill my father."

"We will help you. I'll call ahead and have my plane and some of my men waiting." Cillian follows me out onto the front steps. "Keep a calm head about you. Going in there is going to be anything but easy. Killing your father is going to feel wrong."

I spin and face him. "No. After taking the woman I love and threatening her, killing my father is going to feel like a relief."

Cillian says nothing else as I get in my car, already dialing Christian's number.

He may have told me to stay out of Tennessee, but he can go fuck himself.

Ava is in danger, and I'll be damned if anything stops me from getting to her.

30

AVA

Declan's hot breath skates across the back of my neck as he tightens the ropes. The rough material bites into my wrists, blood pooling as I try to wriggle free.

I move my wrists faster, trying to keep some slack in the rope.

Declan growls and pulls the rope tighter, pinning my hands in place as he finishes tying me back up to the pole.

I've been trapped in a single room for a day.

My wrists ache, and my stomach is growling. Declan's only untied me long enough to use the washroom, before securing me back to the pole.

I don't know how I'm going to get out of the ropes.

Hell, I don't even know how I'm going to survive this entire experience.

I can't free myself, and even if people know that I'm missing now, how long is it going to take them to get to me?

I'm going to be dead long before Finn ever gets here. If he is even coming.

Declan smacks the back of my head. "Enough of the shit, Ava. You're the one who got yourself into this mess.

What did you really think was going to happen when you left me? Did you think that I would just forget that? Allow you to leave? No, I've been waiting for you."

"Sounds pretty pathetic." I spit out the words like venom, knowing that taunting him is a dangerous game.

Declan's hand wraps around my throat, and he slams my head back against the pole. "How many times do I have to teach you how to speak to me?"

My heart races even as I try to stuff down the fear.

There isn't time to be afraid. Adrenaline courses through my body, but it's going to wear off soon.

"I'm not your fucking property." Pain circles through my head, making stars dance across my vision. "I never have been, and I never will be. I'd die before I'd be with you again."

I have to do all that I can to get free or die trying.

Though, I know it's useless.

I have no way of knowing how many men are guarding the apartment. I don't know if someone is waiting for me on the other side of the door—if I could get past Declan in the first place.

Finn is my only hope, and I don't know if I can rely on him anymore.

I'm dead.

Declan laughs and lets go of me, rising to his full height. He kicks my thigh hard before turning and striding out of the room.

Tears roll down my cheeks, the cut from yet another slap to my cheek stinging.

I can't count how many times Declan has hit me in the last couple of hours alone. My cheek is swollen and cut, and my lip is cracked, though it stopped bleeding a while ago.

I don't know how long I'll be alone for, and I don't have time to cry.

I look around the dust-covered room, searching for something to help me cut the ropes.

There isn't enough slack in the binds to work my way loose, and there isn't anything close enough that I can use.

"Fuck."

I groan and tilt my head back, closing my eyes and trying to chase away the helpless feeling.

Declan and his father might kill me, but I'm not going to make it easy on them. They're going to have to work to get rid of me.

Finn would want me to go down fighting.

I open my eyes again and look at the base of the window. There isn't any broken glass. Even a small piece of it within my reach would have been enough to saw through the rope.

When I squint, I can't even see so much as a nail hidden beneath the layer of dirt on the cracked tile.

Disappointment eats at me as I search for anything else.

On the other side of the room, there is a nail sticking out of the wall, but I have no way of getting there.

Declan must have thought of everything before he brought me here. And there is only a short matter of time before he comes back into the room.

I don't know what's going to happen to me when he does.

None of my bones is broken yet, and I'd like to keep it that way for as long as possible.

Heavy footsteps thud down the hallway.

A shadow darkens the doorway as Finn's father stops and glares at me. He hasn't said anything to me since he arrived this morning.

It's shocking to see how much he looks like Finn. They have the same dark hair and green eyes, but while Finn keeps a closely groomed beard, his father is clean shaven.

Seamus Byrne is the kind of man that most people would cross the street to avoid.

Tattoos of Celtic runes cover his arms and most of his neck.

His jaw tightens as he takes a step into the room.

He smirks and kicks the bottom of my foot.

I grit my teeth against the pain, not willing to give him the reaction that he wants.

Eventually, I'm not going to be able to hold back the screams, but I want to delay his satisfaction as long as possible.

Seamus's eyes narrow. "I'll give the boy credit, he picked a tougher woman than I would have thought he wanted. That stubborn nature is only going to get you hurt."

"Seems like I'm doing just fine so far." I jut my chin out, challenging him with a hard stare.

"You're going to regret your impertinence. Finnigan's going to kill you. He doesn't know how to live without being part of the family, and he values his own life. If you keep pushing me, I'm going to kill you long before Finnigan gets here."

"That's an empty threat, and we both know it. You're a cruel bastard. It doesn't matter, though. Even if you do kill me, Finn isn't going to care."

Seamus shrugs and crouches down. "Two dead bodies is no more bother to me than one. Finnigan has always been the weak link. My life would likely be easier without him."

My stomach lurches. It twists and turns, tying itself into tight knots as I try to figure out whether Seamus is bluffing.

When I dated Declan, I did everything I could to avoid

his father. There was always something unsettling about him, and that hasn't changed since I left Virginia.

Seamus wraps his hand around my ankle, pressing against either side. "I want information about what my son is planning with Cillian."

"I don't know anything."

Seamus digs his fingers deep into my flesh.

I grit my teeth, holding back a scream.

He could easily break my ankle if he wanted to.

I meet his amused gaze, glaring as I sit straighter.

"You really are a stubborn woman." Seamus shakes his head. "It's in your best interest to tell me the truth, Ava. I wouldn't expect you to know much about the world that you keep walking into, but you know something. You lived with my son."

"I don't know anything." I kick out my leg, trying to catch him in the jaw.

Seamus drops my ankle for a moment as my foot stops short of his face.

He laughs and shakes his head. "You're going to get yourself killed long before Finnigan gets here. Now, tell me the truth. What is he doing with Cillian O'Reilly?"

"Working for him would be my guess."

Declan enters the room, rolling his eyes to the ceiling before looking back at me. "I told you that she was difficult years ago, Dad."

"Yes, well, at least she would obey you then. All it took was a hit or two to make her compliant." Seamus grins, showing off his gold canine tooth.

A shudder rolls through my body as he grabs my ankle and yanks me toward him.

The ropes feel as if they're going to rip through my torso, knocking the air from my lungs.

Seamus laughs and lets go of my ankle. "You need to have a rougher hand with her this time, Declan. Some women just need to learn their place."

Terror rolls through me in waves, but the anger overrides it, keeping me alert.

I clench my jaw, biting back a response.

I take slow breaths, trying to fill my lungs once more.

Declan turns and grabs a chair from the hallway, bringing it into the room. He sits backwards in it, his arms dangling as he looks down at me. "If you tell us what Finn is doing, you can be my wife. You don't have to die."

"I'd rather light myself on fire." I give him a sweet smile and shift back into the most comfortable position I can find. "Just shoot me now and get it over with. I have nothing to tell you about your son, and based on what you've told me, I'm going to die either way."

Seamus strides to my side and takes me by the hair. He yanks my head back as hard as he can.

I scream, trying to pull away from him.

He laughs, holding me in place.

"Get your hands off me." I can only hope that my glare is enough to make him spontaneously combust, even though I know it's impossible.

Why did I listen to Zoe and turned back to try and talk to Finn?

I should've told Zoe no and waited until she got through the traffic and then gone home with her.

But knowing these two, Declan and Seamus would have found a way to get to me even if I did.

I know what they're like. I watched them kill people. I saw what they did to anyone who dared cross them, and it was worse than death.

Even if I did know what Finn was up to, I wouldn't tell them.

It may be stupid, but I can't bring myself to betray Finn, even after what he said to me.

There is a little part of me that wants to hang onto the good moments.

If this is where I die, then I want to remember. I want to see his smile when I close my eyes and hear his laughter in my dreams.

Seamus slaps me, snapping my head to the side. "Enough of your insolence. Tell me what the fuck my son is doing behind my back."

I spit out the blood in my mouth, grinning when the droplets stain his gray slacks. "Fuck you."

Declan sighs as Seamus hits me again.

"Ava, you're never going to learn, are you? We don't want to hurt you."

"Bullshit, you sadistic fuck." Tears pool in my eyes, rolling through the blood trickling down my cheek from the newest cut. "I don't want you. I'm *never* going to want you."

Declan laughs and gets up, walking over to me. He crouches, his face inches from mine. "This has never been about what you wanted, Ava."

I take a deep breath of air before his hand closes around my neck.

His fingers dig into my pulse, making me feel lightheaded.

The world around me spins.

All I can do is hold on and hope that by some miracle Finn saves me, and we both make it out of here alive.

Even though I know that the hope is unrealistic, it's what I hold onto as my world goes black.

31

FINN

I take a deep breath and look over my shoulder.

Christian stands in the shadows, Jovan and Alessio flanking him.

The three men met me at the airport after my call with Christian, prepared to do whatever it takes to get Ava back.

"I'm going in on my own." I glance at the building before looking back at them. "I'm the only one my father is expecting, and his men are going to let me through. The three of you work your way around the perimeter and kill anyone you see."

Christian frowns. "This is a shit plan. You shouldn't be walking into a trap without backup."

Alessio nods and crosses his arms. "Give us more time to get more people here."

Jovan shrugs and eyes one of the men circling around the corner of the building. "There isn't much movement inside that I can see."

Christian puts his hand on my shoulder, pulling me back a step. "We're right, and you know it. Take a moment.

Cillian's men are getting in position, but we don't know what we're about to walk into."

I whirl around, invading his space.

Right now, I don't care who he is.

Ava is the most important person in my life.

If Christian wants to punish me for disrespecting his authority, he can do it after I've rescued her.

"I appreciate your being here, but if anyone gets in my way, I will kill them too." I pull out my gun and check the magazine, snapping it back into place and flicking off the safety. "Do as I say and stay out of my way."

Before any of them have time to argue, I creep through the shadows to the abandoned apartment building.

Stars shine overhead, and a dim light comes from the window on the right.

I'm coming for you, Aves. Just hold on for a little while longer.

Declan's laughter booms from inside the house, followed by Ava's scream.

I fight the urge to race into the abandoned apartment building, taking my time to get closer to the wall.

If I go in there without thinking, Ava is going to die.

I know my dad and my brother. They're going to be waiting for me to make a mistake.

This is a trap, and it always has been.

I know that someone isn't making it out alive.

I pull out the gold necklace hidden beneath my shirt, wishing that my mother was still here. The relationship with my father and brother would have never gotten this bad if she was.

After tucking the necklace back into my shirt, I round the corner of the building.

A door is propped open with nobody standing outside

it. I'm not foolish enough to think that my father doesn't have any guards.

I grab a crumbling brick from the ground and toss it at the door. The heavy thunk would be heard by anyone close to the door.

When nobody comes out with a gun raised, I creep to the door. I keep low and pressed to the wall.

As I push the door open a little wider, Ava screams again.

I'm going to find my family, and I'm going to kill them for what they've done to her. Nobody is going to be making it out of this building alive.

My heart pounds, but my grip on my gun is steady.

I approach a doorway on the right, checking the first room.

Before I have a chance to shoot the two men sitting there, Christian's face appears in the window at the other side of the room.

The gunshots come quickly, quieted by the silencer on the end of his gun.

He nods to me as the bodies slump forward in their seats, blood trickling to the floor.

Christian disappears, leaving me alone.

As I turn back to the hall, a fist collides with my face.

My head whips to the side before I duck, dodging another punch coming my way.

My knuckles turn white as I hold onto the gun.

The attacker lunges at me before I can get out of the way.

His shoulder slams into my stomach, knocking the air from my lungs.

We tumble to the ground, and my gun skates across the floor.

The man moves quickly, righting himself on top of me and trying to slam his fist into my face.

I catch his fist, my other hand slipping into my pocket.

His upper lip curls as his other fist comes flying. "You're a bastard. Did you think that you could turn against your father and not pay the price?"

The metallic taste of blood fills my mouth as I pull the butterfly knife from my pocket and flick it open.

I slam it upward into his torso, slipping beneath his ribs.

The man's eyes widen as his blood runs over my hand, staining it crimson.

I roll us, getting on top of him and cutting his throat.

Other voices in the building grow louder, boots stomping above me.

I glance at the ceiling before looking for the stairs. There are none near me, and the footsteps are growing softer.

The men on the floor above me have to be on the other side of the building.

The attacker's body is forgotten as I get up and spit out the blood that fills my mouth.

It takes only a moment to grab my gun from the floor and kill another man trying to sneak up on me.

By now, my father has to know that I'm in the building. Knowing him, he's going to drag this out for as long as possible. He's going to want to hurt me.

Killing Ava is the only way to do that.

Dad will want me to be there to witness the moment.

With quick and quiet steps, I make my way down the hall, checking the empty apartments as I go.

It's only when I reach the door to the management office that I see Ava through the streaky glass.

Bruises cover her face and blood seeps from a few cuts.

She glares at my brother like she plans on killing him where he stands.

That's my girl.

Ava spits at Declan's feet, and his fist pulls back.

My blood boils, making me ready to combust as I take a step back before kicking the door in.

Dad laughs and shakes his head. "You always did have a flair for the dramatics, didn't you, Finnigan?"

I keep my gun level with his forehead as I glance at Declan. "Get the fuck away from her right now."

Declan raises his hands, his smirk only growing. "Or what, baby brother? Cormac isn't here to protect you anymore. Not like he was all those years ago. Who is going to save you now?"

Red tints my vision as I turn on my brother.

Out of the two men, he's the bigger threat right now.

Dad is predictable, but Declan is unstable at best.

"Don't bring Cormac into this. He's dead and has nothing to do with it." I tuck the gun away, my hands balling into fists. "You're going to let Ava go, and then I'm going to kill you."

Dad chuckles and leans against the wall near Ava.

He pulls out his gun and flicks off the safety.

Ava's eyes narrow as she turns and presses her forehead against the metal barrel.

Despite the brave show she is putting on, tears still stream down her blood-stained cheeks.

I promised to protect her, and I failed her.

Declan clicks his tongue. "I think Cormac should be brought into this, don't you, Dad? I mean, he did come up with the ridiculous plan to escape and take Finnigan with him."

I look between the two of them, my jaw clenching.

Dad chuckles, pulling his gun away from Ava and tucking it into his waistband. "Oh, I believe he should be. In fact, I think it is the perfect way to kick off our little family reunion. Why don't the two of you settle what's between you before the real show begins?"

He watches Ava like a hawk, even as he takes a couple steps away from her.

My gaze cuts toward Ava. "We're going to get out of here, Aves, and then everything is going to be alright. You just need to hold on for a little while longer."

Declan barks out a mocking laugh, taking measured steps toward me. "You're not getting out of this betrayal, just like I didn't allow you to get out of the first one. It's finally time that you were punished for turning on the family."

My heart screeches to a halt.

The final pieces of the puzzle that I've been trying to solve for years are finally clicking into place.

When I look over at my father, he grins and nods, confirming my fear.

I see red as I step toward Declan. "You were the one who told Dad that we were escaping?"

"Loyalty to the family, Finnigan." Declan cracks his knuckles and rolls his shoulders. "It comes above all else. You and Cormac were traitors. Cormac had to die for that. When I told Dad what you were planning, I asked if I could be the one to kill Cormac. It's such a shame that he wanted to do it himself."

Ava gasps, struggling harder against the ropes that bind her. "You fucking bastard!"

I lunge for my brother, my fist swinging.

His nose crunches beneath the hit, blood pouring down his face.

Declan grins, his fist already slamming into my gut.

It's been years since I fought with him last, and he moves quicker than I remembered.

He grabs the back of my head, trying to pull me down low enough to slam his knee into my face.

I lean into the hold, slamming my shoulder into his stomach and driving him back.

Declan groans as I slam him into the wall, old plaster falling down around us.

"You fucking bastard." My voice is chocked as I fight my way out of his hold, punching his sides until he lets me go. "You got our brother killed!"

"He had it coming!" Declan sweeps his leg out, catching me behind the knee.

My knee slams to the ground, sending me off balance.

I roll out of the way before his boot can connect with my face.

The roll has me pressed against Ava.

I give her a smile and pull out the knife, cutting her ropes. "Get the hell out of here. Christian is waiting outside."

She scowls and takes the knife, scrambling to get out of the way as I stand and duck Declan's punch.

She moves into the corner, her grip on the knife tight. "I'm not leaving you, Finn."

Declan's fist finds my face, splitting my lip and snapping my head to the side.

I spin quickly, throwing my weight behind the punch to his temple.

He falls to the ground, and I pull out my gun from my waistband.

Declan groans and rolls over.

I slam my foot down onto his knee, his scream filling the room.

I spit a mouthful of blood at him before pulling back the safety. "This is for Cormac and Ava, you sick fuck."

My finger curls around the trigger, and the bullet lodges itself in Declan's head.

Even in death that mocking sneer is still on his face.

If I could kill him a second time, I would.

Dad laughs and shakes his head. "You've surprised me again, Finnigan. I didn't think that you'd have it in you."

His hand moves fast, and Ava lunges across the short distance between the two of them.

My eyes widen as I spin and aim at my father.

Ava's knife sinks deep into his shoulder.

Dad drops the gun he tried to pull as Ava holds onto the knife, driving it deeper.

He throws her off, roaring with pain. "You fucking bitch. I should have killed you long before now."

Her body slams into the wall, and she groans as she hits the ground. Her eyes shut, her breathing shallow.

I don't know what else they've done to her here, but I'll be damned if my father ever gets near her again.

Despite the pain radiating through my body, I cross the room in quick steps.

I kick away the gun at his feet, sending it sliding across the room.

Blood pools around the hilt of the knife as Dad glowers at me. "Do you really think that she is going to want a life with you after seeing the monster you are?"

I press the gun against his forehead. "As long as she's safe from you, I'm happy."

I squeeze the trigger.

As his body drops to the ground, my chest constricts.

My family is dead. Not a single member of it remains.

I move over to Ava, wiping away some of the blood on my face before kneeling next to her.

Her eyes flutter as she shifts.

Bruises and blood cover her, but it's hard to see how much of that blood is hers after she attacked my father.

"Hey." My voice is soft as I help her into a sitting position. "I'm getting you out of here, okay?"

"You're here?" Ava's eyes water. "Why?"

"I'll explain everything later, Aves. Right now, I've got to get you to the hospital."

I scoop her up and hold her close as we head for the door.

My body screams in protest as I take her back the way I came, knowing that the path is clear.

As soon as we get outside, I run for the waiting cars.

Ava groans as I put her on the back seat, checking to make sure that she'll be okay for the trip to the hospital.

"We're going to get you checked out and make sure that everything is fine." I kiss the top of her head before slamming the door shut.

I drive as fast as I can without jostling her too much.

My gaze moves between the road and the mirror every few seconds, making sure that she is alright.

When we get to the hospital, nurses whisk her away from me the moment I bring her in.

She's barely conscious when they disappear through a set of double swinging doors with her.

I follow her, not wanting to let her out of my sight for another moment.

My heart pounds as she disappears through another set of doors.

A nurse steps into my path, her hands on her hips. "Sir, you have to stay here. Please go sit in the waiting room, and

I will find you as soon as the doctors know what's going on. You should get checked out too."

"I'm fine. Just take care of her." I look to the doors where she disappeared again before going to sit in the waiting room.

I almost lost her.

Trying to keep her away was the biggest mistake of my life and I'm never going to forgive myself if Ava isn't okay.

A COUPLE OF HOURS LATER, A DOCTOR MEETS ME IN the waiting room.

I spring to my feet as soon as his gaze meets mine.

I cross my arms, trying to keep my voice level. "Is Ava alright? Is she going to make it? I don't know what happened to her but please tell me that she's going to be alright."

The doctor eyes me for a moment before nodding. "Follow me. She's going to be just fine. There are several cuts that need bandages and stitches. Those will have to be changed every several hours. The stitches should start dissolving within a week, but they could take longer to completely disappear."

"But she's alright?"

"She will be, yes." The doctor stops in front of an open door. "I'll have someone bring you discharge papers within the hour."

I stare into the room, my gut wrenching at how small Ava looks on the bed.

When she glances up and sees me, tears fill her eyes. "Finn, what is going on? Why are you here? Where's my sister?"

"Zoe is going to meet us back at the house." I enter the room and take the chair beside her bed. "Dawson should be here in a couple of minutes to watch over us until you're good to be moved."

Ava nods, her fists clenching the thin hospital blanket that's draped over her. "Thank you for coming for me. I'm sorry you had to kill your family."

"There was no way I'd let them keep hurting you, Aves."

"Thank you. I'm okay now. You can go back to Oregon."

"I'm not going back. Not until I say what I need to say." I hold her hand, but she pulls away.

My heart breaks at her distance.

"We don't need to talk. You said everything already. I thought there was something between us. You told me that there isn't. What else is there to say?"

"So much, Aves. Like, I'm so sorry. I'm so sorry that I didn't get here sooner. I'm so sorry I made that call. Aves, you had to know that I didn't mean a word of it."

A LUMP SETTLES IN MY THROAT. I TUCK A STRAND OF her hair behind her ear. "I had to say those things. I thought that if you didn't go back, you would be fine. Dad would leave you alone if he thought you meant nothing to me."

"And how did that work out for you?" She swipes away the tears that dare to fall as the sound of boots on the floor thuds down the hall.

I glance over my shoulder as Dawson appears in the doorway and nods to me. He turns his back to us, his hands in his pockets.

Even though I want to have this conversation in private, it's clear that he isn't going to leave.

"Aves. I never wanted you to get hurt. I thought I was protecting you."

"Thank you, but I really don't need any more of your kind of protection. Like you said, our deal is done."

Hearing my words thrown at me as she is lying on this hospital bed, so close to me yet so far is like a knife through the heart.

"Yes, our deal is done, but *we* are not. We can't be. This hasn't been about our deal for so long now."

"It doesn't matter anymore, Finn." She turns her head away from me.

I'm losing her. I can't. I won't be able to live without her.

"I started working for Cillian to try and overthrow him for my father. I thought that it was the right thing to do at the time, but I changed my mind. Cillian made me an offer for a better life, and I took it. For us. I wanted us to have a good life. You and me, Aves. As a couple."

No reaction. I want her to look at me, look into my eyes. I need her to see how much she means to me.

"I made that call because Dad found out I turned against him, and he threatened you."

Ava's jaw tightens. "So you decide to what? Make it a game of who can hurt her more and break my damn heart?"

"No, of course not, I was doing what I thought was best for you. Now I know the best is for us to be together. Always." I find her hand again. I need to feel her. This time she doesn't pull away. "Aves, please, look at me."

For a couple of seconds, I don't think she will, but I'll wait for as long as it takes.

Then her beautiful dark eyes meet mine.

"I love you, Aves. So fucking much. You have to know that. At that moment, I believed hurting you was the only way to keep you safe, but I do love you. I want to spend the rest of my life making it up to you. Please, just give us another chance."

"Why? You were pretty convincing on your call. I thought that you didn't love me. I thought that you had used me the entire time. How am I supposed to move on from that?"

"I hated myself when I made that call. I was so scared and devastated. I knew that it meant losing you, Aves. I knew it, and I still went through with it because having you at home and safe with your sister was better than having my father kill you. I thought that pushing you away would make him think you meant nothing to me. But I couldn't fool him. I couldn't fool anyone." I shake my head. "Except you, apparently. And I hate myself for that. That for even one second you could doubt how much you mean to me."

"How much is that?" Her voice breaks, her gaze dropping from mine.

"Aves, you are my entire world." I choke down the lump in my throat, trying to form more words.

I almost lost her today, and the thought is making me sick to my stomach.

"If I hadn't gotten to you in time today, I wouldn't have been able to go on. You mean everything to me. I would give up my life a thousand times over just to protect yours for one more day. I love you, Ava."

I squeeze her hand, softly, afraid of hurting her.

"That call hurt me. It cut deep. And then there are a thousand more questions that brings up. What if something else becomes a threat to me?" Her bottom lip quivers as she looks at the cut in my lip. "What if something happens to you? I'm not going to survive you dying, Finn."

I kiss her bruised knuckles and run my thumbs lightly over her raw wrist. "Nobody is going to be a threat to you again. I'll kill them before they get the chance. I love you, Ava."

"I love you, Finn. You're my world too. Don't ever do that to me again."

I get up and hold her tight in my arms, my hands running up and down her back as she sniffles, her arms snaking around me, her tears soaking my shirt. "I'm never going to do that again, Aves. You're the best thing to ever happen to me, and I was an idiot to push you away. If I had lost you, I don't know what I would have done."

Ava kisses the base of my neck. "You would have been fine."

"No. I wouldn't have. My life hasn't been the same since you walked back into it in those scrubs, calling me an idiot for getting in a fight on my first day of prison. Reconnecting with you when I went to jail was the best thing that's ever happened to me."

Her sobby laugh wavers as her fingers curl into my shirt. "You *were* an idiot."

"I was. I can't regret that, though. If it had never happened, I wouldn't get to call you mine."

She pulls her head from my shoulder to look at me. "Can we go home now?"

"Sure. Let me just talk to Dawson for a second and then I'll see where those discharge papers are."

I kiss the top of her head before getting up and going over to the door where the man that has become a friend stands guard.

He turns to the side, keeping one eye on the hall.

I clear my throat. "I have a lot of things I need to tell you."

Dawson shakes his head. "None of that is important.

You're with us now, and you're loyal to Cillian. Let's just get your lady home."

"We'll talk about it later, then."

He rolls his eyes. "The two of you are perfect for each other. You can explain the rest of the story to me later. And trust me, I'm going to want all the details, but she needs you right now. I can wait."

It takes a few minutes to hunt down the nurse with the discharge papers and bring them back to Ava.

As soon as they are signed, the nurse takes them back. "I'll be back in just a moment. Don't leave until then."

Ava scowls at the door. "She's probably going to go get a wheelchair. I'm not being wheeled out of here like a damn invalid."

Dawson snorts from his position in the doorway.

I sigh as I gather the stack of her clothing from the other side of the room. "Aves, you *are* an invalid. Just let her get the wheelchair."

"Finn, if you don't help me out of here, I'm going to do it myself."

I go over and help Ava to her feet.

She stumbles, her legs almost giving out beneath her.

I scoop her up, holding her close.

Though every scrape and bruise in my body is screaming at me to put her down, I'm never letting her go again.

32

AVA

Finn carries me from the car to the house, his arms wrapped around me as tight as he can.

Zoe trails behind him, her eyebrows knit together.

I inhale the scent of his cologne, trying to ignore the metallic tang of the blood soaking his shirt.

All I want to do is go to bed and try to forget that all of this happened.

Although, I doubt sleep is going to be possible with the way my body is aching.

Between being tied up and the abuse at the hands of Declan and Seamus, I don't think I'm going to be able to shut my eyes again. Even if I do, I know that nightmares will haunt me.

Declan and Seamus might be dead, but their memories are still alive to torment me.

I sigh as Zoe darts forward, opening the front door for Finn. "Zoe, really, we'd have been fine in a hotel."

Zoe's eyes narrow. "No. You wouldn't. Look at what they did to you. I never should've left the airport before you were in the air. I should've known something was up."

I squeeze my eyes shut, wishing that she would stop feeling guilty. On the drive home, I told her it wasn't her fault, but she still doesn't believe me.

I don't know if she's ever going to stop beating herself up about it.

There was nothing she could have done, though.

If Declan hadn't taken me in the airport, he would have found another way to get to me.

As much as my heart hurts for Finn and the way he had to kill his family to protect me, I can't bring myself to regret it.

We're better off without those monsters in our lives.

Finn sets me down on the couch.

Christian leads him into the other room for a first aid kit.

Their voices fade down the hall, leaving me and Zoe alone.

The couch dips as Zoe perches herself beside me. Her eyes water as she takes in the cuts and bruises. "I can't believe this happened."

I roll my eyes and shuffle back against the cushion, trying to get comfortable even though everything hurts. "Well, if it makes you feel better, I stabbed his father."

Her eyes nearly bulge out of her head. "Excuse me?"

My chest tightens. "I stabbed him. I didn't think that I was going to be able to do it but then he was reaching for a gun, and I thought he was going to kill Finn."

Zoe's laughter eases some of the tension running through me. "I can't believe it. You spend your life putting people back together, and here you are, stabbing someone."

Finn grins as he comes back into the room.

His split lip is only the start of the injuries on his body. "I knew you had it in you. I'm sorry that you had to do it, though. I should've come out here with you. If I had, you wouldn't have been alone."

"You're not upset at me for stabbing your dad?" I shift my weight slightly. The ache in my side only gets worse.

I ignore his guilt about not being there for me.

Even if he had come, his brother would have found a way to take me at some point. Finn knows that as well as I do.

Finn shakes his head and sits down on the coffee table in front of me. "How could I be mad at you for that? You don't know how many times I wanted to stab him over the years."

Christian enters the room, Jovan and Alessio trailing behind him. "We managed to convince Billie and Hadley to stay put since Jovan and Alessio will be on their way home soon, but both of the girls want you to call later."

I groan and squeeze my eyes shut, but my mouth twitches up into a smile.

I have no doubt that the pair of them are chomping at the bit to get to Tennessee just to check on me.

"You let them know that I'll call after I've gotten some sleep." I tilt my head back against the plush cushions, looking up at the ceiling.

My yawn tugs at the corners of my mouth, stretching wide.

Christian chuckles. "You definitely need some sleep. We'll all try not to keep you up much longer."

Alessio nods, tucking his hands in the pockets of his dark jeans. "You get some rest and try to heal up as much as possible, Ava. If I hear that you're not relaxing, I'll send Billie after you."

Laughing, I reach up to offer him a one-armed hug.

I bite back the hiss of pain that comes when he hugs me a little too hard.

Alessio leans down, his mouth hovering beside my ear. "I'm glad you're okay. Get some rest and don't go easy on Finn. He should have told us about the threat long before you were ever taken."

I roll my eyes and give him another squeeze. "He did the best he could. I don't blame him, and you're not going to either."

Zoe crosses her arms, nudging me with her foot. "And what are the two of you talking about over there?"

My cheeks warm as Alessio pulls away. "Nothing important. He was just telling me to get better."

Christian rolls his eyes. "Clearly, that's what she should be doing. You just said that to her before."

Alessio winks at me before pulling a bottle of water out of the fridge. "I must be forgetting things in my old age."

Jovan claps a hand on Finn's shoulder. "I have to get back home. If there is ever anything you need out in Oregon, contact me. I have a couple connections up there."

Alessio nods. "I'm going too. If I don't get home to Billie, she is going to come out here and insist on staying until Ava is fully healed."

The pair of them leave, the door slamming shut behind them.

Christian takes a seat in one of the chairs, his smile faint.

"Glad you're okay, Ava, though I wish that you would've told me who it was that you were going to Oregon with." Christian's gaze narrows as he turns his attention to Finn. "I would've been watching for signs of his father coming around from the beginning."

Camila breezes into the room, rushing over to pull me

into a tight hug. "I swear, with the way he talks sometimes, it sounds like he forgot that he handed control of the cartel over to me."

I grin and hug her back, wincing when something pulls the wrong way. "Everybody didn't need to rush over here to deal with me. I'm not an invalid."

Camila rolls her eyes and grabs a bottle of water from the fridge, holding it to my mouth. "Sip. You look like you've seen better days, but water is going to make you feel better."

Finn rolls his eyes and takes my hand, his fingers lacing with mine. "Glad everybody is so happy I'm alright."

I stick my tongue out at him. "You're fine. You only took a couple hits. Honestly, I was expecting better from an assassin."

His laugh is warm and deep, his eyes shining as our gaze connects. "Yeah, you would think that I would have been able to do better."

"You're clearly not meant to be a field doctor. You rushed me to the hospital for a couple scrapes and bruises." I pull away as Camila tries to clean some of the blood from my hair with a rag Zoe brought her. "Everybody needs to stop fussing over me. I'm fine. Everything is fine. The doctor said as much at the hospital. I just need to get some rest."

Finn stands, forcing everyone to move back a step. "Let's go get you some rest then. Everyone else can fuss over you later."

Finn helps me to one of the guest rooms.

He sighs as he shuts the door behind us. "That was a lot."

"How are you doing?" I grimace as I pull my shirt over my head and toss it to the floor. "Are you okay? I know that killing your brother and dad would've been impossible."

Finn's shoulders slump. "It's been a long time coming. I should've done it three years ago before I took the fall for a robbery."

"That's why you were in there?"

He nods. "Yeah. I've spent a very long time being loyal to the people who killed Cormac. Declan never told me that he was the one who turned us in. He went along with the plan to escape. If I had known that he was the one who betrayed me and Cormac, I never would've gone to jail for him."

My heart aches for him.

The anger is clear in his voice, and it kills me that there's nothing I can do to make it better."

"Cormac was the one who wanted us to escape. He wanted a better life and he thought that me and Declan deserved that too. Fuck, Declan was eager. He was the one stealing money from Dad."

"Declan is gone now."

Finn barks out a sharp laugh. "So are three years of my life. He was the one who was transporting the fucking guns in the first place. I met him at a rest stop and the cops showed up while we were there."

"I'm sorry, Finn."

"Oh, that's not even the best part of the story, Aves." Finn paces back and forth, his hands linked together behind his head as he takes a deep breath. "The cops weren't even interested in us until Declan decided to hand me the bag of guns before he left. Right under their noses."

My blood boils.

If Declan wasn't dead, I would find a way to kill him myself for what he's done to his brother. "Why the hell would he do that if cops were there?"

Finn's hands drop to his side. "My guess now that I

know everything is that it was a test. He and Dad likely wanted to see if I was still loyal to the family. The cops saw the bag as I was taking it to my car, and Declan insisted he knew nothing about it."

"How did they even know what you had in the bag?"

Finn rakes his fingers through his hair. "I'm sure that Declan probably tipped them off. After my trial, I saw him meeting with them. Dad gave them an envelope of some kind. At the time, I assumed they were being paid off to stay away from a further investigation into Declan."

"And now?"

Finn turns away from me, staring at the wall. "Now I know that I never should've trusted either of them. Declan probably ran to Dad shortly after I told him I was thinking of branching out of the mob life. I didn't want to be controlled by Dad. And if he told Dad that, then the pair of them would've screwed me over."

I get up and stand behind him, wrapping my arms around his waist. As I rest my head against his back, he lets out a slow exhale.

"Everything is going to be okay. He and your dad are gone now. They can't create any more problems for you."

His shoulders tense before he relaxes. "I know. I just don't want to think about it. Not for the rest of the night at least. I just need a break from it all. I especially don't want to think about it when we have things that you and I need to figure out."

"I know." I sigh. "Where do we go from here, Finn?"

He turns to face me, his arms wrapping around me. "What do you mean?"

"We love each other, but this all started as a game of pretend. And then you said that it meant more to you, but then you ripped my heart out. So, where do we go from here?"

His fingers comb through my hair, working through the knots. "Aves, when I think about you, I can see forever in front of me. I see a family and Oregon. I see weekend trips back to Tennessee to see your sister whenever you want."

"You want a family?" I pull back from him, taking a seat on the edge of the bed. "I didn't think that you'd want that."

"I may come from a disaster of a family, but I know that things are going to be better with you."

He flops onto the bed beside me, tucking his hands behind his head as he stares up at the ceiling.

I lay down beside him, ignoring the stiffness in my body as I curl into his side.

I close my eyes, listening to the rapid beat of his heart. "Is this really what you want? I love you, Finn, and I want to be with you, but if you're going to change your mind in the morning or try to push me away again to keep me safe, then this isn't going to work."

"You are really what I want, Aves. This life with you? It's all I've ever really wanted. I can't promise that there won't be danger at some point, but I'll keep you safe. I'll make sure you know when there's a threat, so you can keep yourself safe, too. I won't make the same mistake twice. I don't ever want to lose you again."

"Good. I need this time to be different, Finn, because if it isn't, then I would rather only go through the heartbreak once."

"No more heartbreak. I promise. This time is different. I'm not going to keep you in the dark."

"Will you teach me how to fight? Make sure that I can shoot as well as you can?" I prop myself up on one elbow, looking down at him. "Don't hurt me to keep me safe. We're a team, Finn."

He rolls onto his side, cupping my jaw.

His thumb brushes across my cheekbone. "I never wanted you to be involved in this world."

"Too late for that. You know who my brother-in-law is. You know what my father did. I've been in this long before you and I ever started our fake relationship."

Finn traces his fingers along the curve of my hip. "I never factored that in, Ava."

Laughing, I rake my fingers through his hair. "When are we going to go back to Oregon?"

"I was thinking that we should stay here for a couple more days. Rest a little bit. Visit with your family now that Camila is allowing me to be in Tennessee."

"You weren't allowed in Tennessee?"

He shrugs a shoulder. "No. Christian wanted me to leave Tennessee and never look back once I was released. He kept me alive while I was in prison, so I honored his wish, and I left. Camila pulled me aside while the doctor was examining you at the hospital and told me I was welcome here anytime."

"Camila is the only one you have to worry about. Christian may still be connected, but he gave up the cartel to be with my sister."

"I'm not giving up on life in the mob." Finn's tone is soft, but it feels like he is building walls between us. "It's the only thing I've ever known, Aves, and I like it."

"I didn't ask you to give it up." I trace the line of the gold chain around his neck. "When I agreed to come to Oregon with you, I knew who you were. I didn't go running then, and I'm not going running now."

"Good." He leans in and kisses me. "I would spend a lifetime chasing you down, though. I hope you know that."

"I know that." I yawn and stretch, peeling myself off the mattress and heading to the bathroom. "I need to soak until the ache leaves my bones. You coming with me?"

He springs to his feet and sheds the rest of his clothing. "What kind of question is that? If there is ever a time I don't want to see you naked, shoot me."

I grin and shake my head. "I'm not going to shoot you."

"Fine, you might stab me." He smirks and weaves his way by me, heading to the bathtub and turning on the water. "I've seen the way you use a knife."

Though the joke is morbid, laughter bubbles up inside me.

It's been a long day, and all I want to do is relax and forget everything that happened.

I strip down and get in the bath.

Finn slides in behind me, pulling me back against his chest.

I sigh and lean back, closing my eyes as the bubbles surround us.

We may have a long way to go in our relationship, but this is a fresh start.

33

FINN

Dawson hauls open the frosted glass door to the jewelry store while I consider running the other way.

It's not that I don't want to be here. I do.

It's that I have no clue what kind of ring Ava deserves.

The one I gave her was beautiful, but it came from a place of us needing to use each other.

The ring I get her now is going to reflect where we are.

I want her to know that when I bought it for her, I was hopelessly in love with her.

Dawson chuckles as I walk into the store. "All the color drained from your face the second you saw those glass cases."

"I don't know how to do this. Last time I just picked one that I thought she would like." I rake my fingers through my hair. "She wears gold and likes things that are understated, but that's all I have to work with."

Dawson pulls out his phone and hands it to me. "Well, lucky for you, I asked Brooklyn what she thinks Ava would be interested in."

"I didn't know that you and Brooklyn kept in contact."

Dawson shrugs. "She's been an asset to the mob. Cillian recruited her to launder some money and repaint some things for him. She's more than willing to keep her head down and work for him."

I shake my head, knowing that this only pulls Ava deeper into the mob.

Although, at this point, everyone she talks to is a criminal.

"Does Brooklyn know the truth about me and Ava?"

I don't want Ava to lose the only friend she has in Oregon.

He stops to look in a tall case with several necklaces. "No. She doesn't have an idea about that. Cillian decided that it would be up to Ava to tell Brooklyn what was important to know."

"Good. Ava doesn't need to get back home and walk into a shit show. It's better that she explains everything to Brooklyn in her own time."

Though I think Ava needs more time to rest and process everything before telling the truth to her friend, half of me thinks it will be the first thing Ava does when she gets home.

Over the last few days since rescuing her from my family, I've been reminding myself that she is more capable than I give her credit for.

She might have been terrified of what my father and Declan could do to her, but she was still willing to fight.

I sigh and blink beneath the bright white lights, glancing at the gold and diamonds glittering in the showcase.

As I compare the rings in the case to the description Brooklyn sent, I only grow more frustrated.

The first time I picked a ring for Ava, it wasn't this hard.

I give the phone back to Dawson, knowing that it isn't going to help me much.

One of the salespeople hovers close to us, watching as I glance from one ring to another. Each ring looks the same as the one before it. Nothing jumps out at me as being Ava's.

I groan and look at Dawson. "How the hell did you do this? I know what Ava would like, but none of these rings are it."

The man behind the counter makes his way over to us. "How can I help you?"

I glance at the black velvet trays in the glass case.

Several gold bands set with small diamonds glisten there. "I'm looking for something like this, but more unique. She's not a diamond kind of woman. I would ideally like it to match with this necklace, as if it were part of the same set."

The man nods as I pull the gold chain out from beneath my shirt.

He leans across the counter, inspecting the links a little closer. "I think I have something in the back that may be perfect. We just got a new collection in that should be hitting the showcases tomorrow."

He hurries to the back while I glance at Dawson.

I shift my weight from one side to the other. "What the hell am I doing? I didn't think that I was ever going to get married. Now look at me."

Dawson shrugs and crosses his arms, the blue fabric over his biceps stretching taunt. "You were already engaged to Ava when I met you. How much worse can it be?"

"So much worse. She expects more from me now. It isn't just about picking the perfect ring anymore. It's about living up to the expectations she has for me."

My stomach ties itself into knots just thinking about our future.

The last thing I ever want to do is disappoint Ava, but I've spent a lifetime disappointing people already.

The man comes back out with a satin box before I can spiral too far.

My mouth snaps shut as he puts the box on the counter and opens the lid.

Several rings are nestled inside, all of them gold with different stones.

The man takes out two of the rings, one with a small amethyst and the other with a sapphire. The bands are delicate, big enough to support the stones but small enough to still be dainty.

I take the one with the amethyst, holding it up to the bright light.

The gold band is a little lighter in color than the other, letting the amethyst stand out as the star of the ring.

I hand it back to the man. "This is the one. This looks just like something she would wear."

The man grins and snaps the box shut before reaching beneath the counter. He pulls out a white velvet box, nestling the engagement ring inside.

Dawson leans over to get a better look at the ring. "She's going to love this one."

I pull out my wallet as the man stands in front of the register to the side. "I hope so."

As I pay for the ring, my mind turns to the next thing on my to-do list.

How the hell do I propose to Ava?

Sweat beads on my palms as I pay for the ring.

The man snaps the box shut and puts it into a small bag, cream-colored tissue paper sticking out of the top.

Declan leads the way out of the store and out into the heat.

I hold the bag tight as we make our way to his car.

He looks over at me, the corner of his mouth tipping upward. "Do you know what you're going to say when you ask her to marry you? Please tell me that you're going to add something about it being for real this time."

"If I can get through the proposal without throwing up, I'm going to consider that a win." I take a deep breath and wipe my sweaty palm on my pants. "She deserves the best, and I'm still not sure that I'm ever going to be able to live up to that."

Dawson unlocks his car as we stand near the curb, staying out of the way of people rushing up and down the sidewalk. "If she wanted anybody else, she would be with them, Finn. Ava is a catch of a woman, and she knows what she wants. If that's you, then you need to respect her and get over whatever makes you think that you're not worth it."

I nod and open the passenger door. "I know you're right. It's just hard to piece that all together with everything that's happened over the last few days. I thought that being kidnapped by my brother would make her less likely to want to be with me."

"Well, she wants *you*." Dawson rounds the front of the car and opens his door. "Now, it's time to go home and start planning your big proposal."

I take long inhales and slow exhales, trying to calm my racing heart.

I don't know when I've ever been this nervous before.

I've killed people without blinking. I rushed into shoot outs and didn't think twice.

For years, I put my life at risk without a second thought,

but when it comes to getting engaged to the woman I love, all I have are thoughts.

Ava is too good for me, that's always been true, and I'm going to spend the rest of my life trying to be good enough for her.

Ava hums along with the music as I drive down a winding road later that evening.

The window is down, strands of her hair blowing around her face. Sunlight highlights the different colors in her hair, making her look like an angel come down to Earth.

She turns down the music and looks over at me. "Are you going to tell me where we're going yet?"

I take her hand in mine, drifting my thumb over her knuckles. "As nice as it has been to stay with your family over the last few days, I thought it was time to head home."

Ava tilts her head back and closes her eyes. "Home sounds nice. I've missed home."

I take in the fading bruises on her face as we come to a red light.

My chest clenches tight each time I look at them.

Those bruises are a reminder of what I will never allow to happen again.

Ava is mine, and I'll be damned if anyone ever tries to put their hands on her again.

Oregon is safe for us.

I bring her hand to my lips, kissing the back of it. "I thought that you would have called Tennessee home."

She shakes her head, shifting to tuck her legs beneath her on the seat. "No. It stopped being home when I moved to Oregon with you. Once we saw those redwoods, I was sure that Oregon was home."

As soon as the light turns green, I head down the road and take a right turn toward the highway.

Ava rolls up her window and leans her head on my shoulder. "I'm going to nap for a thousand years once we get home."

"I don't think Zoe is going to let you do that. She's going to want you to call her as soon as we get there."

Ava's full lips press together in a thin line. "She's going to keep blaming herself for Declan kidnapping me. I've tried to tell her that it wasn't her fault probably a hundred times already, but she won't listen to me."

"She's not going to." I squeeze her hand, trying to offer her what little reassurance I can. "She'll get past it, though. She'll wake up one day and finally be ready to put that behind her."

"I know." Ava shifts, moving her head off me and glancing out the window. "I thought we were going home. Why did you just take the exit?"

I let go of her hand to mime locking my mouth shut.

Ava laughs and settles back in her seat. "And here I thought you hated messing up a plan. Which, speaking of plan, did you remember to grab my things in your leave-Tennessee-without-warning plan?"

"Zoe loaded up your bags before we left. She thought that getting back to Oregon and putting all of this behind you would be good too."

"Of course, she did." Ava's slight gasp rises above the music as I turn into a small town. "Now we're taking an even bigger detour?"

"You wanted to do some exploring the first time we went to Oregon together, and we didn't have time. I was thinking that this time could be different. I've booked a hotel in town, and then several others along the way. We can spend as much time exploring as you want."

Her smile is worth the hours of planning this trip took. It makes the butterflies in my stomach erupt, sending my heart racing.

It's the same way I always feel when I look at her.

It's a feeling I know will never fade.

When we come to another red light, Ava leans over and kisses me. She nips at my bottom lip before her tongue slides into my mouth, tangling with mine.

I groan and grip the back of her head.

The car behind us honks, and she sits back, breathless and grinning from ear to ear.

"I can't believe that you're going to spend the day exploring with me." Ava stares out the window, taking in the old stone buildings and their bright paint colors. "We're going to have to take dozens of pictures. You better get your best smile ready for me."

"Aves, I would do anything for you."

I find a parking spot near our hotel and get out.

Ava follows close behind, her phone already out as she snaps pictures.

She takes off down the street, taking her time to glance in the shop windows. Her long skirt swishes around her calves as she walks while her crop top inches higher up her torso.

I hang back, taking in how lucky I am to call her mine.

Ava turns and holds her phone up, giving me a cheesy grin.

I glance at her over the top of my sunglasses.

Her playful little pout is enough to have me taking off the sunglasses and smiling for her pictures.

Once she has a picture she's satisfied with, she ducks into a small shop with a white stone exterior and deep blue awning.

I follow her in, freshly roasted coffee wafting from the back of the little coffee shop.

Ava smiles up at me as I join her in the line. She leans into my embrace as I wrap an arm around her waist.

"What's going to happen once we get back to Oregon?" She twists to the side to look up at me. "I know that you said you were taking a deal with Cillian, but what does that mean?"

"I'll be stepping back from most of the hands-on things. He wants me to oversee the books and businesses and deal with the lower levels when necessary. There's more to it than that, and as soon as I know more about it, I'll tell you. There are still some things I didn't get the chance to work out with him before I left for Tennessee."

I keep the words vague in case anyone is listening who shouldn't be.

Ava nods at me, her gaze distant as we approach the counter and place our orders.

I don't know what she thinks about the deal, but I don't have all the information yet either.

Cillian's initial offer was good, but after some time to think about it, I want clarification on what my job will be.

And if he tells me that any part of my job will put Ava into direct danger, then I'll ask for another position within the mob. Something that is behind the scenes as much as possible.

As soon as we have our coffees, Ava leads the way back out of the shop. She hops over a large crack in the sidewalk, seeming happier than she has since we went to Oregon.

There's a sense of peace surrounding her that hasn't been there before.

It's nice to see.

After watching her tear herself apart to find out who her father was, I didn't think that she was going to get back to the Ava I've known for years.

When she turns and raises her phone to snap another picture, an impish smile curving her lips, I know that she's going to be fine.

And if she isn't, I'll be there to help her get through whatever finds my way.

I may have lost one family, but with Ava, I'm gaining the family I always wanted.

The sun dips toward the horizon as I loop my arm over her shoulders. "Are you ready to go back to the hotel?"

"Can we explore more tomorrow?"

I kiss her temple. "I booked our room for two nights. And don't worry, I've told the staff not to bring any vanilla whiskey to the room. Don't want a repeat of what happened the last time we shared a hotel room."

Her eyes shine with mischief as she stops and slides one hand beneath my shirt. "You seemed to enjoy what happened."

"You're not supposed to mix alcohol with the pain meds you're taking." I put two fingers beneath her chin and tilt her face up to mine.

Her soft moan as I pull her bottom lip between my teeth has my cock standing at attention.

I pull away from her before we can take this too far in the middle of the street. "Come on, Aves, let's go back to the hotel."

34

AVA

I didn't know how much I would miss Oregon until we got back two nights ago.

The moment Finn and I walked into our house, it felt like all the stress from the last several weeks melted away.

I didn't have to worry about his brother or his father, like I did in Tennessee.

Even though I knew they were dead while we were there, I couldn't stop picturing someone else coming after me.

Finn insisted that it wouldn't happen, but I couldn't chase the nightmares away.

Not until we left Tennessee in the rearview mirror.

Now, I'm standing in the middle of our living room, looking at the stacks of things on the coffee table that belonged to my father.

His notebooks and journals tower high while papers I scribbled on to make notes are scattered around them.

Empty cardboard boxes sit beside me on the floor.

Brooklyn sits on the couch, looking at all the work we did while figuring out the truth about my father. Her eyes are still wide after telling her the story about the sex traffickers.

My chest clenches when I think about telling her the rest of the story.

The words are frozen on the tip of my tongue, but if we're going to be friends, she deserves to hear the truth.

I swallow hard and perch myself on the one clear edge of the coffee table. "I know you're involved with Cillian O'Reilly now."

Brooklyn's eyes widen. "How did you find that out?"

"Finn told me. He said that you were running some of their business through the coffee shop."

Her jaw drops before it snaps shut. "I knew that you two were tied up in this shit, I just didn't know how, and I didn't want to ask. Why didn't you tell me the truth?"

"Finn kept as much as he could from me when it involved his work with Cillian. He didn't want to drag me into things if I didn't need to be. That's not what else I have to tell you, though."

"There's more? On top of everything else you've told me about the sex traffickers and your kidnapping, there's more?"

I sit on my hands, needing to do something to keep them from shaking as I speak. "There is. I was never engaged to Finn. It was part of the plan for coming to Oregon. A few years ago, he was sent to the prison I was working in. We reconnected and were friendly enough. I heard that he was coming to Oregon when he was released, and I begged him to bring me with him."

"And he just did?" Brooklyn leans back in her seat and runs her hand through her hair. "He knew what he was going to be getting into out here, and he just decided to drag you along?"

"No. He was on the fence about it. He finally agreed, but he said that we had to pretend to be engaged. He needed to keep a cover story with Cillian for as long as possible, and I became part of that."

"And this entire time, you've just been lying about who you are?" Brooklyn scrubs her hands down her face.

Her loud sigh fills the room while I wait for her to walk out.

I know that this is a lot for anyone to sit here and listen to. I wouldn't blame her at all for deciding that she was better off without my drama in her life.

I swallow hard, trying to stuff down the lump in my throat. "If Dawson hadn't seen you here, he would've never approached you about working for the mob. It's my fault that you're involved with them."

Brooklyn shakes her head. "I would've gotten involved one way or another. Paying bills is a struggle, and everyone in Oregon knows you go see Cillian if you need help with money."

"I'm sorry about lying to you for so long. Finn needed me to keep the secret."

She bites her bottom lip before nodding. "I'm not happy that you lied to me, but I'm just glad you're alive and happy. I know that you would do anything for him."

"I love him."

She laughs and smacks her hands on her thighs before standing. "I know you do. Now, what do you say we pack away your dad's things like you invited me over here to do?"

"You really aren't upset?"

She grabs an empty box and puts it on the chair before grabbing a stack of notebooks. "I'm not happy about you lying to me, but I understand why you did it. Hell, if a man looked at me the way Finn looks at you, I'm sure that I would do some crazy things too."

My cheeks warm as I grab the yearbooks and pack them into another box. "I just want to get this dealt with before he gets home. Now that I've figured out what it was that my father hid from me, I just want a fresh start."

"You can't run from your past." Brooklyn grabs some of the notes and stuffs them down the side of her box. "Are you sure that you're not just packing this away so you can repress it?"

I close my box and put a thick piece of tape over the top. "It's not about running away from it. I'm at peace with it, honestly. Becca seems like a nice woman, even if I do have some anger to work through where she is concerned. As for the rest of these things, they're just memories of a man I never really knew."

Brooklyn holds her hand out for the tape, sealing away another box of memories. "I'm glad that you're going to be able to move on. I didn't think you would."

"Me neither."

"What are you going to do now that your search is over?"

"I think I'm going to go back into nursing. I love the job, and now that I have the answers I was looking for, there's nothing else to really take up my time."

"I'm proud of you, Ava. You're one hell of a woman."

We finish packing the rest of the boxes before stuffing them in a closet. Brooklyn leaves as I put the last box in the closet.

For a second, I stand there and stare at the cardboard boxes. Though what I found tore me apart, I'm better for it.

As soon as the door is shut, it feels like I've closed a chapter on a large part of my life.

Finn walks through the door moments after Brooklyn leaves. He grins when he sees the bare coffee table before sweeping me up into his arms.

"You're in a good mood." I kiss him before he puts me back down on solid ground. "Did the meeting with Cillian go well?"

"It did. Better than I thought it would. Becca invited us to come over for dinner next week, but I can make an excuse for us not to go."

"No. I think it'll be good. If you're going to be there, it might not be too awkward."

He goes into the kitchen and pours himself a glass of water, taking a long drink before setting it to the side. "The original deal I had with Cillian is going to be changing."

My eyebrows pull together as I perch myself on the arm of the chair. "What do you mean? I thought you were going to be his right hand."

"I was. Until he went to see the doctor while we were away. Running the mob is getting to him. His heart isn't as good as it used to be, and Becca is giving him hell for it. He's going to step down in the next year or two."

My mouth almost hits the ground. "What does that mean for you?"

"He wants me to replace him. It's a way to keep you safe. If I'm running Oregon, there are going to be people keeping an eye out in every corner of the state. We won't have to worry about my father's men trying to get revenge for him. I won't have to run around killing people all the time anymore."

"Is this really what you want?"

He nods. "It is, but if you don't think that I should take the offer, then I'll tell him that and see what else he is willing to have me do."

Even though I'd love to tell him to walk away from the mob and leave that life behind, I know that isn't Finn.

He excels at what he does. He's got a head for running a criminal empire, even if that isn't what most people would consider an asset.

"You're going to be the best mob leader Oregon has ever seen." I cross the room and throw my arms around him.

"I'm glad that you think so." He spins me around again, peppering kisses up and down my neck before letting me go. "I have something else I want to talk to you about."

He takes my hand and pulls me into the backyard.

Lights are strung from the trees, and our friends are gathered around the back side of the yard.

Zoe has a camera pointed in my direction as Finn takes off his gold chain and hands it to me.

He clears his throat, looking down at me like I'm the only person in the world. "I wanted to give you this first. I thought that it would be something you could wear your rings on when you go back to nursing. My mom would want you to have it."

My eyes water as he loops the chain around my neck. It nestles in the hollow where my other necklace used to hang.

I haven't been able to bring myself to put the necklace from my father on since we got back from Tennessee. Too many bad memories are attached to it.

Finn smiles and traces his finger along the gold chain before getting to one knee.

My hand flies to my mouth as he pulls out a little white box. "What are you doing?"

"What I should have done when I first asked you to be engaged to me, but this time, it's real."

He gives me a crooked grin that sends my heart racing.

I hold back the tears as Zoe moves closer, her finger pressing down on the shutter button rapidly.

Finn flicks open the box, but I can't tear my gaze away from him long enough to look at the ring.

"Aves, I've been in love with you for the last three years, even if we've only been together for the last several months. Seeing you in that prison every day was what kept me going when I felt like giving up."

I sniffle, trying to fight the emotions flowing through me. "You would have been fine without me."

"No, I wouldn't. You are everything to me. When I told you that I was going to Oregon, I never thought that you would force me to take you. Not in a million years did I ever think that you would fall in love with me."

My smile makes my cheeks ache. "How could I not fall in love with you? Finn, you're everything that I've ever wanted."

"Good, because I want to spend the rest of our lives together. We've spent too many years just dancing around each other. I love you so damn much. Marry me, Aves?"

"Yes." I wipe away the tears as he stands and takes the ring from the box.

My hand shakes as he slides it onto my finger.

I glance down at the amethyst for a second before throwing my arms around him.

Finn chuckles, his arms like vices around my waist as he holds me close.

"I was going to wait to take you somewhere special, but if I did that, I was never going to work up the nerve to propose." He pulls back and kisses me, nipping at my bottom lip in a promise of what's to come later.

"I love you, Finn."

"I love you too, Aves."

He grins as music starts blaring through speakers hidden somewhere in the yard.

Billie and Hadley rush over with Zoe and Brooklyn close behind them, their voices all blending together.

My heart flutters as Finn finds my gaze through the crowd and winks.

This is going to be one of the best nights of my life.

Hours later, Finn whisks me away from the party.

We head straight to our bedroom, clothing dropping to the floor.

He groans as I wrap my hand around his cock and sink to my knees in front of him.

Finn takes my hair, wrapping it around his fist and guiding my mouth to his cock. "You look so fucking good on your knees for me, Aves."

My tongue darts out to lick the head of his cock.

He pushes the tip past my lips as I hollow my cheeks.

His hips rock forward, driving his cock to the back of my throat as I fist the base.

I move my head and hand up and down his length.

The grip he has on my hair tightens as I drag my teeth along the underside of his cock while squeezing his balls.

"Fucking hell, Aves, I'm not going to last long if you keep doing that."

I smirk around his cock, sucking hard and taking him deeper.

Finn pulls me back by my hair, guiding me to my feet. "On the bed. Spread your legs and let me see that pretty pussy, Aves."

"I wasn't done with your cock yet." I do as I'm told anyway, getting on the bed and spreading my legs wide.

Finn stands at the foot of the bed as I run my fingers along my wet slit.

His cock bobs as I slip two fingers into my pussy, his name on my lips.

"You're being a tease." He gets on the bed, crawling up between my legs.

He licks my pussy before taking my fingers and licking them clean. "You know, now that you're my fiancée, I think that you taste even more addictive than you did before."

"Now who's being the tease?"

He pushes two fingers into me, stretching my inner walls.

I moan, fisting the sheets as he crooks his fingers and presses them against the spot he knows drives me wild.

My back arches off the bed as his mouth closes over my clit.

He sucks on it as he buries his fingers deeper into me with every thrust.

I hook a leg around his shoulders, keeping him close as my wetness soaks his fingers.

He groans, his tongue moving faster as my legs start to shake.

As he reaches up to roll my nipple between his fingers, my orgasm rips through me.

"Fuck, Finn, yes. Don't stop."

I writhe my hips in time with his thrusting until the last waves of pleasure roll through my body.

Finn smirks from between my legs before crawling up my body and flipping us over.

His hands roam up my curves, cupping my breasts and teasing my nipples until they're stiffened peaks.

"I love you." I lean forward and kiss him, our tongues tangling as I rub my pussy against his cock.

His hand slides into my hair, pulling my head back. "I love you too. Now ride my fucking cock like you own it."

I smirk and plant my hands on his chest, sinking down onto his cock. "I do own it. Ring on my finger says so."

"Good little slut." He lifts his hips off the bed with each rock of my hips, helping me take him deeper. "Make yourself come on my cock."

I roll my hips, my nails digging into his chest.

He groans, gripping my hips and forcing me to move faster.

My pussy clenches around his cock, milking him as he comes.

Finn keeps slamming into me until my pussy pulsates around him.

His fingers dig into my hips as I come.

When I lean forward, sprawling across his chest, his arms wrap around me.

His mouth finds mine, our kiss lazy as we bask in the feeling of being engaged.

Finn pulls away first, his fingers tracing patterns along my spine. "I didn't think that this would ever be my life."

I prop myself up a little, looking down at him. "Are you happy that it is?"

"Happier than you could ever know, Aves. I love you, and I can't wait to get married to you. What do you think about running away tomorrow and getting married in Vegas?"

I laugh and kiss his chest. "As eager as I am to marry you, I want Zoe and Christian and the rest of my family there. Apart from my mother. I haven't spoken to her since the will reading, and I don't want to."

"You don't have to speak to her ever again." He tucks a strand of my hair behind my ear. "We'll get married when you want to and however you want to."

"You're fine with whatever?"

"Aves, at the end of the day, all I care about is calling you my wife." He ghosts his lips across mine. "However that happens is what I want."

I settle in beside him, already dreaming of the rest of our lives.

EPILOGUE
FINN

Six Months Later

When the back door to Christian's house opens and Ava appears wearing a white gown that hugs her curves, tears spring to my eyes.

I keep my hands clasped in front of me, terrified that they're going to shake.

Her veil trails behind her as she walks down the aisle to an acoustic version of her favorite song.

Zoe grins beside her, tears streaming down her face.

Becca is on her other side, looking like this is everything she's ever dreamed of for Ava.

Ava smiles at me like I'm the only person in the room.

Her eyes are glassy as she clutches the bouquet of flowers to her chest.

She walks down the aisle lined with colorful flower petals until she comes to a stop in front of me.

Zoe lets go of her arm and steps beside me. "If I have to lose my sister to someone, I'm glad that it's you."

I swallow the lump in my throat. "Thank you."

The officiant begins the ceremony as Ava hands off her flowers to Zoe.

Zoe joins Billie and Hadley on the other side of Ava. The three of them look more emotional than Ava is right now.

Becca takes a seat beside Cillian, leaning onto his side as the music comes to a stop.

"Hey." I keep my voice low, barely more than a whisper as the officiant drones on.

Ava laughs. "Hey."

The officiant looks between the two of us. "If you would both like to say the vows that you've prepared."

I turn to Christian, reaching for the piece of paper with my vows.

He hands them over while Jovan winks and Alessio nods.

I take a deep breath, turning back to Ava.

"Aves, I wrote vows, but honestly, they're not that good, so we're just going to wing it."

The crowd of our family and friends chuckles, but Cillian's laugh is the loudest.

Becca elbows him, her eyes brimming with tears as she looks at Ava.

I take Ava's hands in mine, running my thumbs over her knuckles. "Aves, I could live a thousand lives and not find another person who loves me and understands me the way you do. I could wander the earth and never find a woman who is half the person you are."

The lump in my throat threatens to choke me. I swallow hard, wanting my words to be as clear as possible. "I knew when I saw you again four years ago in prison that you were far too good for the likes of me, but you took a chance on me anyway."

Ava reaches up and swipes a tear from beneath my eye.

I turn my head quick, kissing her hand before she can pull away.

"Aves, I love you more than you could ever know, and I will spend the rest of my life showing you that."

Ava's bottom lip quivers, and she lets go of me long enough to swipe away her own tears before they can fall.

"Finn, you set my world on fire in the best ways possible. You came into my life, and you burned down everything I thought I knew, making way for a better life to form."

She sniffles, raising a finger to her eyes again.

Ava takes a deep breath. "We've built ourselves up from the ashes since we've been together, and I look forward to continuing to build with you. I fell in love with you slowly at first, but then it came crashing down around me. My life would be only half of what it is without you."

She takes a moment to smile at me.

I take the handkerchief out of my jacket pocket and hand it to her.

She laughs and wipes away the tears before holding my hands tighter. "I'm going to love you for the rest of our days. I'm going to fall in love with you more and more every day. Being your wife is all that I've ever wanted."

The officiant nods to Christian and Zoe.

The two of them step forward, both presenting our wedding bands.

Ava's hands shake as she slides mine on, grinning up at me with tears in her eyes.

I slide her ring on her finger, my heart pounding in my chest.

"You may now kiss the bride."

I pull her into my arms and dip her low, capturing her mouth in a searing kiss.

Ava grips my collar, holding me tight to her.

When we stand, the crowd is clapping and cheering.

I take Ava's hand and walk with her down the aisle and back into Christian's house.

The moment the door is closed behind us and the curtains drawn, she throws herself into my arms.

Laughing, I hold her close and kiss her until we're both out of breath.

She pulls away and takes a step back. "I have a surprise for you before we have to go back out there and entertain our guests."

Ava disappears into one of the other rooms, leaving me standing in the kitchen.

When she comes back, she's holding a giant canvas.

Ava gives me a tentative smile before turning the canvas around.

My jaw drops as my oldest brother stares back at me from within the brushstrokes of a painting.

In the painting, I stand in my tux in the middle of Cormac and Ava.

She's in her wedding dress, and the greenery of the backyard is blurred behind us.

Tears make the edges of my vision fuzzy. "How did you get this?"

"I found some old photos of Cormac in your things. I got Brooklyn to do the painting. I thought it would be nice to have a picture of the three of us on our wedding day."

She holds out the canvas, and I take it, looking at the detail in it.

Brooklyn did an amazing job, but Ava did even better.

This woman never fails to amaze me.

I set the painting to the side before pulling her into a tight hug.

The lump in my throat keeps me from speaking as I hold her tight.

Ava nestles her head against my chest, hugging me until I let her go first.

"Thank you, Aves. This is the best gift you ever could have gotten. Cormac would've hated missing this." I kiss the top of her head before taking the canvas and putting it back in one of the other rooms.

When I come back, Zoe and Camila are swarming around Ava, bustling her wedding dress so she can dance later.

As I look at my wife, I know that Cormac would have loved Ava.

He would have been proud to see me standing at an altar to marry the woman of my dreams.

Once Ava is bustled and ready to go, we join the rest of our friends and family outside.

Dawson has the music blasting as caterers start to deliver food to the tables.

I loop my arm around Ava's waist, leading her to the dance floor.

She laughs as I pull her close. "We're supposed to have some food before we start dancing."

"Nope, Aves. I'm dancing with you first. And then we are going to have some dinner and dance some more. And then after all of that, I'm going to take you to our plane so you can finally see what I got you for our wedding."

Her eyebrow arches as she sinks her fingers into the hair at the nape of my neck. "You're finally going to tell me where you booked for our honeymoon?"

I nod and dip her low before bringing her back to me. "Yes, Mrs. Byrne, I think I will tell you when we get to the plane."

"Well, Mr. Byrne, I can't wait."

Chuckling, I spin her around. "I love you, Aves."

"I love you too, Finn." Her stomach growls as one song transitions into another. "It's time to get something to eat."

We sit down at the table, eating and talking to our friends.

As soon as the conversation dies down, Zoe gets to her feet. She smiles to the people surrounding her as the wedding planner runs over a microphone.

The moment the microphone is in her hand, Zoe starts to sob. Tears roll down her cheeks, smearing her makeup as she pulls out a scrap of paper.

Zoe looks at Ava. "Would you believe me if I said I wasn't going to cry through your speech?"

Ava shakes her head, her smile stretching from one side of her face to the other.

Zoe shuffles the paper and microphone, trying to see the speech through her tears. "I'm going to keep it short, otherwise I'm never going to stop crying happy tears."

The crowd chuckles as Zoe clears her throat.

Zoe wipes away more tears. "Ava is the best person I've ever known. She is the best sister a person could ask for her. She deserves the best. And with Finn, she got that. Congratulations, you two."

Ava holds my hand tight beneath the table as more people get up to make speeches, each one more sob-inducing than the last.

By the time the last speech is done, Ava's wiped away most of her makeup, the tears still streaming down her face.

I hold her close, smiling as I kiss her and try to ignore the lump in my own throat.

This day is everything that I wanted it to be.

I got to marry the woman of my dreams, and I got a new family.

It's odd to have so many people surrounding us with love after the way I grew up, but I wouldn't change it for the world.

Right here with Ava is where I am meant to be.

Fate brought us together, and nothing is ever going to tear us apart.